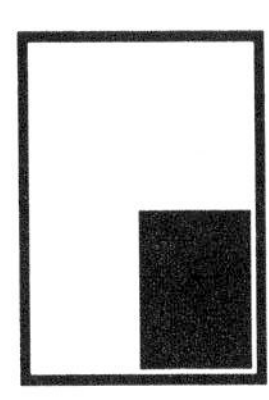

DARK CORNER PRESS
P.O. Box 33046
Riverside, California 92519
(800) 431-1579
www.cfhawthorne.com

This book contains profanity. It is used at the author's discretion, to create more realistic characterizations.

ISBN: 0-9708075-97

First Printing - 2002

10 9 8 7 6 5 4 3 2

Printed in the United States of America

For Every Black Eye

Revenge: When Nothing Else Works

A Novel By:

C.F. Hawthorne

Are you a victim of
Domestic Violence?

You are not alone.
You are not to blame.
You do not deserve to be abused.
Love hurts when it's
coming from the fist.

National Hotline
1-800-999-SAFE

In New York
1-800-621-HOPE

DEDICATION

This book is dedicated to
the Women, Men and Children of Abuse.
Keep your head up, and remember.
Love hurts when it's coming from the
FIST.

If you would like to
contact the author:
www.cfhawthorne.com

ACKNOWLEDGEMENTS

First, I give all glory and honor to Jesus Christ, my Lord and Savior. I thank him for all that I have learned during this process, and all the friends that I have gathered along the way.

To my family, Dwayne, Bradley, and Avari, I have been blessed to have you in my life and I thank you for standing by me, understanding me, and letting me entertain you with my stories of our future and with my love for writing. Dwayne, I especially thank you for standing by me and understanding this was a dream I simply could not let slip away.

To my cousins, Rozelia Felton, Renee and John Harris, Cynthia Richardson and, Cynthia Lee Harris, thank you for giving me a wonderful extended family and being so enthusiastic about my dreams. Renee Harris thanks so much for reading and reading and reading. To my cousin, Tina Gipson, thank you for always asking questions about the novel, your excitement kept me excited. To my Aunt, Ruth Ann Gipson (Fontenot), what can I say but, girl, you can keep a secret. Thank you for your encouraging words, and thank you for always having time for me no matter what time I call.

I have a special thanks for my two Angels: Jacqueline Hamilton and Jacquelin Thomas. Jackie H. thanks for not calling the police as I stalked you on November 7, 1999 at 10:45 in the morning in downtown Riverside. (SMILES) Thank you baby girl for inviting me into your life and introducing me to Miriam Pace and Jaquelin Thomas, who have been my shining light, my inspiration and my best friends. Jackie T, thanks for making room in your FOCUS group, and your life for me, a stranger that you made a friend. Thanks for answering my tons of questions and thanks for educating me on POV. Miriam Pace, I didn't forget about you. Thank you for letting me be a part of your life, and for letting me sit with you at your book signing on November 7, 1999. Christmas came early for me that day.

Deborah Holmes, Carmellia Chavers, Tina Carter, Jacquelin Thomas, Jacquelin Hamilton and Shelby Gordon. If it had not been for you this novel would probably still be a DREAM, but now it's my REALITY. I thank Deborah for getting me into the rehab center for ***comma addictive*** people like me. I have not completely kicked the habit, but I am in recovery. (SMILE) Carmellia, what can I say. You have been in my cheering section since I summoned up the courage to call you and we spent almost three, maybe four, hours on the phone talking about writing. I was in heaven girl. Tina, girl ,thanks for always keeping it real. Thank you for your e-mails asking about the book. You always remind me of the kids (Are we there yet, No, Are we there yet No). Thank you for always asking. (Is is finished yet, No. Is it finished yet, No.) Thanks for your excitement.

My grandmother always told me that we are walking among Angels and she was right. Thank you so much my FOCUS group Angels.

Now that I can say that I have lived among angels, I must say that I have worked among fools! MUCH, much, much thanks goes out to those crazy, funny, caring folks at the Family Law Court: Genette Banks, Tina Hooper-Williams, Raynett Gile, Carolyn Kochek, Suszann Klies, Rachel Chew, and everyone else that I don't have enough room to mention. You guys are so great. Thanks for keeping me excited about this venture and encouraging me to live my dream. Thanks for letting me entertain you with my excitement when I wrote one sentence and jumped for joy because I thought it was the most brilliant piece of work ever written; and you guys jumped for joy as well.

One special thanks goes to Linda Hickman. Linda I never met anyone that could get so excited over someone else's dream. I must say there were days when I asked myself what was I trying to do; and then came you. With a huge smile and big hugs. Saying when is the party. Every time you saw me, you always had a question to ask about the book and I thank you for your encouraging words.

What would this world be without grandparents. I thank you guys from the bottom of my heart for taking me in when my mother turned her back on me. I guess what they say is true. One man's trash is another man's treasure. I pray that I am your treasure. I love you grandma and grandpa.

Chapter 1

"ill him."

I lifted my throbbing head from my knees and glanced around the bedroom. I know I heard a voice.

"Kill him," echoed through the room once again.

I looked to my left, then to my right. Slowly I raised my aching body from the floor. With each painful step I took, the bathroom seemed miles away. I had to lean against the door frame to keep from falling. Jacob, my husband, had beaten me so badly this time I felt drunk. I reached for the sink and propped my hip against the cool white porcelain, closing my eyes momentarily trying to ease the pain and the nightmare of my reality. It was no use. My reality was a nightmare.

I stared at my reflection in the bathroom mirror. My brown eyes were now sunken into dark shadows.

For Every Black Eye

The whites of my eyes had red streaks running through them like a state road map. When I spit into the sink, I watched a tooth dance around the porcelain before descending down the drain. Bracing myself with both hands and closing my eyes as the memory of Jacob's fist surged through my body like a demon, I shook my head.

Staring at my face once again in the medicine cabinet mirror before opening it, I whispered, "He didn't mean it." I told the sad reflection staring back at me. "He told me so, and I believe him, again."

Flinching, I reached into the medicine cabinet. The pain raced up my arm and stopped in my neck. He didn't mean it, I told myself over and over. He didn't mean it.

"Kill him," a familiar voice shouted again, this time sending chills down my spine.

Slowly closing the medicine cabinet door and my eyes, I took a deep breath, held it for a few seconds, and then exhaled. I cautiously opened my eyes.

"Febe! What in God's name are you doing here?" I asked, trying to remain calm.

"You need me, Annie," she spoke softly.

"No, no I don't need you," I said anxiously, shaking my head. "Please go away. I can handle this myself."

"Kill him, Annie."

"I won't kill him."

"He's been slowly killing you for ten agonizing years. Kill him tonight."

"He didn't mean it, Febe. Really, he didn't." I pleaded Jacob's case.

"Kill him tonight when he gets in."

"Febe, stop it!" I shouted and grabbed both sides of my head. "You don't understand. I love this man, and he loves me."

"Annie, you've tried holding on to that dream for far too long. Has it ever occurred to you, the more you love Jacob the more he beats you? He doesn't love you, Annie."

"That's not true. He tells me all the time how much he loves me. Jacob is always confessing his love for me."

"Yeah. As he takes his sweet time getting you to a hospital. You have medical records all over the state of Texas, Annie."

I dropped my head. I couldn't look into her evil eyes any longer.

"As the years move on, Jacob has become more and more violent, and I've sat back and watched long enough. I'm through watching."

"But why now, Febe? Why now? This beating wasn't any worse than any of the other ones."

"Oh, but it was, my dear. I have to save our baby. I think thirty-five is a little old for an ass whipping, don't you?"

I placed my trembling hands over my tiny swollen belly. I wanted so much for Jacob to love us, and he would in time. I looked back into Febe's eyes.

"Jacob is a good man and a great provider, when he wants to be."

"Yeah, but he treats you like a servant."

She frowned. "He's handsome and charming. I need him to survive."

"Annie, the man often reminds you that looks can be deceiving."

"Febe, you don't understand. This man loves me, and I love him."

"Love? Love don't hurt, girl, even I know that, and I don't love nothing."

My hands trembled so violently I couldn't apply the antiseptic to the gashes. I slid to the cold linoleum floor, which felt like ice to my wounds. I covered my eyes and grieved. I wanted a cigarette so badly, but I had none. Frustrated, I yelled, "You think you can just pop back into my life after all these years just because of one lousy fight?"

"Ass whipping, Annie. It wasn't a fight. Fighting is when you hit back. You never lifted a hand, and I never left you. Fear and failure made you a prisoner of Jacob's world, not me."

"Fear! Failure!" I shouted. "What did I ever fail in?"

"Look around you, girl. You're talking to yourself in a bathroom mirror. Now do you see? You don't have a choice. Jacob must die, or you will."

"Febe, no, please don't do this. I need Jacob and he needs me. I can't live without him."

"Annie, that's sick."

"No, it's not. I've become dependent on him, on the attention he gives me when he's sorry for hurting me. I'm dependent on the kisses on my forehead and the..."

"That's sick, Annie."

"No, it's not!" I yelled.

"Yes, it is, and Jacob is a no-good man who deserves to die."

"Febe." I swallowed cautiously, because my throat was bruised. "I've come to accept the fact that a no-good man is better than no man at all, and he's my man. I have to protect him."

"And I have to protect you!" she shouted.

"I can't go on without this man."

"Even if you have to live in fear?"

"Even if I have to live in fear every day of my life." I struggled to my feet, and the pain intensified with each move that I made. I took a deep breath, slowly exhaling, staring into her heartless, cold eyes once again.

"My worse fear is living alone for the rest of my life," I proclaimed, reaching for the eight hundred milligrams of Ibuprofen and the Dixie cup that was on the sink. I though about swallowing the entire bottle of pills as I watched my shaking hand make the water dance around in the cup.

"Don't even think about it, Annie. You are going to live. I will see to that."

I stared at Febe's face in the mirror-not my face but Febe's-closed my eyes hoping that she'd go away. I didn't know many things, but I knew where there's Febe, there's trouble, and I wanted her gone. But when I opened my eyes and she was still there, I knew she wasn't about to go away.

I took a deep breath and asked, "Why are you here?"

"I'm here to protect you."

"I told you I don't need protection. I can handle this myself."

"Annie, that son of a bitch smiles when he knocks you to the floor, and he stands there grinning with those big-ass gold teeth asking you if you're scared of him."

"And Febe?"

"And you answer yes like a frightened child. You call that handling things? I don't think so, sister."

"Febe, this is my life!" I screamed.

"Oh hell no, this is our life. I live in this body too. Jacob put cigarettes out on our thighs. He threw gasoline in our face. He did all those things to us. I let him get away with that shit for too many years by letting you handle it. You didn't handle shit, Annie. You got handled."

I cautiously walked back to my jumbled bedroom, holding my tiny bulge. Turning out the lights as tears rolled down my cheeks, I was able to ease my aching body under the cool crumpled sheets of my bed.

"Tomorrow is another day that I have to survive, Febe."

I closed my eyes as my childhood protector shouted in rage in my head to kill my husband, the father of my unborn child. If only she could understand how much I love that man.

Jumping at the sound of violent pounding that I thought was in my head, I looked around and I was soaking in a lukewarm tub of water with bubbles slowly fading.

"Annie, damn it. Come out of that bathroom," he yelled. "What is in this fucking coffee?"

I had no idea what Jacob was screaming about, but I hurried to get out of the tub. Every muscle in my body was aching, and I didn't want another beating from him, not today. I reached for a towel and saw Febe laughing her butt off. Jacob was on the other side of the bathroom door yelling like a madman about coffee.

"Febe, what did you do to Jacob's coffee?" I cried, watching that unsympathetic expression in the mirror. "Stop laughing!" I screamed.

My heart was pounding so hard I felt like I couldn't breathe, and I wanted to throw up. "What did you do to his coffee?" I cried again. "I don't want another beating from this man, so please tell me." I stopped in mid-sentence. "Why did you make him coffee any way?"

"You always make coffee for Jacob when he's been out drinking all night."

"Me, Febe. I always make the coffee, not you."

"You were in no shape to make him coffee. Hell, Annie, I gotta protect you. Just like I protected you from that son of a bitch father. Remember I told you that I was going to pay him back."

"Pay him back?" I shouted nervously.

"Yes, pay him back For Every Black Eye he gave you and your mother. Jacob ain't no different."

I couldn't help but clench my teeth. "You didn't protect me from my father. You killed my father, Febe. You killed him."

She threw her head back and laughed. "Oh yeah, hell I forgot. You know how bad my memory is."

"Febe, you are so cruel, Jacob is pissed, and I'm scared, and..."

"Like I give a flying pig's ass about Jacob," she interjected quickly. The brief interruption ended with a chuckle.

"Stop laughing. This is serious. What am I supposed to do?"

Her eyes went stone cold, and the smile fell from her face.

I shivered. "If it's so damn serious, kill him," she demanded again. "He has a gun under the mattress. Get it, pull the damn trigger and kill him."

"Febe, I don't know how to shoot a gun."

"Use the knife."

"Knife," I said, glancing at the large butcher knife on the edge of the sink. "How did that get in here?" I asked, grabbing the enormous wooden handle. I examined the huge steel blade and shuddered.

"I brought it in here for your protection," she remarked slowly.

The acid in my stomach rose to my throat. Tears took their position in the base of my eyes. I clutched the towel to my chest and tried to keep my body from trembling so violently.

I knew if I walked out of this bathroom with the knife I was dead. I realized the banging had stopped and calmness descended on my shoulders.

Listening closely I could hear Jacob in the closet searching for his black leather belt. I held my breath and turned to face Febe in the mirror.

"Why did you do this, Febe? Why?"

Jacob rammed against the door and began brutally pounding on it.

He was shouting at the top of his lungs. "You put something in my coffee, you little bitch." I placed my trembling hand on the door, still gripping the knife sternly.

"No! I didn't, Jacob. I promise, I didn't." My voice was barely above a whisper. "Calm down, Jacob. Please calm down."

"Yes, you did. I can taste it," he shouted back at me.

"Jacob, please. I promise I didn't put anything in your coffee."

"Admit it, Annie. You're trying to kill me."

I turned back to Febe. "Please tell me what did you do?" I tried to remain calm. She only laughed.

"I didn't do anything to that simple son of a bitch's coffee. You didn't have anything in the kitchen."

"Jacob! Jacob!" I shouted over his growls. "There's nothing wrong with the coffee." I wanted him to calm down, but once he became quiet I was filled with horror. Suddenly I heard the belt buckle hit the bedroom floor.

"I'm sorry, honey, I don't know what got into me. Come out, Annie, and talk to me. I'm so sorry, baby."

Finding comfort in his words, I slowly opened the bathroom door. Jacob snatched the towel away from my body so fast I didn't have time to think.

He slapped me across the face with the cup before throwing me on the bed. I heard the knife drop on the floor with a loud thud. He was on top of me, with his face only a few inches from mine, his hands around my throat.

"If you want me dead, Annie, you better do it in my sleep, because if you ever try something like this again I'll kill you, little girl."

When he took his knee out of my chest and the air returned to my body. I hustled out of the bed and slid to the floor scurrying to my corner.

"Stop!" he shouted with his back to me. I froze in that spot. I could feel the cold blade of the knife under my knee, but I was too afraid to look down.

We were engulfed in silence for hours, so it seemed. Then Febe spoke, breaking open the gates of hell.

"It was instant coffee," she said, slowly growling and rising to her feet.

"What?" he shouted, facing Febe with fire in his eyes.

"You heard me, you pathetic little curly headed fuck. It was instant coffee."

"Annie! How dare you speak to me like that, and what the fuck do you think you're doing with that knife, and who told you to get up?"

"Oh, this ain't Annie, motherfucker, and you better check yourself because this face is deceiving."

Jacob threw back his head and laughed. "Well you look like Annie to me."

"Well I ain't."

"Who are you today, you insane little bitch?"

"Febe."

"Febe," he repeated. "Well, Ms. Febe, if you think you gonna cut me with that knife--" he burst into another round of laughter and arrogantly pointed toward the blade that was in her hand--"you better think again."

"I'll slice your ass from here to next week," Febe said, swinging at Jacob with the protruding blade.

I didn't move I was so scared. I couldn't move. I was watching but I couldn't see. All of a sudden, Jacob screamed and dropped to the floor, holding a gash as blood streamed down the side of his face. I couldn't believe what had happened. Febe cut him, right before my eyes. She cut my husband!

"Febe!" I screamed, pushing my way through the quietness. "What in God's name have you done? He's hurt. You hurt him," I shouted.

"No shit, Annie."

"Febe, I won't let you kill him. He's my husband, and I won't let him die."

"Annie, you don't have a choice in this matter. I want what I want, and no one will stop me."

Febe and I were arguing when Jacob jumped to his feet. He grabbed Febe around her neck and took the knife out of her hand. I slid away into the safeness of the darkness.

"I'm so glad to meet you, Febe," Jacob said sarcastically. "Annie should have warned you about me," he added, tightening his grip.

"No, Annie should have warned you about me," she mumbled and flipped Jacob over her shoulder, stomped him in his genitals, then ran to his side of the bed. I was horrified as I watched Jacob groaning in agonizing pain.

Kneeling down next to the bed, wild and angry, Febe rummaged under the mattress. She pulled Jacob's .357 automatic out and kissed it.

"Febe, you don't know how to use that thing," I screamed hysterically. She turned to the nightstand, pulled out the clip, inserted it into the bottom of the gun, and flicked off the safety. She cycled the first round into the chamber.

"I took shooting lessons and karate!" Febe shouted. "And I'm gonna shoot this son of a bitch in the middle of his forehead."

"Febe, no, I will not let you take Jacob from me."

"Annie, why are you protecting him?" I could hear the disgust in her voice.

"He's my husband. He said I have to protect him."

"Stop fighting with me. He's getting up." When Febe turned on her knees toward Jacob and raised the gun, it was too late. Jacob kicked her in the head with his black steel-toe boots, and everything went dark.

Chapter 2

Calm down. Just calm down. You don't know where you are, just remain calm and listen. The sounds are muffled and the smells are familiar. If you can smell, that means you're not dead. That's a good thing. So just remain calm and listen, I tried to convince myself, as the voices became comprehensible.

"Is she getting any better, Dr. Harrison?"

Doctor? Oh hell, I'm in a hospital.

"I don't know, Nurse Nelson. She still has some internal bleeding, but the swelling in her head has gone down a bit. However, we still have to keep an eye on her. She has so many broken bones, including her ribs, and she isn't breathing on her own."

Yes I am. I'm breathing on my own. If you take this damn thing out of my mouth, I'll show you!

"We still have a long way to go with her. If she doesn't

come out of this coma soon, she'll slide into a deeper one and die."

Oh shit! How did I get in a coma. But I'm not in a coma, I can understand what they're saying.

"Hello, Harrison and Nurse Nelson."

"Hi, Gloria. How are you?"

"Hello, Mrs. Maxwell."

"Dr. Harrison, you wanted to talk to me about a patient who I might be interested in."

"Yes, come in. What happened to your arm?"

"I fell down the basement stairs."

"Nothing serious I hope."

"No, just a little sprain."

"Good."

"Wow, Harrison what happened to him?"

"Her."

"Sorry, so many bandages, I couldn't tell."

"That's okay, Gloria. She's pretty messed up."

"What's her name?"

"We don't know, so for now it's Jane Doe."

"Jane Doe?"

"That's all we have. We don't know her real name, and she's been in a coma since she was brought to the hospital. Finding out her name was the least of our problems. She was hemorrhaging something awful. I thought I was going to lose her."

"When did they bring her in?"

"A few days ago."

"On the Fourth of July?"

"Yes."

"What happened?"

"Well, she's been beaten up pretty badly. The police say it's attempted murder."

"Harrison! That's a shame. Who would do something like

that to a woman?"

"Gloria, I don't know, and I don't care, that's the police's problem. I just want to help her."

"Is she going to be all right?"

"Let's go to my office. She's not in a deep coma, she's in a twilight stage, and I don't want her to overhear any more than she's probably already heard. It could upset her. Then we'll have other problems on our hands."

"You think she can hear us?"

"Yes, I definitely do. However, some doctors don't think so, but I believe most coma victims can hear what's going on around them. That's why I called you. You can help us pull her through this. She's gonna need lots of attention. Are you up to it?"

"I would like to hear more about Jane Doe before I commit to anything."

"Well this is going to be a long-term commitment, and the hospital is limited as to what it can do and will do without knowing who will be responsible for the bill."

"Hi, Jane baby. How are you doing today? It's me, Nurse Nelson. Dr. Harrison found someone to be by your side almost twenty-four hours a day. You're going to like her, as soon as you come out of that coma. She's very nice and pretty too."

Lady, look I don't give a damn about meeting no pretty, nice lady. I just wanna open my eyes and see what the hell is going on, and my name is not Jane Doe, it's, it's Febe.

"Nurse Nelson, can I come in?"

"Mrs. Maxwell, hello. Sure, come in."

"Call me Gloria."

"Are you and Dr. Harrison finished talking about Jane so soon?"

"Yes, he didn't have much more to say. He gave me a lot of books to read about coma patients, but mostly he wants me to be near her and talk to her, that's all."

"Well that's wonderful, Gloria. I'm glad that you decided to do this for her."

"Do you know anything about her, Nurse Nelson?"

"No, not really."

"What do you mean, not really?"

"I mean I don't know this lady, but I do know that this is not an attack like the police are making it seem."

"Why do you think it's something different?"

"Her body is a temple for old scars and bruises. Her x-rays show that a few bones healed wrong. Somebody's been beating this child for a long time."

"Nurse Nelson, please don't say that. I'm getting goose-bumps just thinking about her pain. Maybe she was in an accident. What are the police doing about this?"

"They think it's a rape, mugging, or something like that. They can't do much now, but when she wakes up, she can tell them what happened. But I don't think she's gonna wake up. I'm surprised that she's made it this long. You'd better start a prayer meeting or something, 'cause she's in pretty bad shape, and there's nobody here to tell her they want her to live. I come in and sit with her when I'm on a break, or if the shift is slow, but..."

"You shouldn't say that. God changes all unpredictable circumstances, and besides, Harrison said when a patient is in the twilight stage of a coma they can hear everything around them, so we have to think positive. She's gonna make it, the Lord will see to that."

"Oh, Gloria. I didn't mean to make you cry. I didn't mean to say that she wasn't gonna make it. Sometimes I say what's on my mind, and it's not always what needs to be said."

"I understand, but we must be careful. We want her to get better, and the only thing she needs to hear is the word of God. Praise your name, Lord."

"Yes, she does. Here's some tissue. Wipe your eyes."

"I've never seen anyone in such bad condition as long as I've been volunteering at St. Elizabeth. Just look at her. Is she in a lot of pain?"

"No. She's not in any physical pain, but that's because of the morphine drip. However, she can be in a great deal of emotional pain and unable to tell us. All we can do is let her know we're cheering for her."

"And praying for her."

"I want you to give her the will to live, so dry your eyes. You have work to do. Go on, get a little closer and introduce yourself."

"If it's true that she can hear us, then I think she already knows my name."

"This is true. However, wouldn't you like to be properly introduced?"

"Well, I guess you're right." "Hi, I'm Gloria Maxwell." Her voice was shaking. "And I would like to be your friend, and God loves you." She whispered so close to my ear I could smell her sweet perfume, and her breath was scented with peppermint. She paused like she was waiting for a reply.

"Do you think she's married?" she asked.

"Don't ask me." Nurse Nelson remarked. "Ask her. Those are the questions that she needs to hear."

"Is someone missing you at home, baby?"

I tried to remember, but came up blank. My thoughts rolled around in an empty space in my head.

Gloria stayed and talked to me until it was time for her to go home. She said that she volunteered at St. Elizabeth Hospital because she and Jackson, her husband, gave a great deal of money to the hospital, and she liked it here. Everyone knew her, and she didn't have to deal with Jackson's uptight friends and all their different charity events because the hospital kept her busy.

She told me that she's 5'6" and 120 pounds. She has skin the color of midnight, with short black hair. Her eyes are dark brown and she has a tiny mole on the left side of her face. She hates her feet, she thinks her toes are too short, and she loves Jesus more than life itself.

Jackson is always working and is never home, and when he is home he's always locked up in his office working on papers for the next big trial.

I don't know how long Gloria rattled on about her life, but by the time she was ready to leave I knew so much about her I didn't need to open my eyes to see her face. Her laughter filled my dull boring room and warmed my lifeless heart. She made me comfortable in my darkness.

The next day Gloria gave me a complete overview of my lime-green room with cement walls and well-polished floors. I was fine until she started to describe the other patient's rooms that were filled with get-well cards, flowers, and baskets of fruits. Some even had tiny teddy bears that hung from the ceiling.

I started to feel that the other rooms were overflowing with love and I was alone. The phone rang crashing my pity party, and Gloria picked it up. I was hoping it was for me, someone who knew I was there.

There was a long pause of silence. Then I heard muffled sounds. I could also hear her sniffling like she was crying or something. I wasn't sure.

"I'm sorry, Jane, but I have to go now," she mumbled softly. "Jackson needs me. I hope that you feel better in the morning," she added right before the room fell into a deep silence.

I was forced to entertain myself, to understand what got me here, and how I was going to leave. I tried to remember what happened, who did this to me, and why, but I couldn't.

Suddenly, I heard screams, horrible screams as if they were

in my room, but they were in my head.

My heart began to race and I wanted to run, but I couldn't move. I couldn't even scream for Nurse Nelson to come back in and help me. I couldn't tell the nurses to make the long wailing cries stop.

The night was long and hard. I realized I didn't like the quietness. I needed sounds to help me through the night, but not the sounds that engulfed my soul, and not the fear that surrounded me for most of the night.

I needed what Gloria was giving me. I needed her company, her presence, and her voice to chase the demons away. As I tossed and turned in my head for most of the night, waiting for the morning noise of the next hospital day, I began to give up and surrender to that demon, when, I heard a voice.

"Good morning, Jane. How are you today?" As soon as Gloria spoke, the demon ran away. I was okay. I was saved by my angel's voice. It was the only way I could keep up with day and night. When Gloria left, the demon came, representing the night, but when she returned with her wonderful stories, her angelic voice would chase the demon away.

Gloria helped my days go by fast. Her visits made each day bearable, no matter what the night gave me. The more time she spent with me, the more I became dependent on her voice and her wonderful stories of the people in the outside world.

Every day Gloria had a different story to tell me. I really liked her tales about the two gray-haired receptionists who sat at the front desk in the lobby.

She said that one of them must be a Mary Kay representative because she had on so much mascara she could barely open her eyes. She called the other lady a lip gloss-queen. She said her kisser was so glossy, her words were slipping off her lips faster than she could speak. Gloria was laughing so hard she said her face hurt.

But one morning when Gloria came into my room she wasn't laughing. And there were no stories of the old ladies in the lobby. She had a story to tell me, and this time it was about me.

"Baby," she whispered, sipping her coffee, "I spoke with Harrison and he's working with a group of doctors around the globe to clarify the definitions of a coma. Harrison feels that you can hear us and it's just a matter of time until your body heals itself. I agree with him and so should you.

However, he said patients like you who have some awareness are more likely to respond to familiar sounds than those in a vegetative state. He said that the brain has the potential to heal. Well, not heal, but reroute information. So you can come to live a normal life.

You have mild traumatic brain injury, which means there's not much damage to your brain. Your brain is responding so he feels you can hear us.

Jane, if we assume you are going to die, without giving you the benefit of the doubt, it becomes a self-fulfilling prophecy. You will die." She was silent, then she took a deep breath. "In a nutshell baby, you need to open your eyes so you can go on living." She grabbed my hand. "Jane baby, if you stay like this much longer, you will run into other complications that I can't even begin to translate. Harrison knows a great rehab center. I want the best for you. So help me help you."

I felt the warmth from Gloria's hand as she gently traced the outline of my healing scars with the tips of her finger. She gripped my hand and delicately squeezed it, like she had done so many times before. "It's almost September, Jane," she said and then slipped into one of her deep praying moods. "You have to move forward," she whispered. "You have to move on, baby. You just have to," she repeated over and over. And she was right. It was time for me to move on.

As she spoke to me that day, something in her voice told me she had more troubles than I realized.

When it came time for Gloria to leave and her hand slipped away from my fingers, I didn't want her to go. I wanted to fight her demons, not mine.

But as soon as she left, I could feel the quietness surround me like a fever. I swallowed traces of fear that tasted like bleach in my mouth. My heart furiously pounded in my chest, making my stomach ache.

I felt as if I were floating around the room Gloria had so vividly described to me, and it all seemed so real. The soft sound of a familiar voice pounded against my skull. Commanding me, willing me to her side, and I felt compelled to follow her. When I finally touched the ground, my feet stroked something hot.

The heat was almost unbearable, but I stood my ground. I walked along the rim of a dead backyard. With unfamiliar thoughts mixed in my head, I kicked around tiny pebbles and a large gray stone. I gazed at the hot earth once more and saw a strange black rock. I kicked it and from underneath it grew a ten-foot monster.

He tore at my inner soul, and I ran and ran and ran. And nothing around me seemed real. "There must be an alternative to this insanity," I yelled out to no one's ears. I was about to give up and let the monster take me out of my pain, until I heard her voice call out to me. Exhausted I turned to search the darkness.

"Febe." I heard a sweet familiar voice call. I became calm, and I knew that I was safe.

"I brought you some books. I don't know what you like so I brought you what I like. Let me see. How to wash your dog, how to cut a friend's hair. Oh, this one is great, how to grow a magnificent garden right from your hospital bed.

We are going to have so much fun with this one, I just know it. I also brought flowers, balloons, stuffed animals, and dolls." Gloria's voice sang in my head. It was morning once again.

Each time Gloria left, she returned with a little life for this room, and she described every inch of the article, object, or thing that was for me. But there was nothing I could grab to bring me from my darkness. Nothing gave way to a memory.

Gloria also described everything that went into her mouth. The taste of her first cup of coffee that she always had with me in the morning, and the coolness of the mint tea she spoiled herself with in the afternoon. Still nothing brought back any memories, but I was hungry as hell.

Gloria tried to fit everything she could imagine into my room, and once that was jammed packed with stuff, she had me moved into a larger area. One that could accommodate three or four more patients. She was trying to bring home into my dreary hospital existence.

But opening my eyes seemed not to be an option for me. I felt as though I were slipping away. Gloria said my eyes stopped moving, so was I slipping deeper into the darkness that was near death?

According to Gloria, my bed and respirator was placed on top of a yellow oval rug and moved next to the window where a tiny garden of flowers was growing.

She also brought in a white wicker love seat with yellow and green pillows, and a matching ottoman. Gloria placed the matching rocker and pillows next to my bed so she could sit and hold my fingers. From the way she described everything, the room had more life in it than I did.

She tried her best to bring in something every day, hoping that it would be familiar to me. I recognized nothing.

Over a period of three weeks, Gloria changed the decor in

the inactive, spiritless room into a home away from home. She said if she were in a coma and just opened her eyes she would love the view, and I knew that I would too.

Gloria spent most of her days with me in the hospital, which she said was a relief from Jackson's boring ass. He made her life miserable.

According to Gloria, I gave her a new reason to live. She was getting a little tired of shopping for herself, until I came along.

Nurse Nelson said the place was beginning to feel like a home and not a hospital room. It had all the comforts of a small apartment. It also started to draw attention, which I didn't mind. Gloria and I had many visitors as if they were old friends.

Sometimes the room was so noisy and crowded, security came in. I wanted to open my eyes to see real faces, and real people, anything but the demon that always clouded my vision.

The more people came to visit me, the more I wanted to get out of bed. I knew I wasn't much company for Gloria. I had no voice or gestures to offer her, no expression at all. I had all the personality of a side of beef. But Gloria seemed to enjoy spending all her time with me, she even introduced me as her baby sister.

Her visiting hours were extended from 7:00 a.m. to midnight, with a possible overnight stay once a week, as time permitted. Jackson didn't like it, but there wasn't anything he could do about it.

Gloria had total control over this situation, and she was going to see it through, she told me, and I smiled inwardly, of course.

Dr. Harrison gave Gloria names of a few specialists who might be able to help me, someone whose primary focus was coma patients. She read a list of names and Dr. Bradley Jyrone's name was on the top, middle, and bottom of the list.

Gloria came into my room one day and her presence made my heart sad. She took a deep breath and left. Portions of bandages had been removed from my body, except my face, there was no Gloria to help me. The I.V. was still in my hand, but the breathing tube was gone. Dr. Harrison said that things were looking good for me. I was still inactive, but any improvement was better than nothing at all, but, still no Gloria. I started to feel abandoned, alone, scared, mad and just plain pissed off. I was condemned to this dark hell without her.

Even if I did open my eyes, I knew no one and no one knew me. Then out of despair came her voice.

"Jane, oh my God! Look at you," she cried into my sleep. "I'm sorry that I wasn't here for the removal of your bandages, but I had to do something that was long overdue."

She paused, then kissed me on my bandaged forehead. "I filed for a divorce, Jane. Jackson reverted to his old ways and decided to use my face for a punching bag, and I don't have to deal with the abuse. I prayed about it, then I left. God will forgive me I'm sure.

The good news is I've leased a nice-sized condo that's more than enough room for the two of us, and it's only a few blocks from the rehabilitation center. So you hurry up and get better. I'm lonely in that big place without you."

I was so relieved to hear her voice when she took my hand and held it, it was comforting to me, so warm and so tender. All I wanted to do was to squeeze her hand with all the strength I had in my body to let her know that I was alive. Then suddenly she yelled, scaring the shit out of me.

"Oh my God! You moved! You moved! Doctor, Nurse, Somebody. She moved!" Gloria screamed.

I didn't feel anything, but I believed her.

"Look!" Gloria shrieked. "Pinky finger, moved!"

"Calm down, Mrs. Maxwell, you're getting too excited, I can't understand you. Take a deep breath and begin again," an unfamiliar voice commanded.

Hell, I agree. The way Gloria was screaming, I thought I

hurt her hand or something. She was losing her mind over the tiny movement of my pinky. I was totally disappointed because that took so much out of me to only move my damn pinky.

"I was holding her hand and her pinky finger moved, it just moved," I heard Gloria say.

"Only her pinky," the uncaring voice announced.

"Yes," Gloria exclaimed with excitement.

"Mrs. Maxwell, that's what the doctors call an involuntary movement."

Involuntary! Hell, now I was on Gloria's side. Tell this asshole this wasn't involuntary. I moved it. It wasn't my whole hand like I intended, but I moved it. I moved it, I shouted.

"Involuntary! Nurse, I'm sure she moved her finger. That wasn't involuntary, that was God."

You tell her, Gloria. I did move my fingers. Involuntary my ass, I shouted.

"That's why it's called involuntary, Mrs. Maxwell," the nurse said.

"Well I'll just wait and see what Dr. Harrison has to say about this. I'm sure he won't think it's involuntary. Thank you nurse, and have a nice day."

"Mrs. Maxwell, I was only trying to help."

"Thank you, nurse. Good-bye."

You tell her, Gloria. Don't let her push you around.

"Jane, I know it wasn't an involuntary movement. I know you are alive inside there. I just know it. The spirit of God lives in you, Jane."

"Thank you, Gloria, but get the doctor, I shouted.

"This means that you are on your way back to this world, and you have to keep trying to come back. I can't wait to hear your voice.

I'm trying, I'm trying, Gloria, but it ain't easy.

"Good afternoon, Gloria,"

"Harrison! Hello. Jane moved her finger."

"She did?" The doctor said unexcitedly.

"Yes, she did. I reached for her hand, and she moved her pinky finger."

"Has she done anything else? I mean open her eyes or move her toes, anything else at all?"

"No nothing else."

"I don't see that much has changed on the monitor but we'll keep a closer eye on her. I tell you what. I would like for you to start keeping a record. Write down every little movement with the date and times of her activities."

"So she's progressing, and it's not an involuntary movement?"

"Well, I don't want to get your hopes up, so let's just track her progression over time and then we can tell.

If it isn't involuntary then I'm sure she'll do it again, hopefully in a few days or so. Then I'll be better able to assess the situation

"Thanks, Harrison. I'll keep praying for her, and I'll most definitely keep track of her progression."

"Okay, Gloria, but don't get your hopes up too high. I have seen this in all of my coma patients."

"I know, Harrison. Thanks." Taking my hand in hers she said, "You hear that, Jane. He said that you'll be moving in a few days. I know you can do it, baby. You've come a long way. So what's a few more steps? Let's get to work and start concentrating on moving. I'm going to help you break through this bondage. But you will have to help me."

I'll do my best Gloria. I'll do my best. But concentrating was not easy.

My brain felt like it was on fast forward, moving too fast for me to keep up with my thoughts. I could hardly separate one thought from another.

Dr. Bradley Jyron, a neurosurgeon, arrived shortly after Thanksgiving. Gloria had him flown in from Warrenton, Virginia.

"Gloria, I've seen hundreds of patients with injuries as serious as this young lady, and I've seen many of those patients recover."

As they stood around my bed discussing my crisis, I could detect a slow sadness in Gloria's voice to the response of his findings.

"What do you suggest I do?" she asked.

"I suggest we treat her with severe aggressiveness," he stated, getting right to the point.

"Will that hurt her?" Gloria asked

Yeah, is it gonna hurt? Hell I wanted to know too.

"No, it won't hurt her, but you must be committed to spending hours and hours trying to get a response. Switching on and off lights, clapping and shouting. She will recover, however, she has to have the will to live. It's one of the chief factors in coma recovery."

"My God will give her the will to live." I heard Gloria state with a bit of firmness in her tone. She always stood strong when she spoke of Jesus, but cowered when she spoke of her own life.

"In that case, she's almost home."

"Well doctor, you've offered us a dramatically different prognosis from what we've been receiving from the local doctors. However, she's heading into her fifth month, and I'm getting a little scared. I read that coma patients who went to the third and fourth months could easily slip farther into an irreversible coma and die." Gloria stated.

Oh, shit, I thought.

"Yes, this is sometimes true. However I've read your journal, and I believe there is a ninety-five percent chance that she'll emerge from her state if you keep trying to reach her. But I have to remind you that once she wakes up, you are in for a long haul. A lot of hurdles will need to be jumped before you will see a change."

A few days later, more bandages were removed and Gloria brought in a bottle of oil that reeked of decaying flesh. It was warm and soothing to my sore muscles, but families started to complain about the smell, so she stopped using the oil.

And that was too bad, because one more day of that rotting stench and I was gonna get the hell out of there myself, coma walking if I had to. Wow! What a smell.

"You know, Jane," Gloria said to me while massaging my legs with warm cherry massage lotion, "Jackson is a butt."

The first time Dr. Harrison introduced me to you, I was wearing a cast. I didn't fall down the basement stairs. Jackson pushed me. He was always shaking me or twisting my wrist. But even though he's a butt," she signed, "I still love him. I'm only confiding in you because I feel a special bond with you."

There was a trace of kindness in her voice as we listened to jazz and reminisced about her past.

Chapter 3

"Merry Christmas, Jane," Gloria announced when she entered my room. "I see someone has raised your head for you. Very good." She sounded so cheerful and happy. "I brought in a Christmas tree for us with lots of decorations," she shouted with excitement. "Let me put these bags down so I can take out this special Christmas ornament that I bought just for you, sweetie." I could hear her excitedly rustling through bags.

Gloria had been keeping a dedicated vigil over my lifeless body for months.

Quoting daily scriptures and praying like there was no tomorrow for my recovery. It gave her a special place in my heart. She never stopped believing that I would wake up, or give her another sign that her prayers were being answered. The only sign of life she had to hold on to was so long ago, I was starting to believe it was truly involuntary.

At one point she became so desperate she was talking about organizing a larger prayer group, five times a week instead of the regular two. However she didn't have to, her prayers were answered.

I gave her something. I gave her the best Christmas present anyone could have ever given her. I gave her me.

When she turned around, our eyes met. She dropped the brightly colored Christmas ornament that was lying in her hands so tenderly. "Praise Your name Jesus!" pierced my ears, as she screamed with joy. She covered her mouth quickly with both hands to contain her shrieks of ecstasy, she kissed me, on my forehead, and I could see her eyes were filled with tears. A nurse came running into the room, along with the security guard.

People who were visiting friends and family came to take a peek. They were all standing around my bed gawking at me.

Gloria wiped the tears from her eyes with both hands, "It feels like I've spent a lifetime praying for you, Jane," she said, cupping my bandaged face in her warm hands.

I tried speaking, but only jumbled words escaped my lips. My heart was beating a mile a minute. I struggled once again to speak, but only gibberish could be heard. I wanted to reach for Gloria, just to touch her hands, but I couldn't move my arms.

Gloria screamed, clapped her hands, praised God, and did a little jig. Inside I was dancing right along with her.

My eyes were moving from one delightful face to another. Everyone had tears in their eyes. They were happy for me. For me, I said to myself. They were all excited that I was alive, and so was I.

Then the room seemed to go dark, when I spotted someone in the crowd. That face gave me a chill. I couldn't scream, I couldn't move. I stared, shouting in my head over there, over there, but no one heard me.

Then Gloria stepped aside, and from behind her appeared a tall dark skin man with no hair on his face, and his head was as clean as my hands. He walked right up to my bed and reached out to me.

I felt my heart stop beating for a few seconds, right before I thought I was going to pass out and die right there on the spot.

He touched me. Oh hell no, I screamed. Gloria was staring at me, but she didn't hear me. I was screaming so hard I gave myself a headache.

"Hi, I'm Dr. Harrison," he said, extending his hand a little farther. "Welcome back." He smiled, with horrifying straight, white teeth.

I stared at him. I was in shock. He was the one who had been haunting me in my dreams. He was pretending to be a doctor. I began to scream or make mutated noises. I just wanted him gone.

A familiar voice spoke from the crowd, calming me down. This big lady, with black hair streaked with gray, pushed her thick glasses closer to her face and bent down to kiss me on my forehead. My heart melted. Her voice was the last I heard before I slipped into the darkness.

"Hi baby. I'm Nurse Nelson, and I'm so happy to meet you. This is Dr. Harrison, and he's been taking such good care of you," she said proudly, with a big warm smile.

My eyes followed her face as she moved to stand next to Gloria, then it was back to the doctor's big bald head.

"Everyone out of the room," he said. Panic raced through my body. I wanted to scream, but nothing came out. My eyes moved from one person's face to another, screaming for help. Please don't leave me alone with him. But everyone kept moving toward the door. Then I saw Nurse Nelson and Gloria standing off to the side near the window.

"Please Gloria, please come over here and stand next to me." I tried to say, but I heard gibberish as the words tumbled off my lips. The doctor checked my eyes and my pulse. He looked in my mouth and nose. He passed his repulsive hands over my entire body, and I couldn't do a damn thing about it.

"Can you speak, Jane?" he asked

Well he wasn't too bright. I could speak I would have told him to get the hell out of this room and leave me alone, but since I couldn't speak, I stared at him.

"Blink once for yes and twice for no if you understand me?"

I blinked once. He smiled

"Do you know where you are?" he asked

One blink for the asshole. He smiled again.

"The lights are on and someone is home." Gloria said with a smile, and Nurse Nelson agreed with a nod.

That damn doctor did so much to my body, by the end of the day I was exhausted and wanted to go back to sleep.

"Jane, there will be a detective coming by to visit you in a few days or so," the doctor announced. "We know that you just woke up, but he wants to meet you and ask you a few questions. Do you understand?" he asked with a smile. I blinked once very quickly. I wanted to keep my eyes on that son of a bitch.

Gloria walked to my bed and put her hand on top of mine. "Don't worry. We won't let the detective bother you too much. I promise."

I closed my eyes once, very slowly, to let her know that I understood what she was saying.

That very night, when I thought everything was going to be alright, I had another dream, and this time that ten-foot monster was no joke.

He terrorized every inch of my soul, and when he grabbed me and began shaking me, there was something so familiar about him that scared me even more. I forced my eyes open to see his face and called him by his name. But all I saw was Gloria standing next to me, holding my hand.

"It's okay, Jane. Things are going to get better for you, and there are greater days ahead," she said. "Let not your heart be troubled. the Lord is your shepherd and you shall not want." She quoted those bible verses to me every day and night, I don't know why, I ain't a religious person, and praying hasn't changed my nightmares.

Though my days were hard and filled with horrible flashes of something that scared the hell out of me, and my nights were even worse, I still managed to take each day as it came and hoped for a better tomorrow.

And Gloria was right. I did have greater days ahead. By the New Year, I was in therapy once a day. I started sitting up a little longer and smiling a lot more. I was still communicating with my eyes, which was good, because I didn't have anything to say to Detective Monroe on any of his visits. Gloria kept her promise, and he stayed in my room briefly.

Dr. Harrison thought I was recuperating quite nicely. My ribs were healthy, and my broken arm healed just fine. He ordered solid food for me once I stopped throwing up the warm salty water they called chicken broth.

Gloria slipped in cinnamon, butter, and sugar, which was the only way I could tolerate the oatmeal. Shortly after that she slipped in real food. Thank goodness for people who didn't know how to follow doctor's orders. Fried catfish, hushpuppies with a side of collard greens, and peach cobbler from Mona-Moan's Fish Shack became my main meal.

One day, when Dr. Harrison came into my room, trying to bring me some good news, I cringed, not because I couldn't stand him, and he made my skin crawl whenever he got within inches of my bed. I was hoping that he wouldn't come any closer because Gloria had just returned from a catfish run.

"I arranged for a private rehabilitation therapist." he said, patting my leg. "Her name is Nikkei. She works for her sister at the

Le Day Rehabilitation Center, where you'll be moving as soon as you are able and ready." He paused and smiled. "At your rate of recovery, it might be sooner than we think," he said with an even bigger grin on his dark, round face.

He shook my leg gently, and chills ran up my spine. I hated when he had to touch me. Now he was putting his hands on my body when he didn't have to. I screamed, but of course, no one understood me. Not to mention when he shook my leg, the tiny cup of peach cobbler slipped off my thighs and the juice was sliding down between my legs.

While my mind was on the warm, thick cobbler juice, a tall, thin, light skinned girl, with a bright smile and a cheerful disposition, entered the room. "Excuse me, Dr. Harrison." She grinned.

I noticed that there was an Ace bandage wrapped tightly around her right wrist.

"Nikkei, I didn't expect you so soon."

"Will you be able to work with your wrist wrapped up like that?" Gloria asked.

She glanced at the doctor. "Yes, I'm okay," she answered.

"What happened?" the doctor asked.

She looked down at her wrist. "Skating. Shelly insisted that I wrap an Ace bandage around it just in case."

He chuckled. "That Shelly is something else."

The two of them smiled at each other, then the girl looked away.

"Shelly wanted me to wait another week, but there was no reason why I had to wait any longer. I wanted to get started now or at least meet her. Where is she?" the young girl asked so damn cheerfully, I wanted to scream.

Dr. Harrison stepped back, and the girl stepped forward. She greeted me with a big smile and a sparkle in her eyes.

"Hi, I'm Nikkei."

I closed my eyes slowly.

Nikkei was great. We were instant friends. She was fun and silly. She worked hard with me every day, and as long as I wanted to work she never complained. The only thing that bothered me about Nikkei was that damn purse that she worried about so much. It always had to be near her.

Still it was wonderful having Nikkei and Gloria in my life. I didn't know if I could live without them when the time came.

Gloria was always there for me for anything I needed, carefully putting each spoonful of collard greens or potato salad in my mouth, or catching the pieces of catfish that fell from my lips.

By the end of Nikkei's third week, I was eating by myself and catching my own catfish when it fell.

Gloria seemed thrilled to death with my improvements. Even Dr. Harrison was impressed. Happiness will be the day I can wash my own butt, I thought.

I started getting in and out of bed with the help of Nikkei and Gloria, who were right by my side for each step that I took, assuring me that I had greater days ahead. Even though I was grateful for them being by my side, there was still a large part of me that was so sad and so lonely, and the emptiness that I felt in the pit of my stomach was almost unbearable. I always felt as if I was on the verge of destruction.

CHAPTER 4

By Valentine's Day I was working with a more aggressive speech therapist practically every day, sometimes twice a day if I wasn't too tired. One night while Gloria and I were listening to the radio, I moved over and patted the space next to me.

"You want me to get in bed with you?" she asked.

I shook my head, and she gently climbed in next to me. We laid there side by side not saying a word, just listening to the music. I was exhausted, and all I could do was lay my head on Gloria's shoulder and began to doze off into a peaceful sleep.

"Febe," I mumbled sleepily. The sound of my voice scared me, but I repeated it. "Febe." Gloria jumped out of bed, stumbled to the wicker love seat and sat down with a big grin on her face.

"Your name is Febe," she shouted excitedly pointing toward me. "I understood you." Tears fell from her eyes and spilled down her cheeks. She was so happy to know my name, and I was happy just to say it, but I didn't like hearing that name any better than I liked hearing Jane Doe. But apparently Febe was my name.

Gloria was on the phone with Nikkei, and she also phoned Nurse Nelson at home. Dr. Harrison, who I now called Harrison was delighted with the news. He predicted I was on my way to a speedy recovery.

By mid-June arrangements were made, and I met Shelly Le Day, Nikkei's sister, and the founder of Le Day Rehabilitation Center. I was only saying a word or two, but I was well enough to move to the center.

Nikkei braided my hair into one thick braid that hung down my back, and Gloria went shopping for me. I had a nice wardrobe. She bought me just about everything that I picked out in the Sears, and J.C. Penny catalogs, and a great deal of extra stuff too.

When we arrived at the center, I have to tell you I was scared as hell, but Gloria held my hand as Nikkei wheeled me on a small tour of the rehabilitation center. After sitting through a boring orientation class given by Dr. Shelly Le Day, I was wheeled to my room. Bright pink and yellow colors floated through the room. It had every comfort of a home.

It was a little different from my hospital room. I had no windows, and a big yellow sunflower was painted in the center of the hardwood floor. Gloria's idea, I was sure. It actually looked like a real bedroom. You only knew you were in a rehabilitation center when you stepped outside of my room and saw strange-looking people roaming the halls.

There were only a few patients in the part of the center that I was in, and they were mostly stroke victims and mostly men, so I kept my distance. I felt more comfortable in my room watching TV or listening to the radio. I didn't want the patients to know me, and I had no interest in knowing them. So my room became my comfort zone.

Or at least I thought it was until I closed my eyes and tried to sleep. The dreams were not too bad. I don't know if I could call them nightmares, but it was definitely strange.

One time I found myself standing in the bathroom looking into the mirror, deep into the mirror, and someone was staring back at me. She was crying, begging me to let her come back. I stared back at her.

Then she began to peel layers of skin from her face. She reached out to me from the other side of the mirror, and that was enough for me. I started to get the hell away from her when I saw a cave and slid inside.

Gloria came into the room and found me hiding on the side of the daybed next to the wall. I jumped to my feet, ran into the bathroom, and switched on the light. It never occurred to me to look under my bandages, as I frantically pulled the gauze away from my face revealing the frightened woman's expression that was in my dreams.

"Febe, no!" Gloria yelled, trying to keep my hands away from my face.

I screamed and yelled. The soaring tones that were coming from deep inside of my soul were the sounds that I'd heard over and over in my head.

"My face!" I screamed. The scars were unbearable. I kept yelling and screaming.

Pain bolted through my body like a freight train. Suddenly I felt weak. A horrifying image of someone punching me in my face flashed before my eyes, the pain of his fist breaking my jaw like the speed of light. My knees refused to hold me up. I could hear Gloria scream and feel her struggling with my limp body, but I couldn't help her, I couldn't help me. Then I saw darkness all around me. I felt my body rising toward the ceiling and floating around the room.

When I opened my eyes, Gloria was holding my hand, and Nikkei was placing a wet towel on my forehead.

Gloria's red eyes told me she had been crying. I tried sitting up, but my head ached and my mouth was dry.

"Shelly had to give you a sedative. You've been out since yesterday," Gloria said in a choked voice.

"Yesterday?" I repeated softly.

"Yes," Nikkei agreed, shaking her head.

I looked over at Gloria and back at Nikkei. Shelly was standing with her arms folded across her chest.

"Why?" I asked.

"Why what?" Gloria repeated.

"Face," I mumbled.

Gloria's forehead wrinkled. "Why didn't we tell you about your face?" She glanced at Shelly.

I nodded.

Gloria bit her bottom lip, trying to hold back her tears.

"You never asked," she replied softly.

"Yeah," Nikkei said. "We didn't think it was important to you right now. Besides, you're so beautiful to us," she added with a smile and a kiss.

I looked away because her words meant nothing to me. I still felt betrayed by my friends, and I didn't speak to them for the rest of the day.

Weeks had passed and I was still refusing to see them, but I didn't have a choice in the matter. They kept coming in, bringing me gifts, combing my hair, and painting my nails. I didn't care, I didn't want their charity. I wanted to leave, but the reality was I had no place to go, and no memory of how to get there if I did leave.

Then one day Gloria came in to the room and sat next to me. She put her arms around my shoulders. I recoiled at her touch.

"Febe, I'm sorry that I didn't say something earlier, but Shelly said that you saw the scars on your arms and legs. Eventually you would ask to see your face.

So we were waiting for you to ask, and in time we no longer saw the bandages on your face. We forgot all about them. We only saw you, Febe, the young lady who we have grown to love.

So if you can please find it in your heart to forgive us then we can work this out." She spoke so softly and sweetly. "Forgive and ye shall be forgiven," she quoted.

I wanted to tell her forgiveness wasn't one of my strong points, but I turned my back and sat in silence until she got up and left the room.

A few days later Gloria sent a specialist in to see me. She assured me that plastic surgery would fix what was wrong with my face and body. The specialist said that it would be better to wait and let my blood-stained eyes clear up on their own.

For days, maybe weeks, I moved around the large room slowly, simmering in a funk, not really crying, just sulking all day and staying up all night.

I was afraid to go to sleep. I would only pretend to be asleep when someone came in to check on me so I wouldn't have to face them with torment in my eyes.

I was still refusing all comforting from Nikkei and Gloria, even though I could see the anguish on Gloria's face. It didn't faze me. I knew she wanted to help me, to take away my pain, but she would only end up crying, and I didn't care to see her tears. I remembered Gloria quoting something from her book of salvation. I think it was Job. "Neither shall thou be afraid of destruction when it cometh."

If I were a praying person, I would have prayed for destruction, because I didn't care about anything. I simply wanted to die.

I tried to hide my depression, but Miss I-wanna-be-just-like-my-big-sister-and-become-a-psychologist had to go and analyze me.

"Febe," Nikkei said one afternoon "your condition hasn't improved much in the last few weeks." She patted a bandage that covered a small slit on her upper lip.

I still wasn't talking, so I stared and pointed.

"Oh, I got this shaving my mustache," she said laughing. I didn't find her answer amusing. I rolled my eyes and looked away. She was always coming up with a new bruise or cut or something. I didn't think she was clumsy, although I had seen her fall a few times, but she still appeared to be stable.

"You've been caught up in this funk for days," she continued. "What can I do to help you? I love you, and I wanna help. Really I do."

I wanted to tell her that I didn't like those psycho sessions with Shelly. I wanted to tell her they made me crazy, that Shelly was prying into my head and I didn't want her there. I wanted to say all that, but she would have only heard mixed-up, wasted words, so I closed my eyes and pulled the blanket over my head.

Nikkei snatched the yellow comforter away from me. "Febe, listen," she shouted, "You were doing so well, and it's too late to stop now." Her hands were on her slender hips.

I stared blankly at her. She understood my gaze and calmed down. She spoke softly and touched me.

"I know that you're still upset about your face, but we had nothing to do with that. The doctors told us to wait until you asked about the bandages. So that's what we did."

I looked away from her, because that shit wasn't flying with me.

"Maybe we can start going for walks around the center and reading all those darn encouraging posters Shelly has posted all over the walls. It might raise your spirit.

Then we can go to the cafeteria and read the menu. I'm sure that'll improve your vocabulary."

"No face," I said sharply.

My thoughts were clear until they left my mouth, then they were just jumbled words. I used to repeat what I heard on the television, or songs from the radio, but it never sounded the way they were in my head.

"Febe, your face is fine," she said, kissing me on my forehead. "Now let's tell Shelly about my idea."

Chapter 5

Shelly thought Nikkei's idea to go to the cafeteria was wonderful and so did Gloria. However, Gloria wanted to take me to the mall for an all-day shopping spree instead of walking around the center, but the violent outbreaks and seizures I was still experiencing from the head trauma I couldn't go.

Shelly felt that I needed a little more time before exploring the outside world. And she was right, it was hard enough for me to see the pain on Gloria's face after I had a seizure. I didn't want to witness the fear on a stranger's face. Walking around the center was okay with me.

The next few weeks I played off my depression, but I was losing the game. That damn monster kept chasing me. And each time I turned a corner in my dream, that pitiful girl was reaching out for me. I felt like I was losing my mind. I wasn't getting any sleep. I would catch a nap here or there, but not often. I was afraid of what I might see in my dreams.

Terrified I might hear the roaring utterance of that monster asking me if I was scared of him, making me promise that I wouldn't disobey him again. I found comfort in music, because it was a constant noise, and no one was asking me any questions. I was becoming more paranoid by the minute.

Then one day I just stopped sulking. All my tears were dried up. I felt nothing. Gloria first noticed the change then Nikkei, who brought it to Shelly's attention. Just because I called her a flat foot-bitch and wished she was dead, she had to run and tell. Well, what I said was foot, bitch, and die. She understood.

I told her that I was sorry and didn't mean to say it. Well what I said was, "Sorry, Nikkei," but she told anyway. and that's how all three of us ended up in Shelly's office, sitting there like three bad little girls.

I wanted to tell Shelly that Nikkei was walking funny and that's why I called her that, but it would have taken me the better part of next month to explain Nikkei's limp, so I kept quiet.

A few days later, all three of us were summoned to Shelly's office. She put two fingers on the bridge of her nose, cleared her throat and stood.

"Gloria, and Nikkei," she said, walking around her oak desk and sitting on the edge of it. Gloria and Nikkei acknowledged her with a smile. I stared through the French doors, that led to the balcony where we would often have our sessions, in order to break the monotony of her boring office.

I continued to stare right past Shelly holding my gaze onto the Santa Monica freeway, for as long as I could, wanting to know so much about Los Angeles, but was afraid to find out what was waiting for me.

"Febe is still improving," I heard Shelly say, which caught my attention. "Let me clear the air about that." She looked toward the ceiling, stretching her neck and shoulders. "Coma patient's are almost never the same as before the coma. They are usually meaner than their families have ever seen them, uncaring and unloving, sometimes unremorseful for the things they might say or do."

"Why?" Nikkei asked.

"We don't know," Shelly answered. "But they are. This almost always occurs in a coma patient, especially when there is head trauma, but they do love the people who are in their lives. And that's the reason I brought all of you to my office today. I wanted to place all the cards on the table. If the two of you are planning on being in Febe's life, you are going to have to accommodate her behavior and mood swings until she can get them under control."

She walked over to me and looked me dead in my eyes. "Now that doesn't mean that you can mistreat your loved ones Febe," she said like a very stern mother. Then she turned back to Gloria and Nikkei. "This is all part of her recovery. If the two of you feel that you can't take on this burden, walk away now and let Febe fend for herself. It would be a lot easier in the long run," she said with her hands on her hips.

"I'm here to stay," Nikkei replied, blowing me a kiss across the room.

"Me too." Gloria smiled and kissed me on my cheek.

"Scared," I mumbled and dropped my head. Shelly walked back to me and knelt beside me. She put her hands on my knees.

"Febe, there's nothing to be afraid of. I told you that you're going to feel lost, scared, and lonely, but we're going to be here for you. We will help you to get back home."

When Shelly said, "Back home," the blood in my veins ran cold. I turned to Gloria and squeezed her hand.

Gloria wiped the tears away from her eyes. "We love you, Febe, and we are going to stand by you until the end."

And they did just that. It was a long road, and they stayed on for the long ride and the ride wasn't easy. My attitude made sure of that.

There was no fun in our lives for months. The nightmares and seizures began to take over my life. Sometimes I couldn't tell them apart. They seemed so real.

I became too afraid to close my eyes, even during the day and turning corners scared the hell out of me. Gloria and Nikkei promised not to tell Shelly about the nightmares until I was ready to talk about them, which had to be soon.

One morning after a horrible night of seizures and nightmares, after running from that damn monster with a mouth full of gold teeth and curly black slimy hair, I was tired and meaner than all hell.

Everyone was preparing for a Labor Day barbecue at the center and the opening of the new anger-management class.

I stayed in my room. There were too many strange faces roaming around the building.

I was lying on my back, looking up at the ceiling when I saw him from the corner of my eye. I saw him sneak into my room and slip into the bathroom. He stayed in there for hours, so it seemed. He was making noises, but they were quiet ones. I kept my eyes on that door, because I didn't know what the hell that creature was doing in that room.

Whatever strolled into my soul, I needed a priest to get it out of me. When the stranger finally emerged from his den of inequity, I picked up a lamp and hurled it at his head. Then I charged him like a three-hundred-pound line backer.

Nikkei busted through the door shouting, as I tightened

my grip around his neck. "What the hell are you doing? Get off him!" Nikkei screamed as she pulled me off the frightend man. I left tracks of my fingernails on his foul, evil face.

"What did you do to her?" Nikkei shrieked at the foul little creature.

"I didn't do anything," he shouted back, picking up broken pieces of lamp, keeping an eye on me.

"Why the hell is he in here?" I shouted at the top of my lungs. "Get him out! Get him out!"

"Febe, calm down."

"Calm down, my ass. If he don't get out of here, I'll throw another lamp at his head and this time I won't miss."

"Febe, he works here."

"Not in this room. I don't want him sneaking in here in the middle of the night. No, hell no. Keep that son of a bitch away from me."

"Okay, okay, go over there and sit down." Nikkei ordered pointing toward my bed. I climbed on the bed and sat on my heels.

Nikkei turned to him. "I'm sorry, but can you please leave. I'll speak with you later."

"Yes, leave, go back to hell where you came from!" I shouted, huffing and puffing like someone was chasing me.

"Febe, be quiet. Let me finish talking to him, then I'll talk to you."

I listened carefully as she told him to find Shelly and get someone else to clean up the mess. Then she turned to me.

"Okay, Febe." Nikkei took a deep breath. "Now tell me what's wrong with you?" She asked putting both hands on her bony hips, breathing as if it was her last breath.

"I don't know. He's a freak. He creeps me out."

"He's not a freak."

"Yes, he is. He's a stupid little freak."

"He's not a freak. He's a man, just like any other man you've seen, and you can't go around throwing things at people and calling them names."

"I can if I don't like him."

"How can you not like him? You don't even know him."

"I don't have to know him. All I do know is I don't like him."

"Febe!" Nikkei shouted.

"What!" I shouted back. "Shit, you scared me."

"You're talking!"

"And!"

"And I can understand you."

"Nikkei!" I shouted, sitting straight up on my knees in bed. Then I jumped to the floor, danced around a few times, hugging Nikkei like there was no tomorrow.

"Call Gloria!" I shouted. Nikkei hurriedly and dialed Gloria's number. I was on the phone screaming and shouting with Gloria just as Shelly strolled in.

"Shelly, I can talk!" I shouted. I dropped the phone, covered my mouth, and let out the biggest yell that I could find. "I feel so alive. For once in my life, I feel alive!" I twirled around the room and embraced Shelly.

"That's wonderful, Febe." Shelly said, holding my hand.

"Now you can call me Shelly and stop saying you."

I laughed. "Now I can say what's on my mind."

Gloria made it to the center in seconds flat. She raced into the room grinning from ear to ear, and joined in on the celebration.

"Thank you so much, Gloria," I said. "Thank you for being there for me the first time I opened my eyes. It was so wonderful to put a beautiful brown face to your voice. Thank you so much, my sister."

"It wasn't me, Febe, it was God."

"I'll thank your God later, but now I wanna thank you."

"And thank you, Febe."

"For what?"

"For coming into my life." Gloria smiled and pulled me into her arms. I could feel her warm tears streaming down her face.

"Febe!" Shelly said. "The road ahead is wide open, and now you can move forward. We can get started focusing on your past."

"Focusing on my past?" I repeated.

"Yes, remembering your past to get you back to your family."

"There's nothing for me in my past. This is all the family I need," I said, reaching for Gloria's hands.

"Shelly, I don't think now is the time to discuss her past," Gloria said. "Let's celebrate her freedom from bondage, the here and now."

Chapter 6

I had a small setback, as I held a mirror in my hand, examining the scars that lined my face. It was just another low blow to my sorry self-esteem, and I wanted to cry, but the disgust from my reflection would not allow me to shed one single tear for my past.

I was back at square one, walking and talking in a fog. It didn't matter to Shelly though. She was on me, prying into my past, searching for answers I didn't have.

She was a little tougher on me than usual. I spoke clearer so I should be thinking clearer, according to her.

Each day that Shelly drilled me about my past made my nightmares worse. Each question that she asked drew me deeper and deeper into myself, until I felt nothing.

The nightmares were changing me, and I didn't know what

to do about them. I wanted to tell Shelly, but then I wanted to keep it a secret. I was afraid of the power the dreams had over me.

One chilly morning I found myself sitting on Shelly's balcony staring at her beautiful soft brown skin, wishing I had what she had. She sat up straight and tall, her long black hair was styled to perfection. I admired her beauty and self-assurance. I knew she had to have confidence because she was wearing a spring dress in October, and Joan Rivers said that was a no-no.

I, of course, had on a long-sleeved black turtleneck sweater and baggie jeans. I would have covered my face if I could. I had no confidence, so it didn't matter to me what I wore as long as it covered the scars of my past.

"Febe, are you listening to me? I'll be leaving for Sacramento in a few hours, and I need to talk to you before I go," she said, breaking my train of thought. "What has gotten into you? Is there something that you need to tell me?"

"No, why?" I asked, suddenly looking at her.

"It's something in your eyes, Febe. The joy and happiness that was once there has vanished. You're covering it up with that false smile and that deceitful little chuckle. But I can see that you're trapped in another world, deep in thought, pondering something. Now, what is it?"

I dropped my head and twirled my thumbs in my lap.

"Tell me, Febe. I know something's there. Let's talk sister to sister," she said, setting down her pen and pad. She clicked off the tape recorder and stared at me.

I cleared my throat, and stared at my thumbs. "It's my nightmares," I uttered.

"Nightmares? You never told me anything about nightmares. Gloria and Nikkei never said anything about you having nightmares."

"I know, Shelly," I said softly. "I made them promise not to tell you, then I started keeping them to myself as much as I could."

"Why didn't you mention the nightmares to me before now?" she asked and got up to sit next to me and seized my twiddling fingers in her hands. "Why haven't you told me?" she asked again.

"I don't know. The nightmares are so frightening and controlling."

"How does that make you feel?"

"What?"

"To be controlled by your dreams. I know you once said that you would never be controlled."

"I don't know. They feel so much a part of me, I can't explain what's going on."

"So they feel real?"

"Yes, so real that when I'm sleeping I feel awake."

"Tell me about one of them, Febe," she said.

I shifted in my seat and looked away. I really didn't want to tell her, but I knew I needed help. I cleared my throat and looked back at her.

"They're always the same," I spoke softly. "I'm powerless. I cry out and no one hears. I speak and no one listens. I struggle to be free, then I realize that I'm only struggling with myself. I die over and over in my dreams, only to wake up and start over again fighting for survival."

"What do you mean that you struggle with yourself?"

"I mean the person that I am fighting with is a demon and someone who looks like me."

"Febe, you have a grieving process you have to go through, and you're fighting in order not to go through it."

"Says who, Shelly? Some damn book? Well this ain't no damn book, it's my life." I slammed my fist down on the glass tabletop. "I've done the grieving act and I put it behind me a long time ago," I shouted. "The old me is dead, and the new me has been reborn. I feel like Gloria when she found Jesus. Alive. I've accepted that part of my life, and now it's time for me to move on."

"You've been a victim of something horrible, Febe."

"No, Shelly, you're wrong. I'm a survivor of something hideous and I'm not denying that. The part of me that was injured will never hurt again. My life has been thrown out of balance."

"You need to know who did this to you, and why. Maybe that's what your dreams are telling you. You can't possibly live the rest of your life unbalanced. You have to put your life into the right perspective. You have to find yourself."

"That's where you're wrong. I don't have to find myself."

"Yes you do Febe. You have to put your life back together, put it back in balance."

"I'll never be the same, Shelly. I have no fears, only nightmares. Some people live far worse than I expect to live, and they're surviving, and so can I."

"What if you were a fun, loving mother or a cherished sister?" Shelly said with conviction.

"Your point is, doctor?"

"What I mean is. . ."

"What you mean is, what if I was a person who let everybody walk all over me. Would you want to return me to that person? The person who I'm fighting so hard to get rid of."

She was silent for a moment. "But what if you were a person who understood you can't always be right."

"What if I were a person who never fought back, then I'd be no better than Nikkei, screaming for help, but too afraid to ask for it. And what about your crazy-ass brother? According to Nikkei, JayR is killing up the world for a fast buck."

"Febe, that's not fair."

"No, you don't tell me a damn thing about what-ifs and fairness. You've got enough fucking what-ifs in your own life. So leave mine alone."

Shelly's face went blank, she stood and walked back to her seat. I stared at her with so much disdain it was unreal, then as fast as the contempt came it disappeared.

I reached across the table for her hand and she gently pulled it away. "Shelly I'm sorry. I didn't mean to be so rough with my words, but I don't think you understand what rehabilitation means to me."

"Maybe I don't, Febe," she said coldly. "But I'm here to help you, not hurt you."

"I know, but I don't want to bring back the old person. I want to create a new one. I have no intention of resetting the balance, and if anyone tries to, the consequences can be catastrophic. There's something frightening in my past. I can feel it and I'm not ready to face it, not yet. I know it's there, and I'll wait until it finds me. Shelly, I'm sorry for what I said about JayR. I know you don't like what he does for a living. I guess I was only trying to hurt you."

"That's okay, Febe. Let me ask you a question?"

I rolled my eyes and looked out over the smoggy city, then back at her. "Go ahead, I'm listening."

"Why didn't you speak with Detective Monroe?" she asked, looking me right in my eyes.

"I did. It's just the questions he was asking, I didn't have any answers. Besides he was so damn mean and rude, I lost interest in his questions."

"You were so mean and cold to him, he was only doing his job. If you don't help him, he can't help you."

"Shelly, once I can help myself I can be of help to him, but until then, I simply don't have any information for him or you."

She slowly shook her head in agreement and sipped her cold tea. I tried not to sound angry, but I was and I didn't even know why.

Chapter 7

Late one night when I couldn't sleep, and as always, I wandered to Shelly's office to sit on the balcony to enjoy soft music and the great night view of Los Angeles city lights. Suddenly, I became paralyzed with fear. As I approached the door, I could hear voices. My heart sank. Was it that crazy lady who was chasing me in my dreams? I quickly thought.

Then I heard a man speaking softly. My heart fell a little farther, and my shoulders drooped, as his demands continued.

"You have to stop seeing him, he's not right for you," The stranger commanded.

"He didn't do anything," she answered him sympathetically.

Realizing it was Nikkei's voice, I began straightening my shoulders and curling my fists into a ball to hold in the rage that was racing through my blood as I looked around for something to bash in his head.

"You can't come into my life and tell me who I can and cannot see," Nikkei spoke softly.

"Yes I can, and I will," he replied firmly. "He's no good, and I don't want you to get caught up with him."

"We're just friends, and I like his company."

"Nikkei, Kenny Blue is a thug. I know him. I ran with him." His voice was becoming dangerously loud.

I didn't have anything to defend her with, but I had to give it my best shot. I exploded into the room like a kung-fu master, slamming the door against a statue of a black-and-gold Siamese cat, breaking it into a million pieces. I knew Shelly was gonna be pissed, but I did have a memory problem, so I could forget about this little incident.

"Nikkei, is everything all right?" I shouted, trying to peer into the darkness for a weapon, with my hands in a karate pose and legs spread evenly apart.

"Yes, I'm fine," she answered, wiping the tears from her eyes.

"Stand behind me," I commanded. I couldn't see the man's face, but I could tell he was big—like the monster in my dreams. I really began to search the room for something to beat his ass with. I couldn't find a damn thing to knock him to the floor. His shoulders appeared so large in the moonlight, there was no way I could tackle him like the other tiny creature who slid into my bathroom.

This one was too big.

He stepped toward me, and I took one step back, still in my fighting pose.

"Hi, I'm JayR," he said. All I saw was a large hand stretching out to me through the darkness.

At that moment I felt trapped. I couldn't move, I couldn't scream. I was frozen in that damn Ninja stance. I better stop looking at those Bruce Lee movies, I thought.

"Febe, this is JayR, my brother, the one I've told you so much about," Nikkei said, stepping between us.
She put both of her hands on my arms and brought them to my side and sort of kicked my legs together.

"He came for a short visit. He won't be staying long," she said calmly. "Shake his hand, Febe. It's okay."

I took his clammy hand in mine and gave it a quick shake.

"Nice to meet you, Febe," I heard him say.

I nodded in response and headed for the door.

"I'm sure we'll meet again, perhaps on my next visit," he shouted. I knew he was laughing at me, I just knew it.

"Yes, perhaps," I answered and hurried back to my room.

Forty-five minutes later I emerged from my safety nest and headed back down to Shelly's office, where I found Nikkei looking through Shelly's file cabinet.

"Is the mercenary gone?"

"Independent bounty hunter, Febe."

"A murderer for hire," I corrected.

"Call it what you want."

"I'll call it the truth. And what's wrong with you anyway?"

"Nothing, I'm just tired that's all."

"Well come sit with me on the balcony. We'll listen to some of Shelly's CDs." I smiled and hugged Nikkei.

Around three or four in the morning I slid into my bed, with Gloria soundly sleeping in the day bed on the other side of the room. As soon as I closed my eyes, that damn monster started chasing me again. This time he caught me. He didn't waste any time with conversation. He slapped me with his large powerful hands, then punched me in the face.

He threw me to the couch and then dragged me through a dark house like a wild animal.

I couldn't get free. He picked me up and tossed me across

the room. I fell to the floor out of breath, I could feel sweat dripping down my back and beads of it forming on my forehead. My mouth was dry, and I wanted to cry. I wanted to be free. "Free, free, free." I shouted.

I saw a door in the distance and began to run toward it. I made it, but it was locked. I began to bang my head on the wood. And the demon disappeared.

Then I felt a heavy pressure on my shoulders. It was Gloria. She said nothing. She stopped me from thumping my head and laid on the cold floor next to me, holding me for what seemed like hours.

"I want to leave this place, Gloria. I want to go to your house, to that room you have waiting for me. I don't belong in this place. These people are. . ."

"I know, Febe, but you're still having those seizures."

"They're not that bad, Gloria. I haven't had one in a long time."

"What about the nightmares?"

"Nightmares ain't never killed nobody, Gloria."

"Febe, you have to take all those pills."

"Why are you making excuses? If you don't want me to go home with you, then just say so."

"I am not making excuses. What if I forget to give you your medicine? Then what?" she asked.

"We won't forget, Gloria. Please take me home. Take me away from here." I buried my head in her chest.

My pleas were soft and gentle.

"If I leave the center, then I can leave the nightmares."

"Febe."

"I only want to get out of here and start living, Gloria."

Chapter 8

Two weeks later Shelly returned from her trip, relaxed and pumped up. I had continued my daily sessions with another female psychologist during Shelly's absence and was doing quite well. She informed Shelly of my desire to leave the center. Gloria was the one who came up with the brilliant idea of letting me leave for a few hours a day, once a week.

Agreeing that was an excellent way to start the transition from rehab living to independent living, Shelly signed the papers. Gloria's place was enormous. The living room was stark white and gigantic. A large white leather couch sat in front of a colossal fireplace, and live green plants surrounded the room. I took off my shoes and walked around on the white carpet. It felt like I was walking on clouds.

White and cream candles were practically on every table. Pictures of Shelly, Gloria, Nikkei, and myself sat next to them. I immediately felt at home, like I belonged.

Gloria took me by the hand and led me to my bedroom. My mouth dropped open. A brass king-size bed sat in the middle of the floor, covered with lots of bright colorful pillows. There was a large, yellow wing-back chair like the ones Nikkei and I were always raving over in the Victorian magazines. It sat in a corner next to a table piled high with presents.

A CD player was in another corner of the room next to an open patio door. I let go of Gloria's hand and walked out onto the patio. I immediately felt the cool breeze of my sister's love hit my body. My emotion was so intense, I wanted to cry.

"Do you like it?" Gloria asked.

I nodded, because of the huge lump in my throat I could barely swallow, let alone speak.

Nikkei took my hand and we roamed from room to room, looking, gawking, and admiring the beauty as if we were children.

We walked up a staircase, with a black winding rail, that led to the second level.

"What's this space for?" Nikkei shouted downstairs to Shelly and Gloria, who were having tea in the oversize kitchen.

"It's not big enough for anything so we're gonna use it for a prayer room," Gloria shouted up to the loft.

"Oh," Nikkei replied and glanced at me. I shrugged. Hell I didn't think Gloria needed a special place to pray.

Nikkei and I ran down the stairs and out onto the atrium that gave me the impression of being the best view in the whole building. We were on the fifth floor, and when you gazed down you could see several large carp in a pond, right in the middle of the building surrounded by beautiful plants and flowers of all colors. I could stare down at that picturesque landscape for hours.

Soon, I was allowed overnight visits once a week. After another month, my overnight rendezvous rolled into long weekends. I was cheerful and happy in my new surroundings, but I became glum and moody when it was time for me to go back to the center.

One night while on one of my weekend vacations, a young man came to the door with a curly wig and bright gold teeth, looking like a New York pimp on drugs.

I froze, as fear ran through my body like a thoroughbred race horse, but Gloria handled it like a champ, reminding me it was Halloween, and the kid lived in the building.

By December, my condition had improved immensely, and the day arrived when Gloria took me to her three-bedroom condo, permanently.

After moving into Gloria's place, I did have a couple of little episodes, seizures, and violent outbursts, but Nikkei and Shelly often came by to visit and to help Gloria.

Watching TV and renting movies were my greatest aspirations in life at the time, until Nikkei broke her ankle skating and couldn't go to work for a while. Then talking on the phone became another one of my passions.

"I'm gonna teach you how to skate," Nikkei said.

"I don't think so."

"Why not?"

"Hell, you can't seem to stay off the ground enough for me."

"I hit a rock," she said, giggling.

"Yea, well, you always seem to be coming in with different cuts or bruises because of those damn skates. No thank you, I'll walk."

"Well suit yourself."

At that time Gloria entered the room, returning from volunteering at the women's shelter. "Gloria, what movies are you getting today?" I asked, after hanging up the phone.

"Febe, you need to learn to drive. I'm tired of getting movies and ice cream for you. Let me take a shower, and we are going to start your driving lessons today."

CHAPTER 9

Gloria learned to put up with my mouth, and I learned to control my temper through anger-management classes at the women's shelter where Gloria volunteered twice a week.

The first meeting was a joke and the shelter was an even bigger one. First of all, it was a huge two-story Victorian house built in the twenties or something like that. It reeked of sour piss and garlic. The women there were disgusting, plain, and pitiful. Snotty-nosed kids were always crying. That place was a mess.

The director of the domestic violence shelter, DeAnna Roberts, conducted the classes. After about a month of attending, some of the women at the shelter almost had me convinced that I was a victim of domestic violence, like them.

That was a joke. As far as I was concerned, my scars were from a very bad accident because there was no way a man could beat me and get away with it. I loathed men so much I would kill one before I let him touch me. So that discussion was dropped.

I stopped attending the anger-management classes, but there was something that drew me back to that place where I felt most comfortable. Gloria offered to pay me a salary if I volunteered, which I agreed to do, eight hours a day. DeAnna, the shelter director, was excited because she was in desperate need of volunteers.

Early one morning as I stood in DeAnna's office, which was the size of a small bedroom. My chest felt tight. I stared out a full-size picture window at a backyard that was cluttered with broken toys and swings.

The window was right behind what she called her desk, which was piled high with papers, books, old coffee cups, and empty diet soda cans.

To the left of me, as I stood facing the filthy window was a bookshelf that was built into the wall where the closet used to be. It looked as if a blind man had hung the shelves, and it was jam-packed with tons of books, magazines, and soda cans. There was even a baby shoe stuck between a cookbook and a housekeeping magazine.

There were no pictures on the walls, and the trash can overflowed with papers and more soda cans. The carpet desperately needed a good shampoo. Maybe then I could determine the color.

As I reluctantly took a seat on the steel-gray chair with a huge stain on the cushion, DeAnna and I talked about the shelter's rules and what took place behind the scene. She told me how many people she had on staff, and how they tried to build the women's self-esteem.

I tried to listen and pay attention, but I blocked her completely out of my mind as I tried to figure out what the hell I was sitting on, as something wet seeped through my jeans.

The next time we met, DeAnna led me into a room where a group of women sat around a large oak table crying, sniffing, and wiping their eyes. Their attention was focused on a tiny bleached-blond woman. Well I guess she was a woman, but she appeared to be only fifteen or sixteen years old. This group was much different from the anger-management classes I attended.

The young girl was giving a description of abuse by her boyfriend. Captivated by her story, I eased down in a clean chair and listened to the tiny blond child, who had a large black eye and one missing tooth. I felt nothing for her pain. She sort of made me sick just listening to her mushy voice.

"It was like a fix for him," she said, moaning miserably, as she ripped her tissue to shreds. "Like a junkie who needed a line of coke or a shot of heroin, he always needed to kick my butt in order. . ." She took a deep breath, sniffed and continued. "In order for him to feel better about himself, he was always beating me up for something." She sobbed into the shredded tissue.

Oh, brother, I thought as I listened to story after story. For the life of me I simply couldn't understand why these pathetic women stayed with men who beat them almost every day.

When I arrived home I told Gloria what I observed. She kept quiet as I rambled about these poor, pathetic critters.

"It just didn't make any sense to me. Why didn't they just leave, Gloria?"

"I don't know, Febe, but I thought that's why you went back, to help them."

"I thought so too, but their weakness makes me sick."

"Then don't go back."

"Maybe," I answered and went to soak in a hot bath.

A few nights later, as I slept, that damn monster started chasing me. I hadn't had that dream in weeks.

I could see his big black arms reaching out for me, and I ran for dear life. He was shouting, telling me that he controlled everything, I only had what he allowed me to have, I was nothing, and he was everything.

Forcing myself awake, I sat up in bed drenched in sweat. The darkness that I wasn't afraid of surrounded me. I eased out of bed and went into the kitchen to make a pot of coffee. I was too damn afraid to close my eyes, so I sat on my balcony and waited for the sun to come up, thinking about those poor women at the shelter, who I had spent almost two weeks with.

I realized that I was hooked on their pitiful, sorry lives. I would wake up in the morning thinking about them and go to bed at night hoping that things would change for the better. Gloria said I should stop hoping and start praying, but since I wasn't a praying woman I didn't waste my time. And there was nothing she could say or do to change that, but she never stopped trying.

On one particular Friday when I returned to the shelter I was informed that Judge Phillip Ranch denied a restraining order because there wasn't sufficient evidence. The victim went back home to her abuser. She was shot later that day. I sat up all night thinking about her.

By morning I had had enough of the shelter and agreed to go shopping with Gloria and Nikkei, Shelly tagged along as well. I wasn't in a good mood but I tried to make the best of the day.

"Febe, are you alright?" Shelly asked.

"Yes, I'm fine."

"You know, I think I'm gonna remove myself from your case and reassign it. I'm getting too close to you, and I don't think I'm doing you any good."

"No, Shelly, I'm fine. Besides, I know you only want to help."

"Maybe if you lighten up, Shelly." Nikkei interjected.

"That's what I'm talking about. I'm going to give her case to someone else."

"You don't have to give her case to a total stranger, just. . ."

Was all I heard, as we walked passed a black leather belt hanging from a hook. I cringed. A vision of being whipped and beaten in the face sent chills down my spine. I started to shake.

"Febe, are you alright?"

"Here, sit down."

"Let's just take her home," I heard Gloria say.

"But Nordstrom is having a shoe sale," Nikkei cried.

"This girl is about to have another seizure. Let's get her out of here." I heard Gloria yelled.

I was fine by the time we reached the car. I hung my head out of the window and let the air hit my face. The sun was gentle, allowing me to breathe again. On the way home I told them what I saw, and what made me shudder so violently.

"Did someone at the shelter tell you that story?" Shelly asked.

I tried to remember which woman told her tale of being beaten with a leather belt; I simply couldn't recall.

After Gloria opened the door to the condo, I ran right for a big bowl of Chunky Monkey ice cream.

"Maybe you should stay away from the shelter for a few days," Shelly suggested.

"Why?" I asked, dropping down on the sofa with the bowl of ice cream cupped in my hands.

Nikkei sat down next to me with a spoon. "Febe, that bowl is too darn big. You need to share." She smiled.

"Because," Shelly continued, cutting her eyes at Nikkei for interrupting her, "I think you're falsely identifying with the victims who you are trying to help, which is causing you not to be able to identify with your own reality."

The three of us sat in silence and stared at her, because we didn't have the slightest idea what Shelly had just said.

"Anyone wanna go fly a kite?" I suggested. They gave me the same look that we were giving Shelly.

"It's too cold outside, Febe," Nikkei said, with a mouthful of Chunky Monkey.

"And?" I replied.

"And you just had a crisis in the mall." She raised her eyebrows.

"Fuck a crisis. I wanna fly a kite." I grabbed my jacket and was out the door.

As time passed, layers of fear slipped away, and I began to come out of my shell, especially around strangers. I accepted an invitation to go to the beach and skate with Nikkei. Well, she skated, I walked. I didn't worry about my face when I was with one of the sisters or at the shelter. I just didn't think about it.

Nor did I worry about the horrible scars on the back of my hands when I reached for my change at the stores. I was stronger than ever before, and I wanted to start enjoying life and stop hiding behind fear.

My scars were my victory, and they made me fearless. Hell, I even said hello to the postman right to his face. I mean I stood right in his face and talked to him. I must admit the conversation wasn't very long, but it felt like an eternity to me.

Men still gave me the creeps, but I didn't hate the sight of them as much as I used to; I could tolerate them, if I had to. But the husbands and boyfriends of the women at the shelter was another story. I wanted them dead.

Every time I stared into my friends' battered faces, anger surged through my veins like hot lava. I knew something had to be done about this abuse and quickly. Especially when the realization hit me that Nikkei's boyfriend was the one putting all those bruises on her body and not her skating accidents, or the car door, or her lame excuses of just being clumsy.

The painful truth was told when Gloria and I received a phone call around two in the morning. I, of course, was awake because of those damn nightmares.

By the time we made it over to Shelly's and entered the house with our key, I spotted Shelly sitting on the floor with her knees bent and her head hanging down crying, sobbing like a three-year-old.

Gloria ran to her, and I headed for the guest room. I opened the door to the bedroom. The light from the hall gave way to Nikkei lying on the bed with her back to me, her shoulders moving up and down very slowly.

"Nikkei, I'm gonna turn on the light," I said softly.

"No," she replied.

"Nikkei, I have to. I gotta see your face."

"Febe, no."

"Why?"

"Because I don't want you to see me like this."

"Girl, I've seen your naked ass, and you're telling me I can't see your face. Give me a break," I said, walking over to her.

"Febe, it's bad, real bad," she cried.

"Let me be the judge of that." I reached for the tiny lamp that served as a night light, but somehow it changed into an illusion lamp because I couldn't have possibly seen what I thought I saw when I clicked the switch.

My hands immediately covered my mouth. I ran to the main light, and nothing had changed. Nikkei's face was a mess.

"Nikkei! You look like you were hit with a bat." I reached for the ice pack on the nightstand and applied it to her split lip. "I thought you were going to a barbecue."

"I did."

"Then what happened?"

"A fight broke out, someone hit me, and that's all I know."

"I can't believe you're telling us you don't know who hit you." She was silent and listened to me jump from question to comment. "Nikkei, I'm sorry, I can't imagine a total stranger walking up to you and punching you in your face. I mean your eye is swollen and your lip is split."

"He did, Febe, so leave it at that," she said softly.

"And you let him!" I snapped.

"What was I supposed to do?" she snapped back.

"You were supposed to pick up something and knock the shit out of him."

She turned her back to me. "Febe, please just go away."

"Go away my ass. What's his name?"

"Who?"

"Who! The person who took out half your face, girl. Who do you think I'm talking about?"

"I told you I don't know him."

"Nikkei, you're lying. Ain't no way a total stranger is gonna pop you in your eye for no reason and walk away. So what's his name, or what's the reason?"

"Well, that's the way it happened."

"Fuck that! Where was your date?"

"Hey, hey," Gloria shouted. "Why are the two of you fighting?"

I turned to Gloria who was standing in the doorway, with Shelly right behind her. "I'm fighting because I don't believe her lies." I turned back to Nikkei. "What's his name?"

"I told you I don't know. It was a fight and I got caught in the middle of it."

"Bullshit, Nikkei." I turned back to Shelly. "He's gonna kill her."

"Febe, calm down. What do you want me to do?" Shelly shouted, throwing her hands in the air. "Nikkei's a grown woman. I can't tell her what to do."

I kicked the wall with my foot so hard a picture of the four us, at the park, fell to the floor. "You gotta do something."

"What?" Shelly shouted, again.

"Hell I don't know. Go over there and kick the shit out of

that son of a bitch, kill him, do something to him, don't let him get away with this shit!" I screamed. "Nikkei, who is he? What's his name?" I charged at her. I don't think I would have done anything except shake the shit out of her, but she was making me so damn mad, playing the helpless victim, I could have screamed.

"I don't know. I don't know," she cried, curling up in a ball.

"You do know!" I shouted at her. "You do know."

Shelly grabbed my arm and turned me around to face her. "Who is he, Shelly?" I asked, my fury almost choking me. "Just tell me who is he?"

"I don't know," Shelly replied, shaking her head. "What are you going to do if you did know his name?" she exclaimed in irritation as she crossed her arms in front of her.

"I'll go over there and smash his fucking face in."

Shelly looked at me with surprise, blinked a couple of times, and then spoke. "You gotta be kidding."

Gloria tried to suppress a giggle as she rocked Nikkei in her arms. "She's not kidding. She punched the bag boy in the face just the other day."

"What!" Shelly's lips trembled with the need to smile.

"He wanted to take her bags to the car," Gloria continued. Shelly looked at me as if I had lost my mind.

"Maybe that's what that son of a bitch needs," I said, folding my arms across my chest and rolling my eyes.

"Who needs what?" Gloria asked, looking over the top of Nikkei's head.

"Maybe we need to find that stranger and beat the shit out of him. I mean do the same thing to him that he did to Nikkei." Nikkei sat up straight and looked at me with one eye.

"What are you talking about, Febe?"

"All I'm saying is do unto him as he has done unto you."

"Oh, so now you quoting bible verses," Gloria said.

"No, all I'm saying is smash his face in like he smashed hers in. Let him walk in her shoes just one time, then he can see how it feels to live in fear, to walk around with a gun always pointing at your head."

"Febe, please."

"No, Shelly. If he can be treated like a second-class citizen for one day, then maybe we can get a handle on this domestic violence, bullshit."

"So just what are you suggesting?" Nikkei asked, holding the ice to her eye.

"I'm suggesting that we take matters into our own hands and whip a little male ass. That's all I'm saying."

"Febe, please, go take your medication. I think you're hallucinating. Maybe even a little delirious," Nikkei said, waving me off.

"No, I'm serious."

"We know. That's what's so scary," Shelly added.

"No, listen. If these violent men can be treated the way they treat us, then maybe we might see a difference in their big, bad attitude."

"Febe, please. What movie did you see that on?"

"I didn't see it on no damn movie. I've been thinking about this for a while."

"Maybe too long," Nikkei added.

Shelly touched me on my shoulder. "What good would that do? They mistreat you, so you mistreat them."

"Yes, exactly!" I shouted with both hands in the air.

"And?" Shelly replied with her arms folded.

"And what?"

"And I don't get it. You are just exchanging one violence for another one."

"No, it's called self-defense."

"I still don't get it," she said and walked back to Nikkei.

"What is there to get? Work with me, Shelly. You're the

psychologist. It would do a lot of good. The women won't feel so helpless, so powerless, so damn scared all the time."

"Febe, you don't even have a man to treat you bad, so how can you say that?"

"And I don't want one—they are all no good."

"And how do you know?"

"Oh no, no, no, Shelly," I said, shaking my finger at her. "I know what you are trying to do."

"What?" she answered.

"You're working that psychology shit on me."

"I don't know what you're talking about."

"Be quiet, Shelly. Go on, Febe. Why do you think they're no good?" Gloria asked.

"It's just something in my gut that keeps spinning out of control when they get close to me." I walked to the window and looked down on the street. "I can sense only pain and destruction when I'm near them."

"Maybe it's something from your past, Febe," Shelly said.

"You think?" Gloria added sarcastically.

"Gloria please," Shelly replied softly.

"I don't know Shelly, but I just don't like them."

"Well we know that by the way you treated the man at my center. Poor guy, he didn't know what to do when you threw that lamp at him," Shelly remarked sadly.

One corner of Nikkei's mouth was pulled into a slight smile. "You should have seen her come at JayR with her karate stance," she added, trying to keep the focus off her and on me, and she was doing a pretty good job because all of them sat and laughed at that memory, but I wasn't amused.

"Well y'all can laugh if y'all want to, but I still can't stand most of them."

"Maybe you'll change your mind once you get more of your memory back," Shelly announced.

"There you go again, Shelly, wanting me to remember something that I want to keep hidden."

"I know, but you have to think about it at some point in your life."

"All I gotta remember is my medication every day."

"Don't you want to know who gave you those scars? Who did this to you?"

"Why?" I turned around to face her. "So I can beat the shit out of him for every black eye he gave me."

"No, so you can heal," Shelly said sorrowfully.

There was a peaceful calm surrounding me. Then Nikkei spoke, shattering the illusion.

"Maybe you were kidnapped. Maybe your family didn't pay the ransom and the kidnappers who were men stuffed your body in the back of that truck."

"Nikkei please," Shelly said in a whisper. "How many black people get kidnapped and held for ransom?"

"I saw it on TV," Gloria said.

"Turn off the darn TV, Gloria. You are the only one with money. The rest of us have to work for a living."

A cold chill ran down my spine with Nikkei's words. "What truck?" I asked. Silence fell on the room once again. This time it wasn't peaceful. I looked from eye to eye. No one said a word. I slammed my fist into the wall this time, rattling the windowpane.

"What fucking truck are you talking about Nikkei?"

"The one you were found in," she answered.

"I was found in the back of a truck?" I shouted. No one said a word. Suddenly a vision hit me with such force I fell to my knees. My body began to shake, as frightening images rushed through my head.

Gloria came to where I was crouched on the floor and put her arms around me. "I can see it," I said to her. "I can see someone stuffing me in the back of a truck. I can see through a tiny hole in the blanket. It's a man. I can hear him grunt as he pushes and shoves my body into something soft. His heavy breathing sounds like a beast, and I can taste the blood in my mouth, and it's running down my face." I felt my body shake as the quietness began to surround me. The bile in my stomach rushed to my throat. I felt an acute sense of loss and emptiness that was almost unbearable.

"Febe, you don't have to do this now," I heard someone say.

"Yes, she does, Gloria."

"No, she doesn't. She's shaking."

"That's okay, we can take care of her."

"Why is he doing this to me? Why is he hurting me like this?" I screamed as I felt his piercing claws jabbing at me.

"Can you see his face, Febe?" Shelly shouted above Gloria's rage.

"No, I can smell his cologne." The fragrance was choking me until I was breathing only his aroma. "Nooo!" I shrieked.

"What?" I heard someone say softly. Then everything went black. I didn't see anything anymore, no more visions and no more trucks, nothing but the shadows of three people standing over me. I began to focus on the silhouette of their faces. Their mouths were moving but I didn't hear what they were saying.

I held my breath, and closed my eyes, as one of Gloria's bible verses danced in my head. Her angelic voice was the first one I heard, then slowly Shelly's and Nikkei's voices filtered in.

"I'm sorry, but I have to take her home and put her to bed. Maybe you can have one of these séances another time, but for now she's going home, and if this is how you treat her when I'm not here, no wonder she hates your sessions."

"Gloria, if you move her she might clam up and never remember anything."

"I'm going to take my chances. I don't like seeing her like this. Look at her. Her eyes are all dark and sunken in, she's trembling. No! She has to do this another time, but not tonight."

"She's not your child," Shelly shouted. "She's a grown woman."

"I know she's not my child, but I will not stand by and watch her go through this."

"Gloria, take me home. I don't want to think about this shit tonight," I managed to say. "And Shelly, you concentrate on Nikkei—she's the one in trouble. I'm gonna be alright."

As I lay in bed wide awake with the covers pulled up to my nose, I tried to get my mind off that horrible image of my body lying in the back of a dark, cold, and lonely truck slowly dying. But I couldn't shake the vision.

For the life of me I couldn't imagine that person being me. I could see my face but it didn't feel like me. I thought as I eased my body out of the bed. I walked into the kitchen and heated a small bowl of gumbo, hoping that my past would vanish and leave me to my future.

One minute I wanted to know about my past, but at the same time, I was too afraid to face the truth.

I knew that truck and these scars had something horrible to do with my past, but the person in the back of that truck was helpless and scared, and that was not me. But there was no need to keep denying what my soul knew to be true.

I am a victim of domestic violence. The realization hit me with such force, it felt like someone had a foot on my chest. The gumbo began to taste foul and the smell made me sick. I put the bowl into the refrigerator, closed the door. I slowly walked back to my room and crawled into my bed and pulled the blanket over my head. I knew what I had to do. Find my past.

I'd find the fucker who stuffed me in the back of that truck. Shelly was right, black folks don't get kidnapped. Besides, I wasn't buying that shit. He had to be found.

CHAPTER 10

Gloria wants me to take my pain to her God. I thought as I sipped hot coffee, but hell, if her God was so big on helping folks,why wasn't He helping me to regain my memory? What did I do to get Him so pissed off that He had to put a curse on me? I refused her solution of praying. I was going to handle this my way. Hell had no fury like a pissed-off black woman. I sat my cup in the sink and clicked off Good Morning America. I headed right to Shelly's house.

Ringing the doorbell, and not waiting for an answer, I let myself in with the key. Yelling for Nikkei, who was on the phone in the guest room crying like a baby, I stood there listening to her conversation. I heard her apologizing for something she probably didn't do in the first place. My blood began to boil.

"Nikkei!" I shouted. She jumped and turned toward me.

Silence loomed between us like a mist. She blinked softly, and tried to ignore me, but she was caught between a rock and a hard place.

She couldn't hang up on him, and she didn't want to continue the conversation with me in the room. I left and went into the kitchen, poured two glasses of orange juice and waited by the bar for her to join me.

Moments later she walked into the room with her bathrobe hanging off her shoulders. Her hair was a mess. One sock was pulled up, the other crouched down around her ankle.

"You look like hell," I said.

"Good morning to you," she replied.

I didn't know if she was still mad at me because I demanded we do something about her situation, but her attitude wasn't sweet. I realized that Nikkei always had an excuse and it always made sense regarding the bruise that appeared on her arms and legs, or where ever they hid on her body. But this excuse I could not accept. So I took it upon myself to pay her a little visit today.

Shelly, of course, choose not to see what's right in front of her face and insisted that I was associating Nikkei's situation with the victims at the shelter.

"Nikkei, you know and I know that your mystery man is hurting you. Why can't you tell us who this person is?"

"Febe, it's too darn early to deal with this stuff this morning."

"It wasn't too early for you to apologize to that asshole who was on the phone." She turned away from me with tears in her eyes. "So why can't you tell me his name?"

"Just let it go." She grabbed the glass of orange juice.

"I will not let it go!" I shouted. "Just tell me his name."

"I can't,"

"Why?"

She fell to the floor sobbing into her hands. The drama was something else. "Because he's married," she cried.

I ignored her little performance, drank some of the orange juice, and continued, "Listen, I don't care if he's married to the queen of Egypt. He shouldn't be hurting you like this. Look at you."

"Let it go Febe, you don't understand," she wailed, hitting her fist on the tile floor.

"Oh, somebody give this fool an Oscar," I said and clapped my hands, staring at her. "You're right, I don't understand and no, I will not let it go."

"If he finds out that I've told you this much he'll kill me."

"Then let's call JayR."

"No, no, we can't call JayR," she said, struggling to her feet. She seemed almost out of control, as tons of tears poured out of her eyes.

I continued my interrogation anyway. "And why not, Nikkei? You said JayR could handle any problem, and this is a problem."

"No, we can't get JayR involved." She threw the words at me like stones. "I will not have his blood on my hands." Her nostrils flared with fury.

Oh, hell no, I thought slamming the orange juice glass on the counter so hard it shattered. "Damn it, Nikkei! I won't have your blood on my hands. You think I give a shit about some married man. Hell, his wife should be grateful that I'm gonna stomp a mud hole in his ass. If he's hurting you, then he's hurting her."

I stared into her pitiful brown eyes with so much contempt I could have strangled her. When she backed down, I realized my stance so I dropped my shoulders.

"Febe, just give me a little time to think," she said, grabbing my hand. "I have to figure a way to get out of this situation."

"Just leave."

"It's not that simple."

"Why?

Just stop seeing that son of a bitch."

"I can't. He loves me."

"He doesn't love you, Nikkei. He controls you with his promises that it'll never happen again, then he sweet-talks you back into his bed."

She lowered her head. "I know," she mumbled.

"If you know that's what he's doing, why do you go back?"

"I can't explain it. He's a wonderful guy as long as I don't make him upset," she added, cleaning up the broken glass. "He's helped me out a lot more than you know." We stood in silence.

"Did you cut your hands?" she asked in a low, tormented voice.

"No, I didn't," I snapped. "Why don't you go to the police?"

"Because."

"Because what?"

"If I go to the police, he'll destroy this family."

"This family!"

"Me. He'll destroy me."

"JayR can handle it, you said so yourself."

"You don't understand. If you go to JayR, I. . .I just don't know what will happen. JayR is a crazy man. He pretty much stays away from us because he knows Shelly doesn't approve of what he does for a living."

"And you approve?"

"I understand JayR. He was a bounty hunter a few years ago. He walked into the wrong house, a man was killed, and he served his time."

"Now he's a mercenary. Some rehab."

"I don't care who he is. He's my brother, and besides, I know he won't hurt unless someone hurts first."

"And if the money's right?" I added.

"Well that goes without saying, Febe." She spoke with a light bitterness and rolled one eye because the other one was still a little swollen.

"Well whatever. The point is, what are you going to do about your problem? I mean I can't sit back and watch you keep getting hurt like this. You may have the others fooled by your lies, but you're not fooling me. So what are you gonna do?"

"Febe, I just need a little time."

"Nikkei, you're running out of time. I gotta get you some help. Come to the shelter and talk to some of these women, then you'll see what you're up against.

"Oh no, that's not for me, and I can't have anything like this getting out. Think what it will do to Shelly's business. Just give me a little time, Febe, please."

When she touched my hand, fear and anger knotted up inside of me. "Please, Febe, just a little more time." I also saw the pain in her eyes. So I backed down.

"Okay, okay. I'll give you some space, but the next time I see one mark on your body, I'm calling JayR, and we'll deal with the consequences. And that's a threat, baby girl. Oh, and if JayR calls first, then it's on, all bets are off," I said folding my arms across my chest.

Nikkei was silent for a while, her head hanging down. She mumbled something.

"Excuse me, what was that?" I asked. "I didn't hear you."

Tears were blinding and choking her. "I love him. Why can't you understand that I love him?"

"Love, love!" I shouted. "Love hurts when it's coming from his fist, Nikkei! Why can't you understand that?"

"Febe, I'm not like you. I need a man in my life to make me whole. I need the warmth of his hands."

Once again I was assaulted by her sick yearning for this son of a bitch. Her words felt like a fist in my chest. "Those are hurtful words, Nikkei. I would rather not feel the warmth of his hands if it leaves my face stinging, sister."

I kissed her on the cheek, smoothed back her hair, and walked out of the kitchen into the dining room, where I saw Nikkei's purse sitting on the table. I was suddenly overwhelmed with rage from her statement. I knocked it over, spilling everything onto the floor, smiled, and walked out the door.

I made it to the shelter as the first group session was about to end. There were more women than last week sitting around the table sharing their stories. As I listened to them crying and consoling one another, I couldn't help but think about my conversation with Gloria and Shelly. What if we could turn the tables on the men and make their lives a living hell?

What would that accomplish? Nothing, I answered my own question, but it sure would make a great deal of women happier. I simmered in that notion until DeAnna broke my train of thought.

"Febe, do you have anything you would like to add to the group before we close?" she asked.

I stood slowly, adjusted the sleeves of my sweater, and searched so many wet faces in that tiny room I wanted to cry. I cleared my throat before speaking. "Do you want to know what I see?" I asked, and no one said a word. "I see a room that's filled with terrified women, women who have let men take control of their lives. You let them tell you what to do and when to do it, what to say and how to say it."

I pointed to a beautiful overweight lady in her mid-forties. Her eyes were cold and unresponsive. Her left eyebrow rose a fraction.

"Dora, you made a comment to a few of us last week after the group meeting, and we agreed that you should share it with the rest of the women today. Can you please do that now?" I asked softly.

She cleared her throat and mashed her ruby-red lips tightly together. You could barely see the dimples in her chalk-white cheeks.

She spoke softly. "Well I said that I didn't want to lose

weight. If I did, then my husband would be able to throw me around even more than he does now. So my weight is my comfort zone, it protects me from him." She looked down at her stomach which was lodged into the table. The room was quiet as everyone stared down at their hands.

"Thank you, Dora," I said, winking at her. She smiled, and her lips became a thin red line.

"Sylvia, you said your husband held your hands in scalding hot water until they peeled, and your family did nothing to help you."

"Yes, yes, he did," she replied, holding up her hands so the group of women could see the pink healing flesh. "And my mother asked me, what I did to cause him to hurt me," she added.

"By applause, if any one of you had the chance to get back at those who hurt you without them knowing you had anything to do with it, would you?"

Some of the women started clapping and cheering, while others looked frighten, as if their other half might overhear them.

"Febe!" DeAnna shouted.

I could hardly hear her over the women's enthusiastic approval. DeAnna held up her hands to regain control over the group. They started to calm down a bit.

"That's not what this group is about," DeAnna added peacefully.

"I only wanted to know how they felt if we could make these men suffer for just one day, to live in fear for just one moment of their lives."

"We are not about revenge, Febe."

"Then what is this bullshit about? Teaching women how to survive in a domestic violence relationship, how to turn the other cheek, only to be hit again?"

"Yes, I mean no. I mean. . ."

"What you mean is, you don't know, but you want to help."

"Febe, this isn't right. We can't preach violence." DeAnna was shaking her head. "We just can't preach violence."

"I'm not preaching violence. I'm simply asking a question."

"And I like the question." A dark skin woman jumped to her feet. "My old man has taken a gun to my head many nights, and I finally got the courage to leave him. Granted, I'm practically homeless and my kids live with my sister, but I'm free of his bullshit. Now, I have to free my soul so my mind can follow."

The room burst into a roar of cheers, and DeAnna went ballistic.

"No! no! no! This is not right. We are not learning anything if we treat violence with violence," she shouted over thundering screams that came from a group of excited women.

Sulee, a little old Indian lady with a red dot in the middle of her forehead and a black scarf around her face, began to speak. She came to every meeting along with a few other women from another shelter, but she never said a word. It was house rules if you lived in the shelter, you had to attend the meetings. So she attended, but never spoke.

The women quietly stared at Sulee.

"My husband has been beating me for years. He dragged me around the house by my hair and demanded I not cry. When I couldn't stop the tears, he threw me to the couch and shouted words in his native tongue that I didn't understand. Last month he got angry with me, after I found out that we had been divorced for two years.

I told him I didn't want to live with him if we were not married. I wanted him to leave the house. I was going to let everyone at his practice know what he had done to me for so many years, but he beat me up and put me out on the streets. The shelter took me in."

Sulee kept her head down the entire time she spoke.

"He said that he had already married someone else and was

building a new home for her, and he was going to move in with her as soon as our home sold. I was no longer appealing, and he needed a pretty face to look at in the morning."

She stood and slowly removed the scarf from around her brown round face. There was a large scar right above her left eye just like mine. I reached up and felt my scar. Large plugs of hair were missing from her head, and something was indeed wrong with one of her eyes. She was also missing many teeth.

"If you ask me if I want my husband to die, no. If you ask me if I want him to be homeless, no. If you ask me if I want him to live in fear every day of his life. . ." Sulee became quiet and dropped her head. She brought her shaking hands to her left eye and then raised her head. She stretched out her arm and opened her hand. In the middle of her palm was her eye. "Yes." She closed her fingers into a fist. The room fell deathly still. She reached for her coat and began walking slowly toward the door. Stopping and gently turning toward DeAnna, she spoke softly, "I'm only thirty-five." Then she walked out of the room.

I drove home as fast as I could to tell Gloria what I thought was good news. "Gloria, Gloria!" I shouted as soon as I entered the house, kicking my shoes to the side. "I can do it. I can make it happen."

"Febe, can it wait until after dinner?" she asked as she took the tray out of the oven and set it on the table next to the salad. "I made lasagna," she added with a smile.

"Sara Lee made lasagna, Gloria. You turned on the oven."

"Okay, if you wanna be that technical about it, I turned on the oven. Now sit your butt down and let's eat," she demanded, pointing to the empty chair across the table.

"Okay, but let's talk about it now," I said excitedly.

"Let's pray," she added and grabbed my hand. I studied

Gloria chanting to her God, and couldn't understand why she bothered. Then she piled a massive salad on my plate and plopped down a large block of ice with red sauce, cheese, meat and noodles sticking out of it.

"You should take some cooking classes. This mess is frozen." I pushed the plate away. "Sara Lee should come over here and shake the shit out of you for messing up her frozen dinner."

That's when it hit me I wasn't thinking those words I was speaking them, but what could I do? They were out and I knew I had hurt Gloria's feelings.

"Febe." Her tone was disapproving.

I looked up at her. I knew a lecture was coming. She bunched up her lips and shook her head, pushing the plate of frozen food away from her and folding her arms across her chest. She said, "This is the food God has provided for us, we have to be happy with it."

"Yes, Gloria, and I'm sorry. I didn't mean for that to come out."

She smiled. "What's your news?"

I swallowed. "Well tonight in the group meeting I asked the women if they would like someone to get revenge on the men who beat them, and I almost received a standing ovation."

Suddenly she bounced to her feet, and I stood to mine.

"Vengeance is mine said the Lord. Let him handle it," she shouted.

"Well, vengeance is going to be mine for a while."

"Febe! You can't go asking people stuff like that, and you can't go around hurting people because they did something to you. Are you insane? I've never heard anything like that in my life. How in the heck are you going to pull that off, girl?"

"First of all, I think it's a great idea. I'll teach these bastards they can't go around beating on women, making them live in fear all their lives, and get away with only a slap on the wrist."

"They go to jail, Febe. You know, prison," she said, slapping the back of her hand in the palm of the other one as if she believed her words.

"Yeah, if the women ain't too fucking scared to do something about it."

"Watch your mouth."

"Okay, but I think the men should pay. Even your God said an eye for an eye and a tooth for a tooth."

"Febe, what are you talking about?"

"Do unto others as you would have them do unto you," I said, smiling. Gloria grabbed her chest and almost fainted. "Stop being so dramatic."

"Dramatic! Febe, you're about to start killing folks and I'm being dramatic! Do you know what dramatic means?" she asked.

"Gloria, we have to help these women. Some are too scared to call the police and press charges."

"And you think your method is going to stop domestic violence?"

"Hell no! domestic violence ain't never gonna stop, but my method will help to put some fear and pain into these bastards' lives."

"And?"

"And, they might think twice before kicking somebody in the head with their boots."

"So what you're saying is if they think they might get their butts kicked, they might think twice about hitting a woman?"

"No. If they know they're gonna get the shit beat out of them every time they raised a hand at any given moment in life, they will think twice about hitting."

"Yeah right, Febe."

"Stop shaking your head. It can work."

"I know you better think of another way to help these women at the shelter. I mean what if these guys found out who's doing this to them, then what?"

"Kill them."

"What!" she shouted, almost falling to the floor. "You can't go around killing people. What is wrong with you?"

"I can."

"Febe, you're heartless."

"No! That's where you're wrong. Being beat until you don't know where to run and having no place to hide is heartless. Being beat until warm piss runs down your leg, that's heartless Gloria. Wanting to get back at the person who caused the pain is—."

"Let the Lord handle it, Febe."

"Oh, please. Gloria, don't stand there like you're letting the Lord handle everything. I remember you told me that Jackson pushed you down the basement stairs and that's how you broke your arm. Where was your God then?"

"Febe."

"Yes, you did. So don't pretend you don't know how it feels to be afraid. The only difference between you and the women at the shelter is you got out before it was too late. They didn't, I didn't, and that makes me one of those women."

There was a massive amount of silence. Gloria stared at me with her mouth open. I couldn't believe I blurted out something that had been haunting me for weeks.

"Febe, when did you realize you were a victim?" she asked, astonished.

"I've been in denial, Gloria, but the truth is the truth, and I'm going to do something about it. I have to do this, not just for them, but for me. I will find out who did this to me, and he will pay."

"Febe, you can't," she begged.

"Yes, I can!" I shouted through clenched teeth. "Yes, I can."

Gloria took off her apron and very calmly began folding it.

"Febe, if you do I'll have to turn you in," she said, never looking at me.

"You can't," I said matter of factly.

Raising her eyes to me, she asked, "Why not?"

"Because Jackson wants to be a judge."

"And?"

I raised my left eyebrow. "And you don't want his name to be tied to being a wife beater, now do you?"

Her expression softened, her shoulders dropped, and her gaze went down to the floor, as she unfolded her hand and slumped down on a kitchen chair. "You wouldn't."

"Try and stop me, Gloria." Her apron fell to the floor.

"You'll ruin his career for some woman you don't even know?" she asked. "I thought we were family."

"Gloria, we are, but someone has to help these women and that someone is me. I'm their, Joan of Ark." Throwing out my sympathy card to win some brownie points, I said, "Gloria, I was battered, and it took strangers to come into my life to help me. Why can't I be the stranger for them?"

"Febe, we didn't hurt you, we helped you, and we encouraged you."

She was right. They didn't hurt, they helped. I couldn't think of a good comeback line, so I knelt beside her and placed my head in her lap. Whenever I humbled myself to her, she always softened.

"You know your past. I have to find out bits and pieces of mine each day. I have to write down memories and flashes of my past every day, because they might be pieces to the puzzle of my life."

"But vengeance is mine said the Lord," Gloria repeated softly.

"Then I'll pretend to be Him until I'm satisfied."

She was silent, slowly smoothing the stray hairs away from my face, calming me. Breaking the silence, Gloria said, "Why didn't you come to me and tell me that you were hurting this badly? Why didn't you talk to me? Maybe I could have helped you before you got on this vengeance kick."

I raised my head to look into her eyes. "How can you help me, Gloria? Can you put a name to the faceless monster who did this to me, who's still haunting me in my dreams?"

"Forget about him, Febe. Who cares anyway? You can't remember him, and he's probably forgotten you."

"I can't forget him. I don't even know if Febe is my real name, but what I do know is he's taken something from me, and I want it back."

"What has he taken from you, Febe?" she asked softly, taking my cheeks in her hands, as tears streamed down her soft, dark face.

I looked up at her. "He's taken my life, Gloria," I cried. "He's taken my life."

"He tried to take your life, baby, but God gave it back to you."

I removed her hand and placed it in her lap. "What good is my life without a heart?"

"Febe, you have a heart, a wonderful heart."

"I don't have love in my heart, Gloria."

"Yes, you do. It's just a different kind of love."

"No, I want the kind of love that Nikkei is always talking about. The kind of love you have for Jackson. I know you've been seeing him."

She scratched her head and looked away, then back again.

"First of all, Nikkei is a little horny toad and she talks about sex too much. And yes, I have been seeing Jackson and yes, I do love him. But, I love you, too, and I can give you everything you need."

"Can you give me love like a man gives a woman?"

She leaned back in her chair and closed her eyes for a moment. "No, I can't."

"So how in the hell are you going to give me everything?" I shrieked and walked toward the cabinets.

"Loving a man and being loved by a man isn't everything."

"No, but it's a part of life, just not mine."

"I don't know, Febe. I can only do what I can do," she said I slammed the doors to the cabinets and searched through the drawers. "And that ain't shit, Gloria."

"What are you looking for?" she asked.

"What?"

"What are you looking for?"

"My damn cigarettes."

"You're smoking now?"

I slammed the kitchen drawer. "No, I'm not fucking smoking, Gloria, and what if I were? Are you going to tell me what a big sin it is to smoke! Is there something in your bible about smoking, Gloria?" I shouted and stormed out of the kitchen.

Plopping down on the couch, I crossed my legs, swinging my foot back and fourth.

"You've never lifted a finger to help anyone but yourself," I shouted into the kitchen, "until you accidentally stumbled across me, your little charity case. Now all of a sudden you're Florence fucking Nightingale come to save the day."

Gloria appeared behind me out of nowhere. I didn't even hear her enter the room. "Febe, you can't talk to me like that," she said calmly. "I wasn't the one who put you in this situation. But I'm the one who reached out to help you, and every chance you get, you try to make me feel bad about who I am and what I choose to do for you."

"Gloria, I don't want your charity speech," I said and threw up both my hands. "Save it for one of those nights when you and Jackson give something useless to Shelly's rehab center or the hospital, or the fucking shelter."

"You will hear me!" she shouted, pointing her finger in my face, with her left hand on her hip. "I don't have to take this from you. I thought we had something here. Sometimes you act as if I'm the best thing since breathing. Then other times you act as if you hate the world, me included." She crossed her arms over her chest and held back her tears.

"Maybe I do," I remarked, rocking.

"That's fine with me. Go on and hate the world, see if I care, but let me know if you hate me, then I can step out of this drama you call a life."

"That's what you want to do, isn't it? Isn't it, Gloria?" I shouted, jumping to my feet. My heart was racing a hundred miles a minute.

"No, Febe, it isn't what I want to do, but that's what you're making me do. Your attitude has become horrible lately." She uncrossed her arms. "How can anyone love you? It's hard to believe you're the same person who woke up from that coma just a year ago."

"Maybe I'm not the same. I know I'm not the same person who was stuffed in the back of that damn truck. I'm not the same person who took all his shit for all those years."

"Febe, I understand that, but I'm not the one who did those things to you. You have to deal with him, but don't take me through the crap with you."

"Take you through what, Gloria? What am I taking you through?"

"Febe, I know about the abuse in these women's lives, but sometimes living with you, I feel like I'm being abused. Not physically, but mentally and verbally."

"That is not true!" I shouted.

"I fail to see the difference, my dear."

"Gloria, you think you're all that. Running around quoting bible verses, praising God, and giving money to shelters, which you said Jackson only gave for the tax write-off. You think you're so great, so much better than the rest of us." I smirked and threw my hair over my shoulder.

"No, you're wrong. That's your way of thinking. That's why you can judge me so harshly, abuse me, and make me feel like one of those helpless women in DeAnna's shelter. You are no better than the abuser. You need to add your name to that list."

Her words hit me like a lightning bolt. I fell to the floor. She ran to my side, and I looked up at her. "Gloria, I didn't mean to treat you bad. I love you." She reached out for me and pulled me into her tiny bosom.

"It's not just me, Febe. What about Nikkei?"

"Nikkei! What did I do to her?" I asked softly.

"Shelly said you went over there today and the two of you had a big fight. Nikkei cried for most of the day. Febe, we are all trying to help you, but you're fighting us all the way."

"I was only talking to Nikkei."

"Did the two of you have a fight?"

"Yes, but it wasn't anything serious."

"What did you say to her?"

"I told her if she didn't leave that guy alone, I was going to call JayR and tell him how she's letting that asshole beat on her."

"And?"

"And she was a damn fool if she thought I wasn't gonna call him."

"Febe, what did Shelly and I tell you about your mouth? You can't go around saying whatever is on your mind to people, whether you agree with them or not."

"I was only telling her the truth. That guy is going to kill her. I don't understand, Gloria. Why is she so headstrong for him? He's a creep."

"Yes, but he's the creep she loves, and we have to deal with it until she can see the light. Besides, we can't say he's the one who's putting those bruises on her. She is a little clumsy."

"But he is the one who's hurting her. I can feel it."

"How do you know he's the one?"

"Because I overheard JayR threaten to kill the guy if he kept hurting her."

"And that means what?"

"That means JayR believes there's someone behind her bruises and not just her overactive lifestyle. Why can't you see that? Why can't Shelly see that too?"

"What is there to see? Nikkei said no one is hurting her, and you say there is."

"But there is, Gloria, there is," I cried.

"Febe, baby, listen. We have to respect Nikkei's right to privacy, and we have to respect her decision to be with that man."

"Right to privacy, decision to be with that man. No! Hell no! He has to respect her right to live safely."

"We have to mind our business."

"Minding our business will get her killed. She is our business!" I shouted.

"Febe, listen, just call over to Shelly's and apologize to Nikkei. Then maybe we can start fresh."

I thought for a while, and maybe Gloria did have a point. When I jumped on Nikkei, I was a little pissed off. "Okay, I'll call and apologize. Not for calling him names, but for my behavior."

I reached for the phone. Gloria turned and walked over to the fireplace.

"When are you going to buy another phone?" she asked.

"What are you talking about." I frowned.

"You were the one that threw the phone across the room and broke it."

"This phone still works."

"Febe, only the speakerphone works.

"Okay I'll buy another one."

"When?"

"I don't know," I snapped, punching in the last digit of Shelly's phone number. I quickly glanced up at Gloria, who was running her fingers through her hair.

The phone rang five or six times before someone answered it.

"Hello, hello." An intense voice spoke into the phone.

"Shelly?"

"Yes."

"It's Febe. Is everything alright?"

"She's gone, Febe. She's gone," Shelly cried.

"Gone where?" I repeated.

"I don't know. She just ran out of here after she finished talking on the phone, and I didn't like the look in her eyes."

"Did you follow her?" Gloria asked.

"No, I didn't. I didn't even think about it," she mumbled softly.

"Did you call the police?" I asked.

"Yes, but they said she is an adult and she can come and go as she pleases."

"If she's not back by tomorrow, call the police again," Gloria demanded. Shelly was quietly sobbing.

"Shelly, did you hear me?" Gloria asked.

"Yes, I heard you," she sobbed into the phone.

"Do you want us to come over?" I asked.

"Yes, please. I don't want to be alone."

"Okay, we'll see you soon."

She hung up the phone before Gloria and I could say good-bye. Gloria walked up to me and I hugged her. I buried my head in her shoulders.

"I'm so sorry, Gloria," I cried. "I'll do better, I promise. I'll find Nikkei and make it better. And you don't have to take no crap from me. I'll try to be good."

"That's more like it," she whispered warmly in my ear.

"Friends?" I added.

"Family," she corrected.

"Sisters," I replied.

"Sister to sister." She grinned, and I shook my head.

"Well don't you ever criticize my cooking again."

"Okay, but I think I've had all the flavors of ice cream, and I don't think lasagna is one of them."

CHAPTER 11

One Saturday afternoon, I arrived at the shelter a little later than expected. It was a gorgeous day outside. I had decided to go shopping without Gloria or Shelly. I wanted to surprise them with gifts.

I might not know where I came from, but good weather always made me think I knew where I was going. I placed my purse in my desk drawer and stared out the window. It had been four weeks, and we still hadn't heard anything from Nikkei. We were almost in August and no phone calls, letters, or postcards, nothing. Gloria was stressed, and Shelly was a wreck.

"Febe." I jumped and turned to see Stella sticking her head through the door.

"What! Shit, you scared me."

Her eyebrows raised, surprised at my tone. "You must have

been in one of those deep thoughts of yours." We shared a smile and she came into the office.

"Yeah, I guess I was."

Stella sat on the oak chair that was at the front of the desk. DeAnna was taking a break from the shelter, and I was helping out until she returned. Stella didn't want the job. Arranging donations for the shelter and setting up group meetings were her main focus, and that was what she liked to do.

Examining the uncontaminated room with a twinkle in her eye, she didn't say anything, and neither did I. She sat with her hands folded in her lap, gazing behind me.

"Did you come in here to say something, or to stare out the window?"

"Oh, I'm sorry. We took in two women last night, each with kids. We had to send one of them to the hospital. She wasn't in any shape to be here. She didn't want to go, but I explained to her she had no choice."

"Good, Stella. How old is her child?"

"Three."

"Okay. What about the other one?"

"She's upstairs in one of the bedrooms. She doesn't want to eat, and she doesn't want to leave the room."

"Who's been taking care of her child?"

"One of the other women."

"Who?"

"Joyce."

"Extend Joyce's stay by another week."

"Okay, but you know DeAnna said we have to kick them out when their time is up."

"I'll talk to DeAnna, because that defeats the purpose of helping these women, now doesn't it."

"What?"

"Kicking them out in thirty days."

"Tell it to DeAnna," she said as she got up to leave.

"I will." I winked.

"Febe?"

"Yes."

Her words were dismal when she spoke. "DeAnna is thinking about giving up the shelter."

"Giving it up?" I panicked, staring at Stella like she just told me she found my memory or something.

"Yes, she wants to close it down. She's been talking to a few people about selling the house, that's why she's been away so long."

"Are you serious? She can't do that. We need this place and more like it."

"I know, but she said it's too expensive to run. She feels it was stupid for her to open up a place like this because we can't help these women. They always go back to their abusers."

"So that's why we need more shelters, and she knows abused women go back to the abusers several times before they can walk away."

"I know, Febe, but we're not getting enough donations. She can't afford to carry the load on her shoulders any longer."

"Why not?"

"Because there are so many organizations that need help."

"Like who?"

"Like Save the Whales or cats or dogs. We are in desperate need of a lot of things."

"Why do we need donations?" I asked coarsely.

"That's how we operate, on donations."

"Really?" I asked softly rubbing my chin.

"Yes, really. Why?" she asked.

"Oh, nothing, but thanks for the information. I'll think of something. What's the new person's name, and how old is her child?"

"Her name is Justine, and her child is only a few months

old. The child's name is Megan. Here's their chart."

"Thanks, Stella. You're in the groove of things."

"I'm trying to get it back."

"I think you got it, girl." I winked.

"What's Justine's story?" I asked, reading her chart.

"I picked her up from the mini mart down the street. A man handed her over to me. He said he was a friend and wanted his name to remain a secret."

"Is she married?"

"Yes, and from what the friend said, the husband's a real butt hole."

"Has anyone talked to her yet?"

"No, I waited for you. Justine needed time to cool down anyway. She's a real hot head."

"Do we know anything about her husband?"

"Other than he's a butt hole, not really."

"Well that's to be expected if he beats his wife."

"Oh, he did more than just beat her."

"Oh! So we have an even bigger butt hole on our hands. What you got on him? I want everything."

"Not much. The guy did give me a brief description of him, and I had an eerie feeling that we were being watched. But as for her, I wanted you to talk to her before anyone else did."

"Okay, I'll talk to her, if she'll talk to me," I said, circling a few key words on her chart.

"Do you want me to bring you some tea?"

"Yes, please. Thank you."

"Oh, by the way," she said, turning back.

"Yes," I answered, looking up from Justine's chart.

"This office is fantastic. You can actually see through the window," Stella said, giving me a thumbs-up before she closed the door.

I took a deep breath and glanced at my watch. It was later than I thought. I really didn't like this part of the job. I was self-appointed to victim advocate, which meant I spoke to the women to find out their stories and needs. I took Gloria's advice and kept a list of the men I wanted to teach a lesson about domestic violence. They were going to be my experiment. If it worked, then I would go into mass production of ass kicking, but if it failed, then I would have the satisfaction of kicking a few tails.

Sometimes I put myself on a pedestal thinking that I'll kill a man before I let him beat me down to nothing. However, talking to the women shortly after the abuse, always yanked on my skirt tail and snatched me off that damn pedestal, forcing me to remember I'd walked in these women's shoes. That's why I suffer from CRS, can't remember shit.

I have to constantly remind myself that I don't know where I come from, and I can't remember how to get back. But I'll know when I arrive, and that's the only thought that keeps me alive. I will arrive, and the fact that I'm gonna kick the shit out of that son of a bitch when I get there, keeps me thriving as well.

As I approached the stairs, the horrible smell of stale urine, from where babies had soaked mattresses, rushed up my nostrils and landed in the pit of my stomach, making me sick. I made a mental note to talk to DeAnna about getting new mattresses. The place had just gotten a new coat of paint and a new refrigerator but someone forgot to put in for new mattresses so that would be first on my wish list for Christmas.

I placed my hand on the doorknob and took a deep breath. I remembered DeAnna's comments that because of my scars the women were more likely to take me more seriously than the other advocates who had never been beaten.

I glanced over my shoulder at the room to my right. All the beds were full with women who thought they were getting involved with Mr. Right, who turned out to be Mr. Do What I Say or I'll Beat the Shit Out of You Because I'm the Man and I Own You.

As I was shaking off that soul-biting thought and clearing my throat, my heart was pounding in my chest. My palms were sweating when I turned the doorknob. I'd done this a thousand times, and I still couldn't get use to it. I mean, I was a stranger asking questions about someone's private life, not to mention their most embarrassing moments. But I had to do what I had to do. I smiled at the two women and their two children who shared the first room.

My smile told them that I understood the hardship of their lives. The kids fought all the time, and sometimes the ladies, but for now they had to endure the flip side of abuse. A shelter.

The second room had the same number of beds, except there were three women and two children. The door was closed, so I left them to their peace. The third room, where Justine was sitting, had three beds and no children, except her own. I knocked softly and slowly opened the door; Justine was sitting with her back to me.

"Hello, Justine, I'm Febe. How are you?" I asked, extending my hand. She continued glaring out the window. I didn't blame her. I took a seat on the bed next to her.

"I know this is difficult for you, having to leave your home and take your child away from her environment, but it's for the best."

"Excuse me," she said sarcastically. "I didn't know I was going to get a lecture when I agreed to come here."

"No, this is not a lecture. I'm here to listen to you if you want to talk, but I will not lecture. We can sit in the quietness if you want."

"Umph," she muttered.

Ignoring her sounds, I continued, "Although I must tell you I hate the quietness. It makes me feel sick, so I just might run off at the mouth for a while."

"Like you're doing now," she replied.

"Yeah, like I'm doing now. Let me ask you a question."

She put her chin in the palm of her hand and shrugged her shoulders. “It’s your world, ask away,” she replied, keeping her gaze on the street below.

“If you’re so upset about what he’s done to you, why didn’t you call the police and have him arrested?”

“Why, so he can get out in a few days and come back and really kick my ass? Maybe even kill me. Then he’ll leave the state and the police won’t find him or my child. No fucking thank you. I’ll take my chances right here until something else comes along.”

She had a point. The most he would be charged with was violating her civil rights, and maybe three years probation. Besides, three years probation was nothing to a true abuser, he’d take that and her life.

“You still have to do something to help yourself,” I continued.

“Well putting him in jail sure ain’t the answer.”

“And why not?”

“Because he’s fucking crazy.”

”I understand what you’re going through.”

“How can you understand what I’m going through, or any of these women in this godforsaken place?”

“What makes you think I don’t understand?”

“Well,” she said with one finger on her chin, “let’s start with your nice warm gray suit and matching hose. And let’s not forget those beautifully manicured nails. Shit, the heels of your shoes aren’t even scuffed. I can go on.”

“You sure do pay attention to details.”

“Well, I guess you can say I have an eye for money.”

“That’s great, however, you forgot one little thing.”

“What? The tiny diamonds in your ears.”

“No, the scars on my face, my broken nose, and the tip of one earlobe is missing.”

“And?”

"And you should never judge a book by its cover, nor a woman by her clothes. So if you're finished trying to make me feel like I don't understand, I have the rest of the afternoon and the night to hear your story."

Sitting in silence, I waited for her to swallow her pain, fight back her tears, and gain her composure. I would have waited all day if I had to.

"I don't know where to begin," she said softly.

"I'd like you to start from the beginning, but you can hop around if that makes you feel better."

She lowered her head. "It started when he burst in the room and demanded the baby. When I didn't hand Megan over, he punched me in my face and my head hit the wall. I slid to the floor and that's when he grabbed Megan out of my arms and threw her on the bed. Then he started ripping off my clothes. He didn't like for me to be in the house with any clothes on. That's how I got pneumonia and had to be hospitalized. Megan came two months early."

"I'm sorry to hear that. Is she alright?"

Justine showed a slight smiled. "She's fine, happy and healthy."

Getting up from the bed, she walked over to the dresser with her arms folded across her chest. "I don't understand why he let them do that to me," she mumbled, shaking her head.

I was almost afraid to ask, but I did anyway. I guess I wanted to justify my actions when I caught up to Mr. Ronny. "Do what to you?"

"He let his filthy fat friends rape me."

My heart sank to the bottom of my gray pumps.

She continued, shaking her head. "The doorbell rang while he was ripping off my clothes. He dragged me by my hair into the living room. I was so damn scared, but I couldn't fight back. I wanted to run when I saw Paul, Jack, and Stanley standing with their pale white faces gawking at my naked body."

"Justine, come and sit down next to me. You're trembling."

I reached for her, but she shook her head and continued with the tragedy.

"Jack said they came for the party. I tried hiding behind my husband, but he pushed me to the sofa. I felt like a naked slave girl on the auction block waiting for three white men to make the highest bid, and they did. The highest bid was my body or my kid's life." She sniffed. "I pleaded with Ronny not to let this happen. He was my husband. He was supposed to protect me from people like that," she cried.

I didn't know what to do to help her. Even though I'd heard similar stories a hundred times, I still didn't have a comforting word.

"He laughed at me, Febe. He threw his head back and laughed at me, and then said 'you told me to bring more money into the house, so this is how I plan on doing it'." Justine slid to the floor, her knees to her chest and her arms wrapped around her legs. I had a flashback of me in that same position, rocking back and forth, shaking in agony.

"Ronny made a comment that if I didn't let them get their money's worth, Megan would get hurt. I had no choice. I had to save my child." Wiping her eyes with the back of her trembling hands, she sobbed softly.

"You made the right choice, Justine."

"I just didn't know what to do, so I did what I was told. Jack's fat sticky belly rubbed up against me, and I wanted to die." By this time Justine was in a world of tears, snot running from her nose, hands trembling, and eyes swelling from crying for days. "Jack gave Ronny a wad of money." She held out her hands. 'Here's something for your troubles,' Jack said.

"I could feel fire in my chest and hot tears rolling down my face. I just couldn't believe what I was living. Then I heard the dreadful sound of Jack unzipping his pants. I tried running for the bathroom, but Ronny stuck out his foot and I tripped and fell. Grabbing me by my arm, Jack dragged me to the couch. He picked me up, threw me down, and fell on top of me, forcing all the air out of my body. I could smell decaying meat on his breath as he forced his tongue down my throat. I could feel my dinner rotate in my stomach, as I was crushed under ten tons of bacon fat—."

"I'm so sorry, Justine," I cut in, holding back my pain. "I don't need to hear anymore."

"No, you wanted the story so I'm gonna tell you the whole story."

"Okay." I nodded.

"He slid his fat infected fingers between the folds of my skin. I closed my eyes and bit down on my lips until I could taste my blood. Paul and Ronny were in the corner laughing, like I was entertainment for the evening. I opened my eyes when Jack stopped making those grunting sounds like a pig. Beads of sweat fell from the tip of his nose and dripped on my lip. I could taste the salt and sweat from his musty body. He rolled off me, dropped to the floor by my feet, and stroked my leg with satisfaction. I sat up and moved to the other end of the sofa. I didn't want to let those bastards see me cry."

Walking over to Justine, I grabbed her hand. She jerked it away from me.

"No, let me finish."

I sat back on the edge of the bed and listened.

"I could hear keys jingle," she continued. "Then a loud thud hit the floor. I looked up and saw Paul. The lining around his eyes was red like fire. Cocaine encircled the rim of his nose. He walked toward me with his pants around his ankles and that disgusting piece of flesh dangling in front of him. He tucked his dirty blue T-shirt under his chin. I held my breath and tightened the muscles around my lips, and thought I was saved when Ronny yelled." She closed her eyes, and shook her head.

"What did Ronny yell?" I asked.

She looked at me with her head cocked to the side. "If you want that thing sucked, it's gonna cost extra,"

My heart stopped when Justine spoke those words. I could hear the pain in her voice and see the hurt on her face. Looking up toward the ceiling, more tears ran down her cheeks.

I got up and walked over to her again, but she put up her hand and ordered me to stop. Silence filled the room.

She leaned the back of her head against the wall and hummed. She took a deep breath and continued. "Paul looked down at me and licked his lips. I turned to look at my husband. I couldn't hear him but I knew he said Megan, so I laid back on the couch and opened my legs like a good little girl. Paul fell on top of me and moved inside, squirming like a snake, slipping and sliding into a dark hole. I caught a whiff of his stinking body. The smell stung my nostrils and made me sick. I could smell years of rotten teeth on his breath when he forced his tongue in my mouth, slipping it out and sliding it down the side of my face. I bit down on my bottom lip when that monster grabbed my breast. All I could think about was dying. Then it was all over as fast as it started. Loud cries, followed by short groans, then complete silence. I prayed for a heart attack. The sound of my husband's cheers made me cry."

"Justine, I'm so sorry this happened to you," I said and groaned. But she ignored my sympathetic words and continued her frightful account of that night.

"I lay motionless on our green couch. The leather was sticking to my skin like burning plastic. The smell of my vomit combined with Paul's funk made me gag even more. Then I heard Stanley tell Ronny there was a little extra money for privacy.

"From the looks of him, I thought Stanley was the worst of them all. He looked as if he could be the head leader of the KKK," she said, shaking her head. "Stanley took my hand and lead me to the bedroom, after passing Ronny a few more dollars. While we were in there—." She took a deep breath, "he helped me gather as many things as I could put in a duffel bag. Then Megan and I slipped out the front door and into a cab.

"You left just like that?" I asked, astonished at her ordeal.

"Yes."

"You just walked right out the front door with the three of them in the living room?"

"Yes, Stanley kept checking until all three of them were in a drug-and whiskey-induced sleep."

"How did you find us?"

"After I quit my job, I spent a few weeks at Stanley's house until Paul and Jack started snooping around and tried to break into the place. Stanley took me and Megan over to a friend who gave us this number."

"Was Stanley the one who brought you to us?" I asked.

"Yes," she said, standing. "I can't believe Ronny sold me to his friends."

"You're acting like this is the first time."

"It's the first time he's done some shit like this."

"But he has hit you before?"

She put her head down and started crying. "Yes, he's hit me a lot of times. I didn't want to do anything with Paul and Jack, but I felt he would hurt Megan if I didn't."

"I know, Justine, you did nothing wrong."

"I wanted to kill them. I wanted to go back into that house, get Ronny's shotgun, shoot everybody in the head, and walk out the door."

"That's not how it works."

Justine kicked the door so hard the window rattled. "Fuck how it works! Ronny had no right treating me like this! He had no right!"

"No, he didn't," I agreed. "You didn't do anything wrong. It's him, he has the problem."

She turned her back to me and began to cry. I was silent for a while then I asked, "What if you could find someone to pay

Ronny back for what he's done to you and Megan?"

"What?" She turned to face me with tears in her eyes.

"What if you could find someone to pay your husband back for what he's done to you and your child?"

"I'd give them all the money I have to my name just to see that son of a bitch fall down on his knees and beg for mercy."

"So you don't think it's a stupid idea?"

"No. Maybe that's just what he needs, for someone to put the fear of God in his stupid ass, because this shit doesn't make any sense. Who does he think he is to do this to me? What the fuck did I do?" she shouted. "Look at my face. Look at this place. It's nasty and dirty. It smells like piss. This is all fucked up. I had a nice clean home, nice clean sheets. Now I'm running from place to place hiding like a criminal." She took another deep breath and balled her hands into fists. "So if you want to know if I think someone should beat the shit out of him, yes, I do. They should kick the shit out of him until I start to feel better, and I feel pretty damn bad right now."

I held out my hands to comfort Justine. When Stella knocked softly on the door. "Febe, Gloria is on the phone, she said it's important."

Chapter 12

There was a numbness that weighed me down, and made my stomach ache, the news was making me weak. I rushed out the front door and jumped into Gloria's red BMW. As I glanced at the clock, it was a little after five. Because I only drove the side streets, it was going to take me at least fifteen minutes before I reached the hospital.

I sped out of the driveway and hustled down the boulevard, slamming my fist against the dashboard. Pushing button after button before settling on a jazz station, I gripped the wheel and weaved in and out of traffic, running stop signs and red lights. I would probably go to jail if the police stopped me because I still didn't have a driver's license, but I had to get to Nikkei. My mind was a crazy mixture of hope and fear.

Finally reaching the hospital parking lot, I sat in the car with the windows up, staring at the building that I used to call home. A wave of apprehension swept through me like a tidal wave. My heart was racing, and my palms began to sweat. I rested the back of my head on the seat and took a deep breath, gathering my senses before heading toward the hospital.

I managed to walk through the double doors. Immediately I had a flashback of the makeup queens Gloria used to tell me about. They were perched behind their desks waiting to help, lips shining and eyelashes matted.

"Hi. I'm looking for Gloria Maxwell," I said, dropping her name as if it was going to get me into Nikkei's room any faster.

"Is she a patient?" one of the queens asked.

"No, she's on the board with Dr. Harrison."

"Oh yes, hold on, let me page her."

I sat on the grape-covered chairs that Gloria described to me while I was in the coma. It was all too amazing. I felt like I was reliving a dream. But it wasn't a dream once I spotted Gloria racing towards me.

"Febe, thank God! Where have you been?" Gloria's voice was filled with so much tension it chilled my bones.

"I went shopping," I answered feeling guilty.

"Shopping? At a time like this?"

"Well it was a good time for me. I didn't know today was the day we were gonna find her. Why didn't you leave a message with Stella?"

"Shelly didn't think you should find out about Nikkei through someone else. Besides, Stella was out and someone else answered the phone."

I nodded. "How's Nikkei doing?"

Gloria dropped her head. "She's not good at all. She's critical. Some hikers found her in the woods. She was badly beaten and left for dead."

"Do they know who did it?"

"No, they're waiting for her to wake up. Then the questions

will begin."

Another round of painful memories hit me. "Is she in a coma?" I asked fearfully.

"No, she comes and goes. They have her on some heavy medication so she doesn't have to feel any pain. She's almost allergic to everything."

"Yeah, I know. Remember when I gave her some aspirin and I had to drive her to the hospital? That was terrible."

"It wasn't so bad, she survived," Gloria said, smiling at me.

"Yeah, and shortly after that you gave me your car."

"Febe, I told you that's your car now. It's a gift."

"But—."

"Listen, I gave it to you. You need to stop being so darn pigheaded."

"You don't understand."

"I don't have to understand, and not everything can be understood. Sometimes you just have to let it be." There was a cold edge to her tone. "I don't want to fight about this right now," I said sharply.

Her voice rose an octave. "Well, anyway, when they found Nikkei they gave her a shot of penicillin and she had a terrible reaction to it."

"Where's that tag she usually wears?"

"Apparently she didn't have it on when they found her. So how were they supposed to know?"

I hung on to Gloria's every word as she brought me up on the events of Nikkei's tragedy. I still didn't know much about the man she was seeing, but I knew enough to put him on my list and locate his punk ass when the time came.

I could get into Nikkei's apartment and snoop around. She had to have something lying around that would lead me to him. I chuckled to myself at the thought of my shrewdness.

"Did Shelly get in contact with JayR?" I asked.

"Yes."

"And?"

"And you'll see him soon."

"When?" Gloria pushed the elevator button to the fifth floor.

"In a minute."

"In a what? Is he here?"

"Yes."

"Why didn't somebody tell me he was here?"

"Things were moving so fast we just didn't think about it, besides you haven't been home that much."

"Yes I have."

"Only to change, it's like you've become obsessed with the shelter. You don't like JayR anyway so what's the problem?"

"Gloria, I don't even know him."

"Well you didn't know the bag boy at the Piggly Wiggly and you don't like him. You don't like the ice cream man, the water guy, or the mailman."

"Yes, I do. I spoke to the mailman just the other day, besides JayR is different."

"I don't think saying hi to the mailman constitutes a conversation." Gloria chuckled. "But you're getting better." She smiled.

"When did he get here?"

"Who?"

"JayR."

"This morning, and how is he different?"

"This morning, and nobody told me?"

"You weren't home. How is he different?"

"He just is, that's all. Nikkei used to talked so much about him."

Gloria spoke in a broken whisper. "So are you getting a little soft where men are concerned?"

"Hell no," I answered, stepping into the elevator. "I just wish somebody, anybody, would have clued me in that he was here. I do have to be in the same room with him, don't I?"

"Yes you do, Febe, and I'm sure that you will conduct yourself in the best possible way given the circumstances. JayR is part of this family, and he is a man, so deal with it."

"I understand, Gloria. Does he know we think it's Nikkei's boyfriend who did this to her?"

She looked at me. There were frown lines on her forehead.

"We don't think anything. You think that. We haven't said anything, but for your information it isn't the boyfriend."

"Why is that?" I asked.

"Because JayR checked into that, and he told Shelly that the last guy Nikkei was with has been in jail for almost six months."

Something just didn't add up I thought as we exited the elevator and made a right toward Nikkei's room, where I stopped. My feet would not let me go any farther. "Let's go into the waiting room. I need to take a breather before going in to see her."

I sat next to Gloria and held her hand. Inhaling more of the musty air, I noticed a couple of orderlies walking by pushing a dead body on one of those gurneys. A chill ran up my spine and I shuddered. Feeling a deep, familiar pain in my breast, I turned away moaning with distress.

"What's wrong?" Gloria asked.

"I'm scared to go in there," I replied.

"Oh, Febe, you're gonna be alright. She needs to know that you're here cheering for her, like I cheered for you."

We stood and Gloria gripped my hand tighter and led me down the hall toward Nikkei's room.

"I'm having deja vu," I said.

Gloria patted my hand and pushed open the hospital door.

Squeezing my lips tightly together, I closed my eyes. I didn't want to see my poor little Nikkei lying in that bed.

"Febe, are you okay?"

Shaking my head, I forced open my eyes to take in the

shocking view of Nikkei's face. It was swollen, and there were little slits where her eyes were supposed to be. She was bruised and puffy. My heart melted, making the inside of my body turn to mush. I couldn't believe it was her, my little angel girl. Familiar panic began to mount in my throat.

"Hello, Bruce Lee," a deep baritone called out from the shadow.

I turned toward it as he reached out his hand to me just like he did when we were in Shelly's office. I stared at him for a moment trying to regain my composure.

"It's me, JayR. You answered the phone a few times when I called."

I swallowed, closed my eyes, and summoned the strength to touch his hand. It felt hot and clammy.

"Nikkei has told me so much about you," he said, still holding my hand. "I feel as though I already know you."

"Well you don't," I said, snatching my hand away from him.

He laughed. Shelly growled, and Gloria's moans followed.

"What's so funny?" I asked.

"Nikkei said you were a hellcat, but I already knew that from our first meeting."

"Well, she's told me a thing or two about you."

"I'm sure she's told you a million things about me, and all of them personal," he said with a smile.

"Well I guess you can say I know more about you than you probably know about yourself," I added.

"I guess you're right. She's told me quite a bit about you, but I'm sure you have a lot more to tell," he said, smiling like a lunatic.

"Well I don't think you're gonna find out any more than that," I answered.

"That's not fair."

"It is tonight," I said sarcastically.

"Hey, you two quiet down," Shelly said. "You just met and you're already fighting."

"She started it." JayR winked, turning to Shelly. They

laughed and hugged. His deep laughter made my stomach turn.

"I don't get the joke," I said.

"Febe, that's rude," Gloria called out.

"Well, I didn't get it."

Shelly glared at me. "JayR always wanted a baby sister that he could blame things on."

"Why?"

"Because he could never get us in trouble." She laughed again.

I gave a little smile so no one would have to explain that damn story to me again, because I still didn't get it.

As they reminiscenced, about their childhood, I summoned up enough courage to walk over to Nikkei's bed. The room filled with silence when I began softly talking to her.

Gloria came over and stood next to me, and Shelly stood next to her. "Let's pray."

"I'm gonna go outside for a breath of fresh air," JayR said when Shelly reached for his hand. He quickly slipped out of the room.

"He's not a praying man," Shelly remarked.

"I know," I replied.

As Gloria began to pray, a cold, deep, evil feeling began to creep in my soul, making the hairs on the back of my neck stand up. The air in the room became so thick I couldn't breathe. My saliva was unbearably salty, and by the time Gloria finished praying, I was a block of ice and shivering to the bone. Disgust revulsion had taken me over. I knew what I had to do, and JayR was going to help me.

"I have to get some air," I said softly.

"Are you going to be all right?" Shelly asked.

"Yes," I mumbled.

Gloria grabbed my hand. "Are you sure?"

I nodded and walked out of the room. The elevator was opened and I stepped inside.

"Lobby," I said to the person on my right, pressing my back

against the wall and closing my eyes. I wrapped my arms around my waist, waiting for the doors to slide open.

Once they did, I glanced around the lobby before stepping out. I paced the shiny tile floor before I saw JayR sitting outside on a cement bench with his head hanging down. I started thinking that he had no doubt kicked a few female asses in his lifetime. Sooner or later men always do, no matter how much love they have for you. They all turn on you in a hot flash of a second. I blinked to clear those thoughts from my mind and took a deep breath. I could feel my anger rise, and I needed to remain calm. From what Nikkei told me about JayR I knew he was just the man I needed to help me with my plan, and I didn't want my great dislike for his breed to mess it up.

Taking another deep breath, I filled my lungs with the antiseptic and Pine-sol odors that permeated the hospital lobby. I dabbed at the perspiration from my forehead with the palm of my hand and wiped it on the back of my skirt as I exhaled. Clearing my throat and clasping my hands together, I approached the double doors, which swung open with such force, it startled me. As I moved toward JayR, like a panther approaching his prey, I could smell his cologne.

"Why did you leave the room?" I asked calmly.

Without hesitation he answered, "I just needed to get some air, that's all. Why did you leave?"

He never raised his head as he spoke to me. His eyes were planted firmly on the ground.

"I needed to get some air too. It's hard to see someone you love in that condition."

He nodded. "That's unbelievable."

"She's strong. She'll pull through," I said, waiting on his reaction.

He shook his head in agreement, and water fell onto the cement in front of him. At first I thought he was trying to spit on a bug that was passing by, but then he wiped his eyes. The whole damn thing kind of made my heart jump for joy, to see a man in so much pain that it could bring tears to his eyes. However, I felt something different toward JayR—sympathy. I quickly dismissed that thought because sympathy wasn't one of my strong points, and I damn sure didn't need it now, but when I saw JayR wipe his eyes on the sly, for the second time, a tiny smile did cross my face. I would have fallen to the ground laughing my ass off, but that would have screwed up my plans. So I controlled my delight and glanced away.

"What time is it?" he asked.

"I don't know," I answered. "Why?"

"Do you think they might want a break or something?"

I shrugged.

He licked his lips and stood. "Let's get some coffee and take it in to them."

I stepped back.

"Come on," he said and extended his large hand toward my elbow. I quickly moved away from him because his touch was burning me. He reached out for me again, this time with both hands, and I stepped back, tripping over a potted plant that was right behind me and fell to the ground.

He extended his hand to help me, but I refused, and leaped to my feet like I was in some sort of damn circus act or something. I guess you could say I was a little hesitant. Well, I guess you could say I was shocked.

My heart stopped and everything slowed down. I could see his mouth moving but I couldn't understand a word he was saying.

"No! You go and I'll tell them where you are," I said, practically running back into the building.

I slipped into the elevator, took a deep breath and let my head drop. Maybe this would be a perfect time to get to know him,

I heard a voice say so clearly I looked around the elevator to find I was the only one in the tiny box.

By the time I reached Nikkei's room and slowly opened the door, I became brave. Gloria was sitting with her feet propped up on a chair, and Shelly was lying next to Nikkei.

"Gloria, we're going to get some coffee."

"Who's we?" Gloria asked calmly.

"Me and JayR," I responded.

"You?" she said loudly.

"Yes, me," I said and moved closer to Shelly.

"And JayR?"

"Yes." I blinked slowly.

"Are you sure you are going to be okay?"

"Yes, I'll be fine. I'm gonna drive and he can follow me."

"Bring us something other than coffee," Shelly said raising her head from Nikkei's pillow.

"You got it, big sis," I said and kissed Shelly on her cheek. I touched Nikkei's feet before leaving. On the way out, I bumped into JayR. I kept my eyes on the floor.

"I'll wait for you in the parking lot," I said and left him standing in the doorway.

Chapter 13

Fumbling with the keys, I tried to open the door to the condo. Between the shelter and the hospital, I was delirious from lack of sleep. I had no time for anyone. JayR was in my face every chance he got, which was pitiful because I wasn't very nice to him, and he really was becoming a nuisance to me.

When I finally opened the door, I threw my keys down on the bed and stretched my aching back, as a Sade song floated throughout the bedroom. She was always on. I found her voice so relaxing.

I stripped and walked into the bathroom and ran a nice hot tub of water. On the way out, I caught a glimpse of my reflection in the hall mirror and stopped to examine my scars.

Gloria has been hassling me about plastic surgery. If she could only understand that my body reflects his love for control. If she only understood that these scars were not just on the surface, but deep in my soul, branded in my life forever. Then she would understand why I had to make abusers pay for the pain they have inflicted on others. Why I had to make these basement creatures, we called men, suffer.

I shuddered as revenge seductively surged through my veins. "Hmm," I mumbled and slowly walked into the bathroom with a smile.

Easing my tense and stiff body down into the steaming-hot tub of water, my skin crawled but then relaxed from the top of my head to the tip of my toes. Revenge was my lover that night.

Hours later I emerged from a cold tub of water and my mind floated to the ceiling, still weightless from revenge's powerful love. I didn't close my eyes. I let sleep and the tiredness of the day close them for me. Sleep meant quietness, quietness meant dreams, and dreams meant nightmares. If I never went to sleep, that would be fine with me. I wasn't afraid of the dark, only the quietness. I could feel it sneaking in, like someone who had come to rob me, stealing everything and leaving me with nothing.

I could smell the quietness and it smelled like fear. It was all around me, slapping me, hitting me, and bouncing me off the walls, kicking me in my head, face, stomach, and chest. Stomping on me with big black boots.

I screamed but the quietness was too thick. No one could hear me. My God! Somebody please help me! Someone please help me! Reach out for me through the quietness and I'll take your hand. Speak to me and I'll hear you. Please God, make it stop. I'll be good, I cried to the quietness. I'll do what I'm told to do, I pleaded to the darkness. I'll cook the beans right and make the rice just the way you like it. Just stop hurting me. The quietness reached down into my soul. I could feel it running through my veins. It was taking something from me. It was taking my soul. I couldn't breathe.

As I felt the life of my babies slip away from me, the quietness reached down and dragged them right out of me. Then I heard someone scream.

"Febe!"

The quietness was shaking me into submission. I submitted to the quietness, it was my god, and I would bow down to it. I was nothing without the quietness.

"Febe, wake up. You're dreaming. Wake up Febe, wake up." I heard her shout. I forced my eyes opened as the morning light blinded me. I didn't even remember going to sleep. Gloria was sitting in front of me screaming and hugging me, I didn't know what was going on. My bed was covered in blood and so was my body. Blood and tears were streaming down my face.

"What happened? Who did this to me?" I shouted. "Who did this to me?"

"You did. You did this to yourself. I'm gonna take you to the hospital. Let's go," Gloria commanded.

"No! No! No!" I shouted and shook my head, which was hurting like hell. I closed my eyes and took a deep breath.

"You're not fine. Look at you! Your body and bed are covered in blood," she shouted and jumped to her feet.

I wanted to kick her in her fucking mouth just to shut her up, but the room began to spin out of control and I needed to get a grip before her hysteria landed me in the hospital as a danger to myself.

"Gloria, I'm fine," I said, speaking as calmly as I could. I wasn't, but I had to say something. "Now sit down so I can think," I said, looking up at her. She eased down on the bed like she had hemorrhoids. I took her trembling hands and looked into her eyes.

"Gloria, I'm sorry. I don't know what happened. I didn't have anything sharp in my room. Hell, I don't even have fingernails. See," I said, trying to ignore my shaking hands.

"Then what happened?" she shouted, looking around the room for some evidence.

"I don't know, Gloria. I just don't know," I answered, trying to convince her I was telling the truth. I had no idea what happened. I started to shake, and this time I knew why. I was angry. Angry that my abuser still had so much control over me, and I couldn't even remember his name. I slammed my fist down on my thigh.

Gloria grabbed my hands and pulled me to her. She held me and rocked me. She branded my shirt with her tears, and I stained her favorite silk nightgown with my blood.

"When is your next appointment?"

"What appointment?"

"With your therapist?"

"I stopped going."

"You what?"

"I stopped going. She was getting on my nerves, and she said I could stop any time. So I quit going that day."

"Febe, you need help."

"And when I think I do, then I'll get help, but until then I will do it my way."

Gloria sat in silence and stared out the window.

"Gloria."

"Yes?" She turned to me.

"Was I pregnant when you found me?"

Gloria bit down on her bottom lip and continued to stare out the window. "Febe, baby, I think so, but you had already lost the baby by the time they got you to the hospital."

"Why didn't someone tell me?"

"The doctors said it would be better when you found out on your own, then it wouldn't be so shocking."

"Can I still have babies?"

"I think so, but I think you will need a man for that." She smiled.

"Why didn't you and Jackson ever had babies?"

"It was never the right time," She lowered her head.

I gently placed my head on her shoulder.

"Well, let's get you cleaned up before I go to the hospital. It's my turn to let Shelly go home," she said as peacefully as she could.

"It's Saturday, already?"

"Yes," she replied. Then she got up and went to the bathroom.

"I've lost all track of time," I shouted from the bedroom.

Gloria came out of the bathroom, her hands dripping wet. "You're the one burning your candles at both ends. You need to slow down."

"Gloria, I do what I have to do," I snapped angrily.

"You don't have to kill yourself," she said, as she walked back into the bathroom and became silent.

I looked away. I didn't know what to say. I felt like I was going to lose my mind. I bit my lower lip until it began to sting.

"How did you calm me down?" I asked, ignoring her silence.

"At first, I kept calling your name," she said, with a little tension in her voice.

"So I guess that shit didn't work, did it?" I said, sneering at her.

"No, it didn't,"

"So what else did your ingenious brain tell you to do?"

Gloria drew a deep breath and held it.

"I'm sorry, Gloria."

She exhaled and continued. "I threw a sheet over you so I could get to you, and I shook you."

"You shook me!" I turned towards the bathroom. "Why did you shake me?"

"Shelly said to shake you."

"Well, that was some brilliant shit. I bet her parents are proud of her for that little intelligent piece of advice," I said, looking away. Anger was building up inside of me, I was almost ready to burst. I was too damn scared to admit it, but I felt as if I was taking two steps backwards.

Gloria walked out of the bathroom. "Febe are you still thinking about that revenge stuff?"

"What revenge stuff?" I asked as if I didn't have a clue.

"That get the abuser, because they did it to you."

"You mean that eye for an eye kick I was on?"

"Yes."

"Naw, I guess it was just a phase I was going through.

"Good." She hugged me. "I'm glad that's over. I was getting a little worried about you."

"Well you don't have to be. Besides, I have to worry about getting along with JayR."

"Mmmm, Febe, I have something else to tell you," she said softly.

"What?"

"I also told JayR."

This time I wanted to choke the shit out of her. "Who else did you tell, the freaking brigade?" I shouted. "It was a bad dream, Gloria. That's all, a bad dream. I've had them before."

"And I could help you before, but it was something different about this one, Febe. It was stronger than before."

"Gloria, I don't know what to say. It was a dream, that's all, nothing more, and that's what we are gonna say when we get to the hospital, right?"

She threw her hands in the air. "That's fine with me. Whatever." She mumbled before going back into the bathroom.

By the time we arrived at the hospital, my nerves were on edge. I tried to pretend this dream was just like the others, but it wasn't. Except for the self-inflicted wounds, you could scarcely tell that I had just kicked the shit out of myself.

CHAPTER 14

Shortly after we arrived, at the hospital, Harrison and JayR walked in together. They must have met in the elevator or something. I didn't ask because I didn't give a shit. They both could leave the same way the came. Together.

"Good morning," JayR said with a smile. I rolled my eyes. I wasn't in the mood for his cheerfulness. Harrison nodded as he always did. JayR came over and sat next to me. He didn't say anything, he just investigated my wounds.

"Did you win?" he asked

"What?" I answered

He scooted closer. "Did you win?"

I could feel his eyes burning my skin. I could smell mint toothpaste on his breath, and the stench of man was leaking from his pores, making my stomach churn.

Keeping silent was giving support to my control. I didn't even look his way. Even though I could feel Harrison eyeing me, I remained detached.

I had too much on my mind to give a shit about JayR and his funny faces. Panic was running a marathon in my head.

"What happened?" Harrison asked, unfolding my arms, and examining one of them.

"I don't know." I answered, staring straight ahead.

"You don't know?" he repeated, "You're all cut up and you don't know?"

"No I don't."

"I don't understand."

"I don't know what happened," I shouted, jumping in Harrison's face. "I can't explain it. Shit happens. I mean, fuck it. It's my damn life," I said with my hands balled into fists.

JayR grabbed me and forced me into the chair. Every one was staring at me. I know that Harrison wants to lock me up. I know he doesn't like the fact that I was trying to find out who put Nikkei in the hospital. Turning toward JayR I glared at him, squinting in frustration.

"Ohooo! Did you see how she looked at me?" he shouted pointing at my face.

I couldn't believe that son of a bitch was telling on me.

Gloria shook her head and walked to the window.

My mood veered sharply to anger, as I folded my arms across my chest and stared up at the ceiling.

"I'll tell you one thing, that anger-management class isn't working. You should demand your money back," Harrison told Gloria.

I was about two seconds from his throat, when JayR grabbed me again. "Let's go for a walk and get some fresh air."

As soon as the cool breeze hit my face, I felt like floating, but not before I slapped the shit out of JayR.

"Ouch! What did you do that for?"

"Don't you ever grab me like that again!" I shouted.

"Wow," he said rubbing his cheek as he stared into my scolding eyes. A sudden chill hung on the edge of my soul.

"Yes, ma'am, but why is Harrison so upset with you?"

"He wants me to stop asking so many questions about Nikkei"

"Nikkei?"

"Yeah. According to him, I'm upsetting Shelly with my accusations."

"Well, Harrison has been in this family for a long time. He was the one who helped Shelly with the business and he refers a large portion of his clients to her center. Not to mention that he's gotten other doctors on the bandwagon, as well."

"Are you indebted to him?"

"I do owe the man some of my freedom."

"Really?"

"Yes, really. I was a bounty hunter, a good one at that. One night we ran into this house and got into an altercation with the man who was inside. He ended up shot, and come to find out it was the wrong house. He fit the description, so I didn't verify."

"And Harrison was there to save the day," I said smirking.

"He stopped me from spending my life in prison. So maybe he's just concerned for us all."

"Well, whatever JayR. All I know is he's trying to get me out of the way."

"Get you out of the way?"

"Yeah, lock me up in the nut house."

"Febe, don't you think you're being just a little paranoid?"

"No. I know that freak wants to lock me up the first chance he gets."

JayR didn't say a word, he just stared at me and shook his head.

"What?" I shrugged my shoulders.

"Nothing, I was just wondering."

"Wondering about what?" I asked

"Wondering when was the last time you had any fun."

"Fun? Me?"

"Yes."

"I have fun all the time with the girls at the shelter. We do a lot of things together."

"That's work, not fun. Let's go and have some real fun."

"I don't know about that."

"Oh, come on," he begged.

I don't understand what was going through my head, but I accepted his invitation.

"Let me go and tell Gloria that I'm leaving," I replied.

Little frown lines gathered in the middle of his shiny forehead.

"What?"

"Aren't you over the age of consent?" he asked

"Yes, why?"

"It seems that every step you make, you have to ask Shelly or Gloria if you can take it."

"That's not true."

He raised both his eyebrows. "Yes, you do."

"That's called courtesy, JayR. You should try it, it works." I said and disappeared into the hospital.

Chapter 15

When we entered Miss Dorothy's crowded little café on the outside of town, JayR checked out the restaurant.

"What are you doing?"

"Scanning the room for a good seat."

I crinkled my face and rolled my eyes. He caught my expression, and the show was on.

"Now what are you doing?"

"I'm still searching."

"And you have to move your neck like a snake?" I asked.

"That's the way I search for a good seat."

"Do you have to bulge your eyes out of your head like that?"

"Yes."

"Why?"

"It helps me to see better."

Before I had time to say another word, we were marching through the tiny café at top speed sliding into a booth.

"The sign said wait to be seated," I whispered.

"Oh, really. I didn't hear it say anything," he replied with a chuckle.

I didn't think it was funny. So he cleared his throat and said. "Mama Dot makes the best red gravy and grits you ever did taste."

The smell of bacon on a hot griddle with stacks of blueberry pancakes and scrambled eggs filled the room. I was definitely hungry by the time the beautiful black waitress came for our order. Her dark skin was smooth and flawless. I wanted to hide my scarred face. I tried not to look at JayR as he stared at the young lady, but I couldn't help but notice the sparkle in his eyes. I wanted to order, but I didn't want to look in her face, and I didn't want her to look at mine.

"What's wrong, Febe?" JayR asked.

"Nothing."

"Do you want to go someplace else?"

"No," I sort of groaned.

"Please give us a minute," he said to the waitress, and watched her disappear behind the swinging doors, then he turned to me. "Now tell me what's wrong. Did something jog your memory?" he asked.

"No, I didn't have a memory flashback," I answered, looking out of the window.

"You were fine until that girl came up to take our order, then you went silent on me."

"She's not a girl, she's a woman."

"And?"

"And she's a beautiful woman."

"And you're not?"

"JayR, don't give me that bullshit. The whole damn world can see that I'm not."

"Febe, I didn't think you were the person to worry about what the world thinks about you."

"Well I'm not, but sometimes there's a little part of something that comes out and makes me worry about what other people are saying about my scars."

"Well forget about what they're going to say today. When that girl. . . Marie comes to take our order, I'm gonna pile this table with so much food everybody is gonna stare." He laughed so loud the room sort of went quiet.

I got up and went to the bathroom to take another pill, I didn't want to take it in front of him and have to answer any questions. When I stuck my head out of the bathroom, our table looked like it held enough food for twenty people.

"Oh, my God, Febe, you said you were hungry, but dang girl," he shouted loud enough for everyone to hear then gave a sly smile.

I put my hands on my hips and cocked my head to one side.

"Nikkei is right, you are mischievous," I said and took my seat.

"I try to be." He winked.

The table was filled with home fries and sautéed onions. The grits and red gravy were as good as he said they would be. I wanted to take some home to Gloria. The sausage was cooked to perfection. One forkful after another was shoved into my mouth.

He leaned over the table. "I thought you weren't hungry."

"Well, I wasn't until I saw all this food you ordered, now I can't stop eating."

We exchanged one or two words throughout the meal. I relaxed against the red booth. Silence slipped in, and my mind wandered back to the night before. I was still amazed that I kicked the shit out of myself, and I lost. I knew Harrison was gonna have a conversation with the sisters and try to convince them that I was a danger to myself.

"But I'm not."

"You're not what?" JayR asked.

"Nothing," I said and stared out the window again.
He was quiet for a moment and then he said, "This place is always crowded."

"What?"

He rolled his eyes. "I said this place is always crowded."

"Well I think the owner should be happy."

"Oh, he is. He owns three more just like this one."

"Do you know him?"

"He's a friend of mine."

"Good. Maybe you should think about going into a respectable business."

"Ain't no money in respect." He smiled.

"And you make a lot of money hunting folks down?"

"No, but I get to help people who can't get help any place else."

"And that's rewarding?"

"Yes, very. I'm gonna take care of the bill and check on Nikkei."

"Okay," I replied. Glancing out the window, I saw two people standing in the middle of the parking lot hugging and kissing as if they were alone. The man held the woman so tight I thought she was struggling to be free, which made my blood boil instantly, but then my eyes fell on her gyrating hips.

Throwing her head back as laughter crossed her face made me feel warm inside. Their bodies wiggled together like worms. She definitely wasn't in any pain, and I sat and stared at their bump-and-grind show.

Watching without looking. Wondering without thinking. Did it really feel that good to be held by somebody? A man, that is. Gloria holds me after a bad dream, but did it really feel that good to be touch by a man. I shrugged my shoulders and waved the thought away from my face.

As I dragged my eyes away from the two lovers, JayR was sitting, staring at me the way I was staring at the lovers.

"Febe."

"Yes."

"Can I ask you two questions?"

"What?"

"First you gotta promise me that you won't get upset and go off the deep end."

"How do you know that I'll go off the deep end?"

"Well, I've witnessed a few of your attacks, and Nikkei told me."

I exhaled and said, "Okay, ask your questions."

"How are you doing with your memory?"

"What?"

"Wait a minute. Hold on. It's just a question. You don't have to answer it if you don't want to."

I calmed myself. I thought about his question for a while, then I told him just what was on my mind. "I don't know," I said. "Shelly said my memory will come back when I want it to, but until then. . ."

"Until then you're S.O.L." he added.

"S.O.L?"

"Shit out of luck."

"I guess you can say that, now what's your second question?"

"Why do you have to drive your own car when we go places?"

"Because I don't date."

"Oh, I see." He raised his brow.

I looked out the window. JayR reached across the table and touched my hand. I jerked it away quickly, spilling my orange juice.

"Did I hurt you?" he asked, looking confused as two waitresses rushed over to clean up the spill, which they did in record time.

"No!" I shook my head and lowered my eyes to the drenched red tablecloth.

"Are you okay?"

"I'm fine." His touch felt like a hot piece of metal pressing on the back of my hand.

I wanted to cry, but then again I was always on the verge of tears.

"Did I say something wrong?" he asked.

"No, JayR, you didn't say anything wrong."

"Then what's wrong?"

"It's just that I see how you are with your sisters, so loving and caring. Shelly is all smiles when you are around, and if. . .if Nikkei were able I know she would be smiling too."

"And?"

"And I can't believe you do what you do for a living."

"Febe, what I do for a living is just a job, just like what you do at the shelter. It's a job."

"No, JayR, it's not a job, it's my life. These women need me, they need my help."

"I didn't say what you do is not important. You are doing the best you can, and that's all that you have to offer. Just like me, I do the best that I can. You help people in your job, and I help people in mine. I do what I do because that's who I am."

"I have a question for you."

"Okay, shoot, and I promise I won't get angry." He pointed to me.

"Have you ever hit a woman before?"

"Febe, I have never hit a female in my life, except my sisters and that only happened a few times. Man, when them girls finished whipping my butt I never hit them again."

"Second question."

"Okay, let it rip."

"If I ever need your service, will you be there, even if you don't believe in what I believe in?"

He frowned, looked away, and then back at me. "I'll be there and I'll ask no questions, but don't think you're gonna get a family discount."

Chapter 16

I was sitting at my desk late Tuesday afternoon when the phone rang, and my heart dropped. I let it ring two more times before picking it up.

"Hello." My voice was trembling.

"Febe."

"Gloria, what's wrong?"

She didn't say anything, but I could tell from her silence something had happened.

"Is Nikkei alright?"

"No." She sniffed. "Shelly said something about a test."

"A test," I repeated, and wrinkled my forehead.

"Febe, I don't know, Shelly was talking so fast I couldn't understand her. She wants all of us at the hospital right away."

I was silent. My stomach started to turn, and I felt nauseous.

"Do you need someone to come and get you?" she asked.

"No, no I can make it. Where are you?"

"I'm in Long Beach. Are you sure you can make it?"

"Gloria, I'll manage. You go to the hospital, I'll meet you there."

"Okay, baby girl, you take care," she said and hung up. I grabbed my keys and headed for the front door. I don't remember much after that.

I woke up in a cold sweat, my heart was pounding in my ears, and my vision was blurry. I blinked, trying to adjust my eyes, scanning my surroundings for some familiarity, but there was none. Then I saw a body next to me, I gasped for air as I recognized her face. It was that bitch called Fear, and she wasn't playing with me anymore.

I tried to scream, but she reached up and grabbed me by my throat, choking the strength out of me. I was suffocating, dying right where I lay.

My eyes felt like they were popping out of their sockets. I began scratching and clawing my way out of a steel cage, frantically fighting for freedom. Finally I was able to stumble out into another unfamiliar place. All around me was darkness. No lights, no sound. All I could hear was the thumping of my heart, one loud and slow beat after another.

I began rising to the sky as warm hands lifted me into the air. The light gently made its way through the darkness, and I began to breathe. Fear released her grip, and my body became free. As I struggled to open my eyes, the sweet floating sensation came to a screeching halt when I recognized his big, round, dark face. My body was drenched in sweat and my nipples poked through the silk white camisole like two brave soldiers. Gloria said the camisole would make me feel pretty. It made me feel pretty alright. Pretty naked.

His hands felt like hot metal against my cool skin. I could feel his fingers fusing to my thighs. I partially jumped out of his hands and covered my exposed chest. I examined the side of my thighs to see if this devil man left any marks.

JayR looked at me, with tears in his eyes. He drew in a deep breath and exhaled it slowly. I stared back without any sympathy at all. I couldn't even summon up any. Hell I couldn't even fake it, and I didn't even try, until he shook off his tears and wiped his face with his palms, dragging one hand down his chin. He looked as if he could use a hug.

He walked slowly toward my car, and grabbed my keys and purse.

"Febe, what's going on with you? Why did you come here?"

I shrugged. "I don't know, JayR, I really don't know. I was heading to the hospital, next thing I know you're holding me."

"I picked you up from the ground. I came to my car to get my address book and I found you crawling around on your hands and knees crying. What's going on, girl?"

I turned away from him, as panic raced across my face. I've found myself in places and I didn't know how I got there, but why did I end up here at Nikkei's place? I questioned my actions.

He drew in another breath and released it. "They had to drill two holes in Nikkei's head to relieve some of the pressure that was causing her brain to swell," he said, looking up into the steel rafters of the underground garage.

My head felt heavy and my body went numb. I tried to control the shaking, but JayR saw right through me. He walked closer and put his arms around me. I couldn't stand for him to touch me, and I didn't like what I was feeling when he did.

"Febe."

"JayR, please," I said.

"Okay," he replied and walked to his car, retrieved a black case, and walked back over to me. "Come on, let's go inside and get you cleaned up before we head over to the hospital."

As I slowly climbed the stairs to Nikkei's apartment, I tried to replay the event that led me there. Why would I want JayR's comfort instead of Gloria's?

"Febe!" Gloria screamed, when we exited the elevator. "I've been calling all over the place for you." She hugged me so tight, I thought I was going to pass out.

"How's Nikkei?" I asked.

"Sit down, baby."

"How's Nikkei?" I asked again, a little louder than I wanted.

"Febe, we don't know yet. We're just waiting," Gloria said, picking gravel out of my hair. We sat in silence, staring into space for about two hours. Then Harrison, who seemed to stroll into the waiting room, glared at me. I sat up straight. JayR and Shelly stood. The saliva in my mouth became unbearably thick and salty when Shelly buried her face in Harrison's white hospital coat.

JayR turned to face us with large tears hanging from his eye lashes. I fell back against the chair, looking at my world crashing in on me. My nostrils began to burn with fear, and anger knotted inside of me.

I could see everyone crying and hugging one another. I saw lips moving and tongues wagging, but I couldn't hear anything. No one told me anything. No one was talking to me.

"What happened?" I screamed. "Lord, please tell me what happened to my sister." I slipped out of the chair onto the floor, and Gloria went down with me, rocking me in her warm embrace.

"What happened, Gloria?" I howled. "What happened?"

"She's gone, Febe, Nikkei's dead," Gloria whispered in my ear, and I tried to contain the pain, really I did, but it was too strong for me to hold back. I tried to bury the pain in that grave in my soul, but the grave was too full, and I exploded.

"No!" I screamed. "Nikkei, please don't do this to me.

Please, Nikkei, don't do this to me." Jumping to my feet, I ran to my sister's room, swinging open the door only to find an empty bed. I turned and grabbed the first person I saw.

"Harrison, where in the hell did you put my sister?"

"Where is she?" I shouted. "I want to see her now."

Harrison's eyes darkened as he held my gaze.

"Just take us to see her," JayR shouted over my cries.

Harrison said nothing at first, then he looked over at JayR.

"I'll be right back."

A few hours later he walked back into the quiet arctic room.

"Follow me." He mumbled.

Pushing open a huge steel-gray door, Harrison pointed to a large silver cookie sheet where my baby sister was lying. She wasn't crying, just lying still like she was sleeping.

I turned to stare at JayR, who looked away. Gloria and Shelly were crying so hard their bodies were shaking. But I wasn't crying, I wasn't shaking. I wasn't there, this wasn't happening. I knew it was all a dream, just a bad nightmare, like so many others. I knew that monster was around the corner. It was just a matter of time before Gloria woke me up.

I never did wake up, because a few days later, all four of us were standing at the foot of Nikkei's grave, just like we stood at the foot of her hospital bed. This time it was an everlasting bed of rest.

I was never going to see her again, never going to smell her Charlie perfume or fight over what movie to go and see. I was never going to hear her long, boring stories of her adventurous love affairs, or how those jeans made her butt look so round. I was never going to have the chance to tell her to get out and run for her life. I was never going to be able to warn her of this day, this moment, this very second. Hell yes, I was pissed off and I was gonna do something about domestic violence or die trying.

"Febe," Shelly said, bringing me out of my self-pity. She

reached in front of JayR for my hand. "Thanks for being there for her on so many nights when she needed me and I couldn't come home," she said, squeezing my hand. I could see in her eyes that she was blaming herself for that one time when she should have said something. Now it was too late.

JayR was standing next to Shelly, and he took her in his arms and they cried long, painful tears. Then Gloria joined in. I stepped aside; I didn't want to be a part of the discussion of what they should have done. I knew what they should have done, they should have saved her. She was our responsibility. Our friend, our sister, and our business. They should have helped her, but they didn't, so I didn't see the point in sharing in their pain.

I backed away from my best friend, and my sister, to let her rest. I was almost to Gloria's car before they realized I was gone.

"Hey, where are you going?" JayR yelled.

I kept walking. I needed to be alone to think. I needed to get the show on the road, because something had to give or I was going to snap.

"I don't know, JayR, but I have to get out of here."

"Let me drive you!" He yelled.

"No, I can drive myself." I slipped behind the wheel of Gloria's Mercedes and drove away. My heart was burning with something I couldn't even begin to describe.

I ended up at the only place I could think clearly, the shelter. I sat on one of the cement benches in the backyard. It was a beautiful, wonderful, sun-shiny day. Big fluffy clouds were floating in the sky, and children were running and playing, screaming with so much life.

It was too extraordinary a day to bury somebody you loved. Too perfect a day to say good-bye. Too great a fucking day to put somebody in a cold, hard, dirty ground. I cried deep within my soul for what seemed like hours.

Then JayR appeared out of nowhere and took the seat next to me. He didn't say anything to me at first. He just sat there, then he started to cry like a small child.

"After they drilled the holes in her head to release the pressure, she had a seizure, followed by a stroke, and she died. That's all they told us. She died. Harrison was there and he had no answers for us again." JayR said.

He stopped for a moment trying to regain his composure but his tears continued to flow freely. He had no clue what really happened to his baby sister, to the joy of his life. He leaned into me and put his head on my shoulder and cried even harder. A part of me wanted to push him away, but another part allowed him to stay.

All the stories that Nikkei ever told me about her brother had to be lies. This big-time, fearless man that would take anybody down with a blink of an eye was just a bunch of crap. He was crying like a little pansy. I bit my bottom lip in order to keep my thoughts inside my mouth, because they had already left my mind.

"I just want to kill the son of a bitch who did this to my sister," he shouted, slamming his fist on his thigh.

"JayR, not here," I said. "Let's walk."

We started out on a slow-paced walk not far from the shelter, but far enough as not to upset the women and children.

"When I find the person who's responsible for her death, I'm gonna rip his heart out."

"JayR, that's what they do on TV. Why not do to him what he did to her."

"What?" He frowned.

"I mean why not teach him, an eye for eye and a tooth for a tooth. That's what Gloria said they did in the bible."

"Febe, what are you talking about? You don't even believe in God."

"How can I believe? Look around you, JayR, and tell me what you see."

He turned around and wiped his eyes. "I see mothers playing

with their children, and children playing with their friends, so what." He shrugged."

"What are you feeling right now?" I asked.

A frown line filled an open space right in the middle of his forehead.

"Febe, I just put my baby sister in the ground because some fucker murdered her. What do you think I'm feeling?"

"I don't know, tell me."

"I'm scared. I don't know life without Nikkei. What if this should happen to Shelly, or you, or Gloria?"

"JayR, can you imagine living in fear for the rest of your life, not knowing if you're gonna live or die? Do you realize this is a paradise for all of these kids and some of the women."

"Paradise?" He blinked.

"Yes, paradise," I repeated. "It's paradise to a woman who's beaten every night by her husband for one reason or another. It's paradise for that lady who's standing in the window. She had to leave her jealous husband, her beautiful home, and the wonderful school her children attended. However, this is still paradise."

He looked puzzled. "I don't understand."

"Look over there," I said, pointing to my left. "In the corner of the yard underneath the trees, look at her face, and tell me if you understand. Can you see how much her husband loves her? Do you think he's sorry for kicking the shit out of her a few days ago? No! He's pissed off because she left him. This happens over and over. As we speak, more and more women are being beaten. Each one of them has a different story. Each one has her own reason why she left, and why she stayed. Yet each outcome is the same. They all left because of the abuse, because they got tired of being some man's punching bag. They stayed because of fear, poverty, family, and even the God Gloria speaks so much about."

"What does that have to do with Nikkei?" he asked.

"Nikkei was seeing someone, that I'm sure of, and we have to find out who."

"Febe, I don't know what you're talking about. The only guy Nikkei was seeing was in jail long before she came up missing."

"Are you sure?" I asked.

"Yes, I'm sure, Febe, I mean. . ." He took a deep breath to calm himself. "Why do we have to find out who she was seeing anyway?"

"Her abuse was staring us right in our faces. Domestic violence is real, and it injures and kills more women than car accidents or random acts of violence. It kills our loved ones, and we aid the abusers when we don't help the victims."

"And?" He stared at me, baffled.

"And every nine seconds a woman is beaten, Nikkei was one of them. She stayed in the relationship out of fear and love, two deadly combinations.

"What are you saying?"

"Domestic violence killed your baby sister. It killed Nikkei," I shouted at him. My words hit him in his chest so hard he fell back a few steps. JayR looked as if he saw a ghost. His face darkened, and his body stiffened. He was speechless. Not a word escaped from his lips. We were thrown into another moment of silence before I could speak. I tried touching him, but each time I did his skin felt like hot metal. He looked around, observing his surroundings, then shook his head.

"Shelly and Gloria refused to believe me, and I was giving Nikkei a little more time before I called you. But it's true. She was involved with someone."

"Who! I'll kill that son of a bitch."

"It's not just about killing the one who killed Nikkei. We have to do something to help the other Nikkeis of the world. We have to take matters into our own hands and help these women.

They can't do it alone," I said, adding fuel to his fire. I could see that he was madder than a blind man at a strip show.

"We have to do something, JayR. We have to help. We can't leave it up to the victims. We left it up to Nikkei and look at the result."

I could tell by his eyes that I had the bull by the horns, and it was time for me to take a ride.

"JayR, you have to understand this is not something I know for a fact, but it is something that I believe happened."

"Why do you believe it happened?" he replied, breathing harder by the second.

"Well," I said, turning my face away from him only for a moment. "She was dating this guy, a married man. She didn't want the rest of the family to know about him. You have to understand that Nikkei loved him dearly."

"Do you know him?" he asked with his hands in tight balls.

"No, I don't. I never met the man, but I know that we can find him. Nikkei said that you can find anyone."

He looked away.

"JayR, I'm sorry that you had to find out like this, but what other way was there? I know that Shelly didn't want you to know because she didn't believe it herself. Nikkei was really great at hiding things."

"Yeah, I know, she taught me," he said. "She was good at hiding things that she didn't want you to know."

"Why didn't Shelly know that?" I asked.

"Shelly can't see what's right under her nose. There was never any reason to hide things from her. You can put something in her face and tell her it's not there, and she'll believe you."

"I remember Nikkei saying the same thing when we first met regarding her bandaged wrist."

"Febe, you have to remember whatever you can about this man. If I don't have something to go on, then it's even harder to find him."

"JayR, you know how my memory is. I need time."

"Are you telling me you and Nikkei spent just about all of her free time together, and she never told you about this man?" he questioned.

"No, she didn't!" I replied softly.

"You have to remember something," he shouted.

"Stop badgering me. I can't remember! I just can't remember! People are always wanting me to remember shit and I can't!" My breathing became heavier, my chest expanded, and my shoulders moved up and down two, three, maybe four inches with each deep breath I took. My top lip curved up to the right. I thought my head was going to start spinning. JayR dropped his arms and stepped back an inch or so.

Shit I was starting to scare myself, but he really did piss me off. "I told you about grabbing me!" I screamed.

"Okay! I'm sorry for grabbing you," he said. "Calm down. You shouldn't get upset so quickly. Nikkei warned me about that."

"Didn't you and Nikkei have anything else to talk about besides me?" I screamed.

"No."

"And why not?"

"Because I find you interesting."

"Me!"

"Yes, you." He looked at the ground.

I became calm again. "Why do you find me interesting?" I asked, tossing his words right back at him.

"It's obvious that you have been through something in your life. And from the looks of things, something very powerful. You have too many scars to say otherwise."

His words struck me in my heart, and I turned away. I always forgot about my scars until someone mentioned them or I caught someone staring.

"Don't turn away. I didn't mean anything bad by it." He

touched my arm, once again burning a hole through the sleeve of my black dress. I jumped from his touch and walked over to the pine tree. He followed me.

"I didn't mean to hurt your feelings. What I meant is you are not letting anything stand in your way. Nikkei talked a lot about you. She admired you."

"Me?" I blinked.

"Yes. She wished that she could be like you. "

"And, I wanted to be like her," I said, looking up into the tree.

"Nikkei described a giant of a woman, stronger than the gods, and mightier than their swords. You've been through a lot, and you are stronger because of it. You didn't need anyone to lean on, and she admired you for that."

As he talked about Nikkei, the pain of losing her became so great I couldn't stand it. The pit of my stomach ached with agony. The anguish was making its way to my throat, arriving in my nostrils, setting them ablaze.

I could no longer hold what was inside of me. It all came up, along with this morning's breakfast. JayR jumped aside, and I let it all out. He stroked my back, and this time I couldn't move. Each stroke stung like fire. He handed me a handkerchief, and I wiped my mouth on the corner of it.

I hated that he was helping me while I was in this condition because it made me feel powerless. My emotions had more strength than I thought and pushed the words right out of my mouth. My heart was full of pain and I wanted to let somebody know.

"JayR, I'm not strong," I said, standing straight. "I live in pain and shame every day, and I can't stand it. It's something that's driving me insane."

"I don't understand, Febe. You are strong. Look what you're doing for these women."

"You wanna know about my strength?" I shouted, pounding on my chest. "My fear is my strength! I don't know where I come from and I don't know how to get back. I walk in fear every day. I sleep with the demons of my past. That's how strong I am, JayR. That's why I can relate to these ladies, that's why I wanna help them. I know about their pain, because it's my pain. It's my own fucking pain, JayR, and I need you to help me, you promised me that you would." I stared into JayR dark eyes and at that point I knew that I had to gain my composure after such an asinine outbreak, but I couldn't, so I did what I knew how to do. I ran. I left him standing with his own thoughts. I ran to the front of the shelter where Gloria's car was parked. JayR ran to catch up with me. He wasn't that far behind, yet he seemed like a million miles away.

"Febe, wait!" he shouted. But I didn't stop my pace. I needed to be someplace fast. Any place but there with him.

I made it to the car, but he was right on my tail. "Wait one minute. I'm sorry I didn't know all this. Shelly and Nikkei didn't give me all the details."

"That's because they didn't know all the details." I tried to unlock the door. He reached for my hand, and I moved it away, dropping the keys to the earth.

"Let me help you," he said picking up my keys.

"Help me?" I snatched the keys from his hand. "You know what you can do for me?" I shouted with one hand on my hip.

"You name it and I'll do it!" he shouted with both hands stretched out, stepping away from me.

"Help me help these women. Help me get their abusers the way you're gonna get Nikkei's abuser."

JayR stopped in his tracks, his arms fell to his side. His expression showed a quick panic attack, then he smiled.

"You want me to do what?" He chuckled.

"Help me with a job. I know what you are capable of doing, so don't try and play me for a fool. I know all about you and your skills. And I have money."

He walked closer to me and in a whisper he said, "I will

find Nikkei's killer, but I'll have nothing to do with the rest of these women."

"They need our help, JayR," I replied calmly. "We have to help the Nikkeis of the world."

JayR stood silently for a while. He looked up at the house and saw a woman in the window with one black eye and a bruised lip.

"Have you thought this through?" he asked, squinting to avoid the sun.

"Yes, I have, and I will do this with or without you."

He thought for a while. "It's gonna cost you, ya know."

"I know that, I told you I have money."

"Oh, I don't want your money."

I leaned against the car and put both hands on my hips.

"And just what do I have that you could possibly want?"

JayR's manly face changed right before my eyes into a sheepish little boyish grin. "A hug" he said, unsure at first. Then his shoulders straightened and he stood tall. "Yeah, a hug, that's what I want." He grinned.

"JayR, you know how I feel about such foolishness. I mean I had lunch with you, then we went to that lake, we—."

He interrupted, "You were tense all the time. You hardly ate anything, and you didn't enjoy the beauty that surrounded the lake, and—." he held up one finger—."you drove your own car."

I stared at his big smile. I couldn't help but shake my head.

"So if I agree to a simple little hug, then you'll agree to help me."

He looked down at the ground. "Well if I help you, you have to give me one date with no strings attached except to have a good time, and one hug, and—." he held up another finger—"we ride in the same car and I get to drive."

"JayR, that's a lot to ask. I want to pay you instead."

"And what you're asking isn't? You're talking jail time, assault and battery, possibly kidnapping with intent to do bodily harm. Oh, I think that's more than fair."

"Yes, but, you're asking me to trust you, to let you in, to be humble."

"No, I'm asking you to let me feed you because you're hungry, let me entertain you because your life is boring, and let me hold you because I want to."

"I'll have to think about that. Why not just take the money."

"I don't need your money. So you think about it, and I'll arrange a meeting with my crew."

"What crew!" I frowned. "I thought it was going to be me and you."

"Girl, you gotta be crazy. This ain't no me and you situation. I'm gonna need help from some professionals. So I'll get the crew and you get something nice to wear for our date." He grinned.

We stood for a few minutes looking up at the sky.

"You're rubbing the bridge of your nose,"

"And?" I answered rolling my eyes.

"And what's on your mind?"

I cleared my throat and tried to shake away my thoughts with tears staining my eyes. "Let's talk about this another time." I trembled when I spoke. The sound of my voice was the sound of a wrecked soul, and I think he knew it.

"Well I guess you're right. We can talk about this later. I think we've said enough today," he remarked.

I shook my head.

He stared at me and I tried to look away, but I couldn't. "I know the war is not over for you. I know that you're fighting a battle within yourself, but maybe, just maybe you can use another soldier."

"JayR, you don't understand. This pain is so great."

"It doesn't have to be."

"But I've become used to the pain. I've learned to ignore the constant suffering. It's a part of my life. I don't know any other pleasures in life but pain. And now you're here to mess everything up and make me lose my concentration."

“No I’m not, Febe. I only want to be your friend. Not all men are bad.”

“I have to go,” I said.

“Running away won’t solve anything.”

“No, but that’s what I’m good at.”

I slid behind the wheel of the car and closed the door. JayR stood motionless on the other side of something familiar. I could feel it in my stomach and in my throat. It was my old friend Fear.

Chapter 17

I was back to work in the full swing of things. I had mourned Nikkei's death and used her fate as an example to the women in the shelter. JayR and I spent a few hours together so that I could enlighten him of my plan, an eye for an eye, but he still wasn't satisfied regarding my reason. We were going to meet again later, unfortunately I had nothing else to convince him with. Until today.

I was reviewing a dismissal request on one of the women in the shelter. She was on her last leg. I found out she met with a male friend of her abuser for lunch on the other side of town on several occasions. House rule number one was no outside contact from your past. I was just about to sign the request, when Stella burst into the office.

"He's here! He's here!" she screamed in a state of panic.

I jumped to my feet. "Who's here?"

"Tammy-Tina." She shook her head, trying to catch her breath. "No Theresa, yes, Theresa's husband is here in the house."

"This house!" I shouted, dashing for the living room.

"He has a knife to her throat, Febe!" Stella shouted.

I stopped, picked up the phone, dialed 911, and gave as much information as I could. Then suddenly we heard more commotion, tussling and fighting. Women and babies were screaming and yelling.

"If I can't have her, no one will," the crazed man yelled.

I ran out of the room with a bat in my hand. Two men had him on the floor with his hands cuffed behind his back, strapping something around his ankle.

"Damn, they got here quick," I told Stella. Then I realized it was JayR giving orders and directions to the women in another part of the house.

When I walked into the living room I saw two men dressed in black from head to toe lifting a shackled, deranged, screaming man from the floor. They carried him outside to a waiting black van. I tried to approach JayR, but his eyes told me otherwise. Then in a flash, they were gone.

Ten minutes later the police showed up. The women were still crying and nervously pacing from room to room. The children were screaming and yelling for comfort. It was a madhouse, because no one felt safe. Now they understood why we had house rule number one, no outside visitors.

I finished giving Officer Ray my statement, leaving out the part about the five men in black, the van, and JayR, when Stella grabbed my attention.

"Febe, the phone. It's for you."

"I'll take it in the office," I yelled.

"Excuse me, Officer Ray, I have to take this call," I said,

relieved to be able to walk away from him.

"You go on I have to let these ladies know that this was an isolated incident."

I smiled and put the phone to my ear. "Hello."

"How's everything?"

I looked towards the officer, then closed the door.

"Wow, was that the crew?"

"Yes, some of them. How's everything?" he repeated.

"Fine, but Theresa and her kids left."

"What!"

"She took what she brought and left."

"After all that, she left the shelter?"

"I told you if they don't want to be helped, sometimes we only get in the way."

"But he had a knife to her throat. He was going to kill her."

"And he will."

"He'll what?"

"Kill her."

"You sound as if you don't care."

"I care, JayR, more than you think, but if she doesn't want help, we can't force her."

"Well, I don't think she's gonna have to worry about him anymore."

My heart fell. "JayR, you didn't." I gasped for air.

"Didn't what?"

"Kill him."

"Girl, you must be crazy. I ain't no killer. They kicked the shit out of him. He has a lawn service, so he's gonna do a little community service for a while."

"JayR, that's blackmail, and it's not legal,"

"Yeah, like beating the shit out of someone every month for a year is legal." He added.

"You think a year is too long?" I asked sarcastically.

"Hell yeah. A year is a long time to get the shit kicked out of you."

I became silent, while I tried to tell the maniac that was in my head to keep quiet, but it was no use, she spoke anyway.

"JayR."

"Yes."

"Come by the house tonight, we can talk more about my plan," I said softly.

After I spoke, my heart pounded so loudly in my ear I thought I missed something that he said.

"JayR?"

"I'm here."

"You're not backing out on me, are you?"

"No, no, you're not backing out on me, are you?"

"No, I don't think so."

"Good, because I was coming by anyway."

Chapter 18

When I finally did make it home, Gloria and I gossiped for a while and then said good night. After she found out JayR would be here and I wouldn't be alone, she went to see if Jackass Jackson wanted to go to a movie and dinner. Whatever, I thought, as I slid into a steaming-hot tub of cherry bubble bath, that came up to my neck. I closed my eyes and tried to relax my mind, just as I was instructed by one of my many therapists. As I soaked my troubles away, I had to admit to myself that I was tired of being scared, tired of running, and tired of wondering about tomorrow.

No sooner did I shake that negative thought out of my mind, another one popped in.

Then I remembered the couple I saw in Miss Dorothy's parking lot. I definitely tried to shake that image out of my mind, but it was there. It was stuck on the way they moved their hips against each other, the way he kissed her mouth and neck, how she threw her head back and exploded with laughter.

I shuddered in the water. I couldn't imagine letting a man do that to me. I couldn't imagine feeling like that, or even wanting something like that. I can't even imagine not being afraid that he would turn on me like a wild animal, then I would have to kill him.

"Febe, are you getting out of the tub? That water must be ice cold by now," JayR shouted from the other room.

"JayR?" I replied.

"Yes, Gloria let me in."

"Okay, here I come," I said, stumbling out of the tub, and slipping into a pair of large men's Pajamas.

I walked into Gloria's side of the condo and there he was, with a gallon of ice cream and an armful of movies. I smiled.

I know how much you like karate, so I brought *Enter the Dragon*," he said smiling.

"I love Bruce Lee," I said as I returned from the kitchen with two spoons and two bowls. I sat on the sofa, and he plopped down next to me, gawking.

"JayR, please don't stare at my face. It isn't that bad."

"No, it isn't. I was looking at your eyes." He reached out to touch me, but I pulled away.

"What's wrong with my eyes?"

"I don't know, they look different."

"How?"

"Softer, I guess. Are you alright?"

"I'm fine. Put in the movie," I ordered, changing the subject.

"I still can't believe that you do what you do for a living."

"Febe, what I do for a living is just a job," he said, shoving a spoonful of ice cream into his big mouth.

"Now who's getting upset? I'm not here to judge you. If you want to go around finding some people and hurting others, that's fine with me. My question is, are you willing to help me, just like you did tonight?"

"I don't see what I did tonight is going to stop domestic violence."

"I know it's not going to stop it, but it might help. I just feel it."

"What about mandatory counseling or that anger-management class that Shelly has down at the center?"

"JayR, I'm living proof that anger-management ain't for everybody. Hell, I took the course and I'm just as angry as before, if not more."

"What about the justice system or a restraining order?"

"Women have died on the courthouse lawn, and some have even died after obtaining a restraining order that very day."

JayR dropped his head and stared into his half empty-bowl of Chocolate Cherry Jubilee ice cream. He took a deep breath.

"Febe, you hav'ta talk to the crew and convince them, because I wanna help you, but I don't want to get involved in such a political affair."

I looked away from him and mumbled under my breath. "No one ever wanted to get involved with Nikkei, not even her own family."

"Febe, that was a low blow, and if you're gonna talk like that then we can just stop talking, and I can. . ."

"You can do what, JayR?"

"I can sit here and eat my ice cream, 'cause I ain't gonna leave, you can't make me because I already told Gloria that my VCR was broken and I wanted to watch these movies."

I squinted at him. "You little sneaky bitch."

"Febe." He smiled. "You have to apologize to me, or I will not talk to you," he said, crossing his arms over his chest and poking out his bottom lip.

"Okay, okay, it was wrong of me to say that."

"Good. Now, do I still get my hug, even if the crew says no?"

"Yes, JayR, you still get your hug. But tell me about your crew." I crossed my legs in front of me. "Do I get to see their faces?"

"Oh no, we can't have that."

"Why not?"

"You can jeopardize our entire organization."

"By seeing their faces?"

"Yes."

"Why?"

"Some of these men are very important people in the community."

He had my attention when he said that. "You mean government officials, the chief of police, and men in the CIA?"

"Girl, slow down. I mean like ex-cons who don't give a shit. Ex-junkies who want to make a difference. Men hiding out from the military police, important folks."

"Important hell! You mean criminals," I shouted and sat back.

"Hey, now don't go knocking the crew. They're reformed criminals, good men."

"Criminals just the same. Any of them using drugs?"

"No, except the short one. We think he's on something because he's crazy as hell."

"Oh hell, JayR! I don't need no junkie with no freaking monkey on his back. I'm on a mission."

"Calm down, I'm just kidding. He's not a junkie, but he is crazy."

JayR became quiet and his expression turned serious.

"Febe, when we go out on our date and I take you to meet the crew, you have to let your guard down."

"JayR, I don't know, I'm a little uncertain."

"The crew won't hurt you."

"No, I mean going out on a date with you. It's an enormous step for me."

"I won't hurt you. Besides, we've gone out before."

"Yeah, but not on a real date."

"Febe."

"JayR, let's just watch the movie and talk about that date thing later."

Chapter 19

Time seemed to slip by. It was Friday, and I was wrapping a large yellow towel around my wet body, racing through the bedroom like a mad person, searching for something to wear. I slid into a pair of heavily starched blue jeans, a black long-sleeve, high-neck body suit, black low-cut leather boots, and a black belt.

"Wow! Febe, you look great," JayR said, gawking at me. When I walked into the living room.

"JayR, you promised, no compliments."

"Okay, I take that back."

"Where are the two of you going tonight?" Gloria asked. She and Shelly were smiling like proud parents.

I turned to look at JayR.

"Well I thought we would take a trip down to Riverside."

"Riverside!" Gloria said with a frown.

My eyes moved from one person's face to the next. I had no idea where Riverside was.

"What's in Riverside?" she asked.

"A little amusement park. The three of us used to go there whenever I was in town."

I looked at Gloria for some assurance that everything was going to be alright. She understood my glare.

"Oh, that sounds wonderful. You two kids have fun," she added, rushing us out of the door.

"Yeah, you're gonna love it. It ain't DisneyLand, but it's fun," Shelly smiled.

Once we were outside, I turned to JayR. "Why did you choose an amusement park?" I asked, sliding onto the cool leather seat.

"I thought it would be a great first date. That way you could still feel free and we wouldn't be caught in an awkward position."

"I thought you said this was not a date."

"Why can't we call it a date?"

"Because I don't date."

"Oh, that's right, you don't date, you just go out." He winked.

We took the 91 freeway east to Riverside County, which took forever and a day. I thought we were in another state when we arrived at our destination. The amusement park looked small from the outside. But once we were inside, I was satisfied. We ate chili-cheese dogs and cotton candy. We played miniature golf and video games. We shot hoops and threw darts. I was having so much fun I wanted to do everything twice. We decided to skip the movie and stay until the place closed.

I still had my guard up. I knew any minute he was going to reach for my hand, but he didn't, which made the evening even better.

I was sorry that the evening had to end. For the first time tonight, I thought of nothing except having fun.

A couple hours later, after we were kicked out of the amusement park, I found myself engulfed in darkness as we drove down the longest stretch of highway I ever did see. It was pitch black. No lights anywhere, and the sky was a blanket of stars, just as thick as the darkness down below. The only light was from the front of JayR's black convertible.

"Where are we going?" I asked slowly.

"Can you trust me, just for one night?"

"JayR, I don't like this feeling, and I don't trust."

"That's the feeling of not being in control of this situation."

"Am I gonna like it?"

"Trust me."

"Okay, but you know I know kung-fu or some shit like that. So no funny business."

He chuckled and drove faster. "Okay, no funny business."

I leaned against the door—actually, I was glued to the door. My face was toward the wind. I sat in silence as my heart raced along with my thoughts. I closed my eyes, took a deep breath, and relaxed.

Was I doing the right thing for these women? Was I doing the right thing for their children?

Violence was violence no matter who was doing it or who was receiving it. I pondered that thought for a while, trying to keep my eyes open but it was no use. Sleep slipped in like a thief in the night.

I could feel the monster rise up out of the darkness, but this time I didn't run, I didn't back down.

"I only treat you this way because you're so weak, so gullible, so pathetic. You will always be under my command." The monster said as he began to shake me.

I hit him so hard across his hairy face he stumbled back. "No more!" I cried. "No more pain, no more suffering, and no more damn tears!" I yelled. When I turned to run, he grabbed me, and I took hold of him. I held him tightly in my hands. This time

I was going to fight that monster, beat him down, and kill him like the man that I know he truly was.

Then I felt a warm sensation take over my body, calming me down. I slowly opened my eyes, and it was JayR. He had stopped the car and he was hugging me, rocking me gently.

I wanted to stay in his arms forever, but my stubbornness would not let me. I pushed him away, jumped out of the car, and dashed down the two-lane street into the thick blackness. I wasn't afraid of what was out there in the darkness, but I was terrified of what was in the car—JayR

"Where are you going?" he shouted after me.

"I need some air," I shouted back.

"Febe, the top is down,"

"It's not a monster, JayR. It's a man. A mother- freaking man has been chasing me in my dreams."

JayR got out of his car and walked to where I was standing.

"Febe, get back inside. We still have a long way to go."

"He's responsible for me, for who I am and why I'm here. I wanna take this to the authorities. I wanna talk to Detective Monroe."

"Wait a minute," JayR said, staring straight into my eyes. "Before we do anything, let's think this over. What do you have to take to the police? We already know that someone beat you. Who that someone is, we still don't know."

"But, JayR," I cried, "I know for a fact that he did this to me. I was sometimes unsure, but now I know and I want something done about it."

JayR rubbed his head. "It was you who needed to see the man and not the monster, and it was you who said the police can't do anything about your situation."

"Yes, but this is different."

"How so? Gloria said that Detective Monroe gave you a hard time once before when he came around with all his questions, so what's gonna be different about your statement that's gonna make him change his mind?"

I lowered my head.

"He didn't believe you then, and you still can't tell him much more than you did the last time he saw you, so he won't believe you now. And, your attitude is telling them that whoever did this to you is probably lying someplace dead, and your memory loss is only a cover-up for a much larger problem. So let's sit down, put all the pieces on the table and see what we come up with. Then once everything fits, we can go to the police, but for now you only know that he's a man and not a monster."

"JayR, I don't know. I don't want him to get away with what he's done to me."

"Oh, sweetie, he won't get away. When I find him, he's gonna wish he was dead, but he won't get away."

We walked back to his car, both of us caught up in our own thoughts. He opened the door and I slid inside. He jumped over the door, slid into his seat and started the engine. Then he reached out for me.

The tiny frail voice in my head made me surrender my hand to him. His hand was warm, not burning hot like it used to be. It was alive, like the life that was beginning to brew inside of me, and slowly running down my thighs. I gasped for air, and JayR squeezed my hand a litter harder. The electrifying feeling was now on the dead part of my body, bringing it back to life. Stimulating it, caressing it, melting away the ice.

Part of me wanted him to verify that I was alive. I wanted to be touched by more than my lies. I wanted to feel alive. I laid my head back and enjoyed this new sensation with a smile.

"If this is pleasure, I like it," I said out loud without thinking. I held my breath, hoping he didn't hear me. But he did.

"This is pleasure," he replied, and gently kissed my hand. I felt like a school girl on her first date.

I arched my back, drew in a breath of fresh air, and rode the shock waves that were surging through my body, bursting out the top of my head. Soft music seeped out of the speakers. "Turn up the music please." I said, and adjusted my body as Kenny G played "*Let Go*."

Chapter 20

When I glanced at the clock, it was 12:15 p.m. the usual time things started to slow down. It had been so busy and hectic, I'd barely had a chance to drink a glass of water. Fridays were like that around the shelter, I reminded myself, as I sat at my desk reminiscing over the last few weeks. My list had grown and I still hadn't heard from JayR and those guys he took me to see.

I knew JayR was pissed at me for not keeping my mouth shut. I was supposed to ask questions and not get all in the man's face. Now his little crew probably won't help me get these damn abusers. Shit, I knew that I'd screwed up and I didn't even have a Plan B.

Maybe when JayR returned from this special assignment, I'd apologize. I smiled to myself. Thinking that would never happen.

"Febe?"

"Yes." I answered looking up from my piles of papers.

"Officer Ray called. He's bringing a lady over. I did an intake and cleared her over the phone."

"Does she need medical attention?"

"He said she didn't need to go to the hospital, no drugs and no mental problems."

"When is he coming?"

"He'll be here soon. I told Lesley to let us know when they get here," Stella announced.

"Well I guess I won't be going home early tonight. Call Gloria for me, if you can."

"Okay."

"Oh, any word on DeAnna? Is she gonna close the doors to the shelter?"

"The place is sold."

"Sold."

"DeAnna is coming in on Thursday to sign the papers."

"But why so soon?"

"There aren't enough donations to keep it going, and she wanted to stay private."

"So she'd rather close the doors than have the state take it over?"

"DeAnna doesn't want to deal with the government. Things can get too political. She opened this house because of her daughter, then it just caught on from there."

"They're here," Lesley said, interrupting our conversation.

"Okay, we'll be out in a minute. Take her into the back room and check her in while I talk to Ray. Don't forget to mark down the time."

"Oh, so it's Ray now." Stella smiled.

"Ray is just a nice kid, not too smart, but nice."

"And nice looking too." She beamed. "Tall, dark, and very

big, not fat, I think he goes to the gym." She shook her head.

"I don't have time for a man, Stella, now move so I can see what he wants."

When I opened the door Ray was standing outside, leaning against the banister.

"Hi, how are you?" I shook his hand quickly.

"I'm fine, Febe, and you?"

"I'm doing the best I can. How's your sister?"

"She's fine."

"Good. Come in. How's her situation?"

"Well you know the drill—leave, stay, stay, leave. We just don't know what to do."

"Well just hold on, we'll think of something. In the mean time, just try and stay close to her."

A tiny knock interrupted us.

"Febe, can you and Stella come to the back room, please?"

"Sure, Lesley." I smiled. "Can Ray come?"

"That's fine." Lesley blinked.

"You got time?" I asked.

"Yeah, sure."

"Bring your sidekick," I added looking at his partner.

Stella and I stepped into the room first. My heart melted. I tried to keep my composure as I quickly stepped out of the room.

"Her name is Lisa. Now where did you find her?" I asked Ray, crossing my arms over my chest, chewing on my bottom lip.

"Griffith Park sitting on the grass crying. I asked her if she needed help, and she said no. I asked if she wanted to go to the hospital, and she said no."

"Hmm." I uttered.

"I asked her if she had a place to go. She said no. I didn't see any marks on her, and she said she wasn't hurt."

"Then what happened?"

"My partner and I started to leave."

"Ray-Ray-Ray. You were going to walk away and leave her there?"

"Yeah. She said she was okay."

"So why didn't you. . ."

"Why didn't I what?"

"Why didn't you leave her at the park?"

"She didn't want me and Rick to leave. So I called you. I mean you helped me and my parents out with Whitney. You were the first person who crossed my mind."

"You didn't take her to the hospital? You just called me and brought her here?"

"Yes."

"Ray, let me show you what you missed. Come with me."

I led Ray to the room where Lisa was standing. His partner tagged along. "Let me ask you a question?" I said, stopping in front of the door, with one hand on the knob. "Did you find it to be a little unusual for someone with this young lady's appearance to be dressed in so many coats? I mean, well-manicured hands, clean smooth skin, silky blond hair."

"No, not really, and to tell you the truth, Febe, I didn't pay much attention."

I opened the door to the room where Lisa was standing, with her naked back to us. Lesley was down on her knees cleaning Lisa's wounds.

Ray's mouth fell open and so did the rookie's, who started to lose his dinner.

Black and blue marks covered Lisa's pale little body. From the back of her neck to the bottom of her heels. She was shaking from the pain that engulfed her. Her body trembled and she quivered as the medication was applied to her broken and bleeding skin. She didn't cry, only tiny little whimpers escaped from her lips.

"Lisa, please turn around," I said.

"Ray, when you look into Lisa's face, what do you see?"

He didn't answer me, but looked away.

"I see a beautiful, healthy, young lady," I answered and shook my head. "But underneath her clothes there's years of abuse, pain, fear, and despair. Look into her eyes!" I shouted with anger.

"Febe, I just didn't know. I didn't see."

I turned to Lisa. She held a large beach towel in front of her pale body. "Lisa, my dear, tell these wonderful police officers what your husband does for a living. How does this wonderful man take care of his family?" I asked, looking in the direction of the two speechless officers.

She raised her head, tears streaming down her face and pain running down her back. She uttered, "He's a police officer."

More silence filled the room.

"Did you hear that, Officer Ray?" I asked with my hands on my hips, shaking my head. "He's one of you. One of this city's finest. To protect and serve. While the both of you were out on the beat, your coworker was beating his wife."

"Who is he?" Ray asked with anger in his voice.

"Oh, he doesn't matter anymore, Ray, but as soon as I get the information I'll pass it to you." I said sarcastically.

"But why did he do this to her? What did she do to deserve this?"

"Tell him, Lisa, if you'd like."

Lisa turned her face to the wall. "He found a tampon in my purse. And he beat me with a whip," She grunted through clenched teeth.

"A what!" Ray said with disbelief in his voice.

I put my hand on his back ushering him out the room. "You heard her right, a whip. He didn't want her to wear a tampon. He told her the only thing that was going inside of her was him. So he beat her to teach her a lesson."

"Why didn't she call the police?"

"Why! So he could get fired and beat her even worse, because she caused him to lose his job? No, she did what she thought was best. She ran, but once out of the house fear took over and she was too scared to run back home and too scared to keep going."

Ray's bottom lip trembled. "You see, Ray, when you tell me you really didn't pay attention, I see the little things that you miss. I see the anger of someone's fist, the print of a boot in someone's back. I see a stream of blood that has made a lagoon by her feet. I see black-and-blue marks, colors so real, so vivid, they appear painted on. When you don't pay attention, you miss a lot. Now if you don't mind, I need to be escorted to the hospital."

The day was long and I rode it hard. I had another intake right after I returned to the shelter from the hospital. As I settled my keys into the elevator, turned to the left, and pressed the gold button to the fifth floor. I took a deep breath. I was so glad to be home. I silently surrendered to the upper story, and I slid out of the small elevator like a cat burglar. My bed was going to feel real good tonight, I thought when I slid the key into the lock. I left instructions at the shelter that if I was desperately needed, to ring me but otherwise try and handle it.

Saturday morning was going to be another day and I was going to make it a great one.

I undressed, peeling off the day's clothes and its madness. JayR gave me a little hint of what fun was, and I wanted more of it. Shelly was out of town again, and Gloria said she would go to Disneyland with me, so I needed to try and get some rest before sun up.

I lit a few candles and filled the tub with steaming hot water and so much Cherry bubble bath, I could almost taste the cherries. I stood in front of the full-length mirror in my matching panties and bra examining my body.

My stomach was flat and my thighs were firm. My breasts were a nice size also. My body was okay. Except for the hundreds of scars that lined my frame. I traced the scars with my eyes, down my body around the back of my legs. Cuts and marks on my breasts. I tried to remember what had happened to me and what my abuser had beaten me with, but nothing came forth. I tried to remember his face or the sound of his voice. Still nothing.

It used to be painful to look at my body, but now the scars just kept me going. They held a story that I wanted to tell.

After soaking until the water turned cold and my hands and feet looked like prunes, I rubbed my body with pure vitamin E oil that Gloria gave me, insisting that it would help to fade most of the scars.

I shivered as I passed a gentle hand over my past. I could feel the scars standing high as hills, and they felt bumpy and choppy, sort of like that road JayR and I were on a few nights earlier.

I collapsed in my bed with the CD softly playing. One day I'd get up the nerve to go to sleep without the damn thing on, but this wasn't the night.

My heart came to a sudden halt when I saw the black dress that I wore to Nikkei's funeral. It was in a plastic bag draped over the arm of my chair. The maid must have forgotten to take it to the thrift shop.

Slowly easing off the bed and quietly walking over to the chair, I picked up the dress, slipped it out of the plastic, and brought it to my nose. The dry cleaners had taken all the smell away.

Nikkei's Charlie perfume that I doused myself in was gone and so was my best friend. I blew out the candles and shoved the room into darkness. Me, Sade, and my thoughts of Nikkei were left alone.

I thought about crying, but crying wasn't something I was devotedly attached to. The tears would come to sneak a peek at the world on the edge of my eyes and recoil to their hiding place, deep in my soul.

I began to fall asleep thinking about JayR and his sister, wanting both of them, but afraid as hell of one of them. I slid between the comfortable white sheets with the dress clenched in my fist. Barely breathing.

I wanted to scream so badly for Nikkei, Justine, Lisa, Rachel, Donna, and all the women who had suffered abuse by the hands of their lovers. Yes, I wanted to cry for them, but most of all, I wanted to scream for me, who was so afraid to love.

Suddenly I could feel the quietness near me. I could feel it as I lay still. My body was light, floating in the air. I could hear the quietness sneaking up on me, and I fought to keep my eyes open. But soon the rhythm of my heartbeat closed my lids for me, and I slipped into a peaceful sleep.

Then my heart stopped, I opened my eyes, as a cold fear ran through me, as the pungent nitro powder solvent hurried up my nostrils and stung my eyes. My room reeked of the stuff. Then I heard heavy breathing and smelled men's cologne.

The nitro hit me once again like a ton of bricks, forcing me to remember. It's the stuff you use to clean guns, I shouted in my head. I slowly removed the covers from my body. It couldn't possibly be a dream, the odor was too strong.

I searched around in the darkness until I felt the coolness of the steel bat. I grabbed control of my fears, and with all of the strength that I had in my body, I came up swinging. I heard a few screams and a loud thud.

The lights went on and off again. I quickly saw men standing around my room. That bitch named Fear was on me again trying to secure a place in my heart, draining me dry. I was at her mercy, hoping for a little pity. I was about to speak, but the next thing I knew, a sheet was thrown at me and the lights went on.

Two men were lifting JayR from the floor. "What you do that for?"

he shouted softly. “We just came to get you for a run.”

"What’s wrong with you?” I asked lowering my voice. “Why did you do that?”

“It’s part of the initiation. The crew decided to help so we came to get you.”

“In the middle of the night? JayR!”

“Yes, we were going to take our place then slowly wake you. But nooo!” JayR said pacing around the room, holding his nose. “You had to come up swinging like a crazy baseball player.”

I just glared at him. I really didn’t have anything to say. I wasn’t mad, but how stupid can one person be? I tightened the sheet around me and headed for the closet to get something to put on.

One of the men handed me a black bundle. I looked over at JayR.

“You’re part of the gang now.” He rolled his eyes. “Get dressed, Kung-Fu Babe Ruth.” He smiled.

I emerged from the bathroom looking just like one of the boys.

“Where are my gloves?” I asked.

“I couldn’t remember the size of your hands.”

“Well you sure got the pants size just right.”

“Yeah, I did do quite well,” he remarked, grinning sheepishly.

I waved him away. “Oh, forget you. I have some.”

I reached into the drawer where I kept my underwear and socks and grabbed a pair of gloves.

I glanced over at JayR, who raised his right eyebrow and gave me a little smile.

“Well, that’s all I have,” I said, slipping my hands into a pair of fishnet black gloves.

I grabbed my black leather jacket off the hook, my keys off the counter, and dashed out the door. We ran down five flights of stairs, jumped into a waiting van and sped away. I was breathless and completely out of shape, but determined to keep up with the big boys.

JayR sat calmly next to me. "Do you have any questions?" he asked.

"Yes," I answered.

"What?"

"Where are we going?"

"To Ronny's apartment."

My mouth fell open. "How do you know Ronny, and where he lives?

"We asked around the neighborhood."

"You're lying."

"We did."

"You're lying, because the women are never placed in shelters where they live or work."

"Well I guess we got it off this." He dangled a sheet of paper in my face. "Next question."

"My list!" I almost came out of my seat. "How did you get my list?"

"From your safe," he replied calmly. Combination 11-7-63."

"When did you take my list?"

"A few nights ago, as you slept."

"So you were in my room?"

"Oh yeah, lots of times. Sometimes when I couldn't sleep I would sneak in and watch you sleep."

"JayR."

"Okay, just kidding. I only watched you sleep a couple of times."

Chapter 21

When we arrived at Ronny's house, JayR threw me a mask and we jumped out of the van like a SWAT team. People were already inside waiting for us. I caught a chill when my eyes fell on that green sofa that Justine had described to me. I imagined her lying on the hot, sticky couch with her husband standing nearby as someone violated her.

Looking from room to room, I spotted Megan's tiny crib in the corner of their bedroom and her Miss Piggy doll was on the floor. I turned my attention to the voices that were coming from another direction.

"Tell me, you low-life, no-good son of a bitch. How does it feel?" I heard someone say. Then I saw Ronny shaking his head.

"How does it feel to be at someone else's mercy?"

"I don't like it," Ronny answered.

"You're the big man on campus," someone shouted.

There were two men standing on each side of Ronny holding him up, as the tall guy thrust his fist into Ronny's stomach, shouting question after question. All I could hear were moans and groans, and blow after blow being slammed into flesh.

I stared as punch after punch landed on Ronny's face and stomach. "This is where you hit your wife," the man shouted as he landed another one to Ronny's face.

"What you gotta say for yourself? Mr. Big Man, beating up on your wife, like she's one of the guys. Get your sorry ass up and kick the shit out of me like you did her. Fight back like a real man."

Ronny lifted his head, looked at the tall guy, then toppled back down. He was suddenly overwhelmed by the torture; he burst out crying like a baby. I had no sympathy for him, and it was amazing to see.

"Get up! Get your naked ass up and walk around the house the way you made Justine walk around your friends. Now that I'm thinking about it, go and fry me some bacon. I'm hungry," he commanded.

Ronny struggled to his feet and staggered to the kitchen. He looked liked a brokenhearted kid, as tears ran down his face. His hands were shaking, limp dick hanging in the wind, ass hairy like a baboon's face.

Ronny finally made it to the kitchen, someone snapped on the light, letting him know there was no way out. He was trapped in this nightmare.

He walked slowly toward the stove with a cast-iron skillet in his shaking hands.

"And after you finish, I want some sex. And you better go down on me. Just the way I like it," the tall guy shouted.

Laughter filled the room from all the men who were standing at attention military style.

Ronny was horrified. He dropped the skillet and it landed on his foot. He jumped from the pain and danced around the kitchen.

"Pick it up, and you better not cry or I'll come in there and kick you in your balls." I couldn't help but think that this guy was almost too damn mean.

Ronny said nothing. He just stood in the kitchen naked as a newborn baby, holding the skillet, fighting back his tears, staring in total shock.

"Stop looking at me!" the tall man shouted, causing Ronny to jump, dropping the skillet on his foot again. I could see where his foot began to swell.

Ronny started to cuss, hopping around the kitchen like he was doing the second part of his rain dance.

"You cussing at me? You cussing at me!" the tall man shouted, jumping to his feet, running into the kitchen after Ronny, who ran for cover near the kitchen table.

"I ain't cussing at you!" Ronny cried, trying to explain, falling to the cold linoleum floor with his hands above his head as if this guy was a god.

"Get your sorry ass up. You make me sick, you undeveloped little shit. You ain't nothing, ain't gonna be nothing."

Ronny walked unsteadily into the living room, holding his dried-up penis in one hand and bracing himself with the other.

"We'll be back next month to pay you a little visit." Ronny leaned against the white wall with both hands cupping his haggard little penis and balls.

"Next month?" he mumbled with his head hanging down.

"Yes, bitch, next month, and the month after that and the month after that for the next year or two or three, until you learn to keep your hands to yourself."

Ronny dropped to the floor and started crying, I mean wailing, crying like someone stole his candy.

"Man, I can't take no ass beating like this for a year. Man, this is unreal. Come on man, can we. . .can we work something out?"

"You can't take this for a year! You can't take this for a

year!" he shouted at Ronny.

"How many years have you been doing this shit to Justine? Now you can't take it. Well you will take it and don't try to run." He turned to the men. "Somebody tell this punk where you work?"

A body stepped out of the line.

"Private investigator, sir!" A short man shouted to the top of his lungs, and took one step back into his place in line.

"Don't try to go to the police. Somebody tell this punk where you work."

Again another man stepped out of line.

"This city's finest!" he shouted, stepped back into his place in line.

Ronny looked up from the floor and back down again.

"Don't go to confession," the tall guy said very softly in his commanding voice. "Somebody tell this punk where you work."

Again another man stepped out of line. My eyes widened and I looked in his direction.

"St. Frances Catholic Church!" he shouted just like the other ones before him. "Come to confession my, son. It's good for your soul. Won't do nothing for your ass, but it's good for your soul." He stepped back into his place in line.

"That's the church my mother goes to," a weeping Ronny stated, not taking his eyes off the floor.

"And don't even think about telling your mama."

"My mother?" Ronny said softly.

"You will deal with this on your own," the tall man said, and once again in his commanding voice, "Mother." He shouted.

Oh, this was some crazy shit. "They got this man's mommy?" I asked JayR.

Someone stepped out of line. Ronny looked up in shock, like someone just stepped on his tail. The room broke into another round of laughter. "You thought we had your mama, didn't you?"

I thought Ronny was going to drop dead right where he

was kneeling. A one-word command was sounded, and stillness covered the room.

The crew turned and left the house as quietly as they came, leaving me, JayR, and the tall guy alone with Ronny sobbing in the middle of his living room floor. I looked at him as tears filled his eyes.

I bent down to his level. "Tell me, how does it feel to know that next month this same shit will happen again?"

He spit in my face. Before I had time to react, JayR had a knife to Ronny's throat.

"No!" I shouted.

"Why are you fucking with me? She's my wife," Ronny shouted.

JayR snatched Ronny up by his throat and held him against the wall. "She's your wife to love her and take care of her, not to beat her and sell her body to your friends."

I put my hand on JayR's shoulder. He let go of Ronny's neck. "You don't get it, do you, man," JayR said.

Ronny put both hands in the air. "I'm sorry man, I don't know what's gotten into me."

JayR spoke very slowly to Ronny. "If you feel you have to hit Justine," he spoke through clenched teeth, "it would be in your best interest to leave this house. We will be keeping an eye on you, so don't fool yourself."

"Okay, okay," Ronny said, sniffing.

"Write this address down," JayR commanded.

Ronny hurried to get a pencil and a brown paper bag. JayR recited the address to Shelly's center. Ronny frantically wrote down the information.

"Now I expect you to be at the center every Wednesday night at 7:30 for an anger-management class."

Ronny nodded in agreement. "I'll know if you don't show up. And another thing, Justine doesn't need to know anything about tonight's meeting. This is our little secret. Do you understand?"

"Okay, man, okay I'll be there and my lips are sealed. I won't say a word to Justine."

After Ronny's, we made our rounds to a few other prospective clients. Some were a little harder than we expected, but for the most part I guess you can say it was a very successful night. The crew drove me home, and JayR made sure that I was in my bed safe and sound. Gloria didn't even know I was gone.

About a week later early one Sunday morning, Gloria woke me up to answer the phone.

"Hello," I said softly, bending over the intercom.

"Febe, it's JayR. Good morning."

"What's wrong?" I asked.

"Why do you think something's wrong?"

"The sun ain't up and you're calling me, something has to be wrong."

"I do need to talk to you. Meet me out front."

"Okay, but it better be good."

"It's important."

I hung up the phone, grabbed a quick shower, and was out front waiting when he drove up.

"Good morning, pretty lady." He smiled, peering over the rim of his glasses.

"JayR, don't start with the bullshit this morning. What's up?"

"Accept the compliment, then I'll tell you."

I took a deep breath, opened the car door, dropped into the seat, and looked over at him. "Accepted, now what's up?"

He slid his sunglasses back up the bridge of his nose and stared straight ahead. "Last night while you were out with Gloria, they did Anthony, in his house."

"Anthony! Who's that?" I asked frowning.

"He's Lisa's husband. The cop."

"They did?" I covered my mouth.

"Yeah, hope you're not mad."

"Nah, that's okay, but no more without me."

"I understand, but they ran into a little problem with him."

"What kind of problem?"

"Well they let the little guy get to him, the one I told you was a little crazy."

"Yeah."

"Anthony's in the hospital. ICU."

"Is he gonna be alright? You look worried."

"I don't know, but there's gonna be an investigation, simply because he's a cop."

"Investigation?"

"Febe, there's nothing to worry about. We have enough connections to keep this tied up in lost report hell for at least a year. Anthony only knows he was attacked by the same unidentified person who attacked his wife."

"JayR, the man was attacked in his house and beaten with his own whip, a whip that lands him and his wife in the same hospital. I don't think that's gonna fly."

"Well the good thing is Lisa is not talking to the police, and with Anthony in the same condition, the police are at a loss."

"If you got everything under control why are you telling me?"

"I know how you are about these women, and information is important to you. Besides, it was the only excuse I could use to get you to have breakfast with me." He smiled.

After breakfast I went to visit Lisa who was still in the hospital. I walked into her room where she slept, wishing that I could sleep that peacefully. I touched her on her shoulder. "Lisa." She opened her eyes and yawned. I kissed her cheek and put the flowers in the vase next to her bed. "Did you speak with your parents?"

"Yes, I did."

"And?"

"And they didn't sound too happy to hear that I needed to come home."

"Well did they say you can come?"

"Yes."

"So, what's the problem?"

"I don't think my father wants me there. He didn't want me to marry Anthony in the first place. Now I have to move back home and hear his bitching for God knows how long."

I folded my arms across my chest. "Which one is worse? Hearing your father bitch for a few months or getting the stuffing beat out of you for the rest of your life, which won't be too long if you stay with Anthony."

I saw that my words hurt her. Her face went pale and she rolled her eyes.

I took her hand in mine. "Look, I know that you didn't want to hear that, but the truth is the truth. If you go back, you will die. You may not die the next time he beats you or the next or the next, but you will die. A little piece of you will die each time he hits you."

"So go home, eat crap with a silver spoon, get a divorce, and start living. You have a place to run to, so you run, as fast as you can. And you never stop running until Anthony is so far out of your mind he is no longer a memory."

She started to cry. "I know it hurts. Like you, Lisa, so many women are in love with their abuser. I'm sure I was, but he made me get over it, and so can you."

I tilted her face to mine. "Love doesn't hurt, girl. I know." I patted my chest. "I had to find out the hard way." She nodded. I picked up the phone and handed it to her. "You call your father again, and you tell him that you need him and you're coming home."

I left Lisa to her conversation, and located Anthony. As I stood in the threshold of his room. He was lying on his stomach, blood seeping through the white gauze that was placed so neatly on his back, butt, and thighs.

"He won't be able to sit for a few months," an elderly gray-haired nurse said, interrupting my peaceful thought. The smile dropped from my face and was replaced with a concerned look.

She whispered, "He could have died from all the lashes he took to his back. There must have been more then two hundred of those babies on this poor man's back."

I held my tongue and bit my bottom lip. I tried to make my face seem concerned about his well-being. I personally could have cared less. They should have given him three or four times more than what he received. One for each time he made Lisa feel bad about herself, another for each time he hit her, and another for each time he called her names.

The nurse put a warm hand on my shoulder. "Is he a friend of yours, dear?"

I fixed my eyes on Anthony's back. "No, just passing by."

"That's a shame," she uttered, shaking her head at Anthony's still frame. "You know the same thing happened to his wife—she's on the upper floor—you know, cuts and abrasion up and down her back. The police are stunned, they can't make heads or tails of the whole situation. He can't talk yet, and she won't talk."

"Is he gonna wake up soon?"

"No, baby, not any time soon. This man is on some heavy meds. He ain't gonna wake up for a while." I continued to chew on my bottom lip. I wrapped my arms around my waist and slipped out of Anthony's room just as quietly as I came. I had just enough time to meet with Gloria and Jackson.

CHAPTER 22

I woke with a dark cloud hanging over my head. I sat on the edge of my bed and took a deep breath. I felt like I was losing my mind.

I was not any closer to finding out anything about Nikkei, and my list was growing. Justine went back to Ronnie and I felt like I traded one evil for another.

The old abusers stopped abusing for the time being, but there were younger ones popping up in their places, which made me sick. I even stopped going out and left it up to JayR and his crew to do my will.

Today didn't seem like a day I wanted to deal with, so I decided to stay home. I just couldn't explain what I was feeling. I know things were moving quite fast for me, but I was getting more and more confused each day.

Gloria said that she would ask me to do something and I would agree, but it would never get done. On the other hand, I never remembered her asking me in the first place.

I made a phone call to my new therapist, hopped in the shower, and drove down La Brea in a fog. When I reached her office I just stood in the threshold of door.

"Febe, come in. How are you today?" I heard her ask.

"I really can't answer that truthfully today, Ella, because I really don't know."

Ella gave me a heartwarming smile that only she could give. "Sit, let's talk."

I didn't look behind me. I just plopped down on her soft brown couch with my arms folded across my chest.

"Febe."

"Yes," I answered quickly.

"Sit back, relax, and take your shoes off. You talk, I listen, remember."

I took a deep breath, relaxed and looked up at the ceiling. I went through a truckload of therapists before I found her. Actually I don't remember how I found Ella, I just sort of woke-up in her office. I liked her so I stayed.

Ella was medium height, with shoulder-length natural curly brown hair, complexion smooth as cocoa silk sheets, and her bedside manner was love at first sight.

When she smiled at me, it made me calm. Ella was a great therapist, because she never tried to fix anything. I talked, she listened, but she never tried to fix it.

"Febe."

"Yes," I answered, slowly raising one brow.

"You can unfold your arms now and relax."

I unfolded my arms and held my breath for a few seconds.

"Are you ready?"

"Yes."

"Good. What's new in your life?"

I took another deep breath, exhaled, and looked way. "I had a meeting with Gloria and Jackson a week ago. They turned the shelter over to me. I knew DeAnna had sold the house and we were just waiting for the new owners to give us our kick-out orders, but instead I received the deed to the house. The shelter is mine."

"That's wonderful."

"Gloria said it was Jackson's idea."

"That's still a good thing. Isn't that what you wanted?"

"Yes, but why would Jackson do something like that for me. I mean he knows how I feel about him." I was silent as I thought for a moment. "Maybe it's his way to right a wrong with me as far as Gloria is concerned."

"What do you mean?" she asked.

"Well, he has been very generous to me and to other shelters I'm trying to get off the ground. He's put us on his organization list to receive money on a monthly basis. Donations are flowing in from some of his wealthy clients, new and old."

"Well that's a good thing."

"Yes, but why is he doing all of this for me?"

"Febe."

"Yes," I answered.

"Do you really care why he's being so generous, or do you care that now, you can keep the shelter open as well as open other shelters?"

"I don't know, Ella. It's just that things are happening so fast it seems as if I'm losing days or even weeks. I feel like I'm chasing something I can't have."

"You mean like JayR." She peered over her glasses.

I stared at her, baffled that she would say something like that.

"What?" I remarked, coming to the edge of my seat. "Who

told you about him?"

"You did."

"I told you about JayR?" I answered, pointing to my racing heart.

"Yes, don't you remember?"

"No."

"You called to make the appointment to talk about JayR."

"I called you this morning and I know I didn't mention a damn thing about JayR."

"Not this morning, a week ago."

"I didn't call a week ago. I called this morning."

"No." She shook her head. "You made the appointment a week ago. We talked on the phone for hours. You said that you could not come in—

"Because," I interrupted her.

"Because you were about to start a new project that you really didn't care for, but your job required that it be done. And you made mention that JayR was angry with you and he was supposed to help you."

"Oh, shit Ella! Did I really?"

"Yes, Febe, you did. You also said that you were starting to have some feelings for JayR, but someone was keeping you from him."

"Ella, are you sure it was me?"

"Yes, I'm sure it was you only calmer and no profanity."

"Oh, hell Ella, if I didn't use profanity then that wasn't me."

"Well, sweetie pie, I spoke to you on the phone. How else would I have known about JayR, and your appointment today?"

"But I always get a standby appointment. I always call the day that I need to see you."

"No, Febe, I don't have standby appointments. You've always called in a few weeks ahead. That was our agreement from the first day you decided to come and see me. You make the appointment, and then you call to confirm."

I was quiet, trying to sort some things out in my head.

"Ella, where did we meet?" I asked after a few moments.

"In church. You were praying."

"Praying in church on my knees?" I asked frowning.

"Yes, Febe. You go to confession all the time."

"Oh, shit, Ella. I gotta go. Can I use your phone?"

"Yes, sure. Do you need privacy?"

"No, I'm checking in on the shelter. Did I tell you about the project that I am working on?" I asked, holding the receiver firmly in my hand, hoping that Stella would pick up the phone.

"No, why?"

I remained silent. I didn't want to talk to her until I had time to think. Shit was getting too weird for me. I never pray. I turned my back to Ella. "Stella, hi, it's Febe. How's everything at the shelter? Oh, really. Okay, I'll be there soon. Put her in my office." I hung up and took a deep breath before turning back to Ella.

"I gotta go. Maybe we can do this another time."

"Is JayR married?"

"What!" I turned back to her.

"Is JayR married? You said she would not let you have him. So is he married?"

"No, he's not married." I frowned

"Does he have a girlfriend?"

"No, Ella. He's not married, and he doesn't have a girlfriend. His mama is dead, and his sisters and I are best friends."

"So what's the problem? Who is this other person who won't let you get to him?"

"Ella, I don't know what you're talking about, but I gotta go because there is someone at the shelter who needs me."

"You need you, Febe," she said calmly, smiling at me before I walked out of her office.

CHAPTER 23

J arrived at the shelter, mystified by the conversation I had just had with Ella. I went into the upstairs supply room and retrieved the list. I found that Jackson's name had been crossed off. So that explained his generosity. The crew must have paid him a little late-night visit. I stuffed the list back into the safe and closed the door.

After reading the new client's folder I took a deep breath in order to prepare myself. Stella had forewarned me that this one was not a nice case. I shook off the feeling of violence that always surrounded me when I spoke to a new victim and entered the room.

I stared at the back of Lydia's head. She was sitting in front of my desk, her face resting in her right hand, the other one was in a cast. I could hear her softly crying. Those are the worse tears to shed, I thought. They hurt the worst.

Her long brown hair was pulled up on top of her head, but I could still see bald spots where her hair was pulled out of her skull. There was a dark ring around her neck.

I stood silently behind her letting her have a moment, because I knew that it was going to get a lot worse.

Her tears stopped flowing as quickly as they came. She wiped her eyes with the corner of her cotton striped shirt and sat up straight. I knew from her back, she had calmed herself with her own thoughts of comfort. She probably told herself that she wasn't going to cry over him anymore.

"Lydia," I said calmly, "don't turn around, close your eyes, and breathe. Picture yourself any place that you want to be. Relax, starting with the frown on your face. Let your troubles fall to your neck slide down your shoulders, roll down your back. Let your thoughts glide down your butt and between your thighs, slip to your legs, and flow to your feet.

You're standing on a drain, the biggest drain you ever did see. All that you used to be, all that he has done to you, all that you think you have allowed him to do, is now draining out to sea.

Alex has no control over you. You owe only what he has already taken away from you. You are now free. As of this moment, you are paid in full."

I was standing in front of Lydia when I told her to open her eyes. I reached down to her and helped her to her feet. We embraced, and the tears that she thought she was finished with began to flow freely once again. Her body jerked and her hands trembled.

I cleared my throat and moved her away from me, so I could look into her wet eyes. I didn't try to hide my pain, because

I was hurting for her too. I wanted to let her know that her fears were real.

"Listen, if you don't let go of the past, it will kill your future. I have to tell myself that every day, because letting go is the hardest thing to do if you want to continue to live. Alex can only take what you are willing to give."

Lydia shook her head and wiped away her tears. We sat in absolute silence for a few minutes before heading into the question phase. Stella had already checked her in and had gone over the rules of the shelter.

"I have read your file and I know that you have been in and out of shelters more than you care to count. Now tell me, why do you think this time is going to be different?" I looked her right in her eyes.

"I don't know," she replied softly. "I just don't know. I'm so tired. I want a change."

"Tell me what can we do to keep you from going back to him."

"I don't know." She shook her head.

"Look at me, don't look away. If you don't know, then how can I help you to stay away from him?"

"I just don't know. I'm so tired of him and all the fighting. Every day he has to beat me about something. He has gotten my kids taken away from me. Child Protective Services will not return them. I don't know what more to do."

"Yes, you do, Lydia, but right now you're too frightened to think. I can help you, but the real help must come from within. You have to want to leave before you can leave. He'll never change. He'll continue to beat you until you do something or until he kills you, and he'll only move on to the next victim," Lydia cut in before I was finished.

"It's always about him. What he wants, what he needs. Don't you see what he's done to me?" She pulled her collar away from her neck and exposed what I had already seen, burn marks from a rope.

"Do you see what he's done to me?"

"Yes, I do. Did he try to hang you?"

"No! He raped me. He pushed me down and tied my hands to a chair and the other end of the rope around my neck. Each time he forced himself inside of me, he would pull the rope until I almost passed out."

"Okay, Lydia." I blinked.

"He raped me, and he kept raping me until I was unconscious, and he left me there, bleeding from my rectum tied to a chair."

"How long were you there?"

"Two days. He left me there for two days! Kim, a lady from my job, knew about my situation and when I didn't come to work she and two of her brothers came to my house. They found me, naked, bleeding, and tied to that chair."

A small part of me could relate to her. I couldn't recall being raped, but her story felt so real. And I knew from what she told me, Alex was a good candidate for the crew. Top priority, while it was still fresh in his mind.

I shifted a bit in my chair. "If you want help, we can help. If you want another place to hide for a couple of days, then Stella can find you another shelter."

"Okay." She closed her eyes.

"Now I'm going to call Stella to take you to your room to think about what I just said. If and when you have decided to help yourself, speak with Stella. She will help you with all that you need. She will have more questions regarding Alex. Some will frighten you, but don't worry, we only need answers to help you. What Alex has done, twenty-five to life in prison will never replace what he has taken away from you. No judge or jury will ever give you back what you have lost. We can and we will help you because love doesn't hurt."

I hugged Lydia with all the strength that I had. I called for

Stella to take her to the other room. Before Lydia left she turned back to me.

"I know that domestic violence is a disease." She spoke, looking down at the floor. "But he. . ."

I took her hand. "No sweetheart, domestic violence is control, not a disease."

Chapter 24

The week had taken a toll on my body. I was tired and cranky. I had put almost three hundred hours into the shelter for the month. When I first took the job I didn't understand what it meant to fully run a shelter for battered women. Now I did.

The donations were coming in, and the funds were high so I didn't have the stress of that, but there were still more women coming into the shelter than there were beds. I shouldn't have been stressing out as much as I had been, but I was.

JayR kept bitching that I was breaking dates as fast as he was making them, and I didn't have the faintest idea what he was talking about. Gloria was tripping, saying that one minute I was nice to Jackson then the next I couldn't stand him. I didn't like Jackson, and never will. I don't understand why she couldn't get that through her head.

But all I did know was I had a date with a bathtub filled with steaming-hot water, and lots of cherry bubble bath.

"Febe."

I jumped when Gloria called my name. "I didn't mean to scare you." She laughed. "But you were talking to yourself again?"

"I was thinking out loud."

"Talking out loud, thinking out loud, same thing. Febe. The point is you're doing it again."

"Whatever, Gloria."

"Look what Jackson bought me." She beamed.

I flattened my lips and cocked my head to one side. "A dozen yellow roses, Gloria. He could have at least given you two dozen. It's not like he's hurting for money."

"Febe, you are so anal sometimes." She laughed.

"I'm serious, Gloria."

"Well, I'm going out to dinner with him tonight, and I'll make him pay then."

"Do what you like. I'm going to take a bath."

"Do you want to say hello?"

"No, I don't."

"Okay good night."

"Good night, Gloria."

After Gloria and jackass left, the house was quiet. It was the first time Gloria had ever left me alone. I felt like a teenager when her parents were away for the weekend. Even though being alone wasn't something that I enjoyed and October wasn't one of my favorite months to do it in, I was okay with it.

I wasn't scared, but the house made all sorts of noises. Settling and shit. The clock on the wall ticked exceptionally loud, the ice maker clicked on and off, and the toilet adjusted itself. Hell, I could hear all sorts of things, but I was still determined to stay in the house alone until Gloria got back.

I dried off, dressed, and ran over to Gloria's side of the house. I jumped on her couch and grabbed the remote control. I flipped through one stupid TV show after another. Even though I was tired, I wanted to look at all the things that Gloria complained about. I started with the news and was gonna work my way down. I remembered last week Becky, a pretty blond newswoman, reported that there was another life taken by domestic violence, and it also included a police officer. I wasn't shocked, and I didn't know why everyone else was.

I flipped from channel to channel hoping that something on the news from around the world would offer a memory for me, a familiar face, a familiar place, or something to help me get back to where I came from.

There was nothing on the news except some shit about a cat or a dog. It was even reported that a ferret chewed half a baby's face off. All I could think of right then was a woman getting the shit kicked out of her, and the news was doing a story on the damn zoo. Ain't that a bitch.

The phone rang and snatched me from my thoughts. I let it ring two more times before I pushed the speaker button.

"Hello."

"Febe?"

"Yes."

"Are you almost ready?"

"JayR?"

"Yes, were you expecting someone else?"

"No, but what do you want?"

"Are you almost ready?"

"For what?"

"To go out."

"What?"

"We were supposed to go and hear my friend's band play."

"JayR, what are you talking about?"

"Febe, I can't believe you're breaking another date with me. You said that you would go to the coffeehouse to hear my friend's band play. Now this will be the fourth time you canceled on me."

"JayR."

"No, really, did I do something wrong? First you're nice and understanding, then the next thing I know you've changed on me. Am I supposed to know what the new you is thinking?"

"JayR, I'm sorry, but I made plans to stay inside tonight."

"You know what, Febe, forget it. I can't win."

"No-no wait, I'll go out with you, but know this, I ain't in the mood for no shit tonight."

"I'm on my way."

I pushed the button, hanging up the phone, and took a deep breath before turning off the TV.

I threw the remote control down on the floor. "Shit! Shit! Shit!" I shouted, storming around the house. "I don't know what the hell he's talking about," I complained as I slipped on a black, long-sleeve turtleneck dress.

The black box chimed just as I slipped on my black low-heel shoes.

"Yes?"

"It's me. Let me up."

"JayR, how did you make it here so quickly?"

"I was at the market when I called. Let me up."

"Okay, but that was pretty sneaky." I said as I sent the elevator down to him.

"I know. I get that from Nikkei."

I waited by the door, my heart in my hands.

"Why did you call me from the market?"

"I wanted to get you something." He handed me the large brown paper bag.

"I guess I can never have too much ice cream."

"Yeah, I know." He winked.

I put the ice cream in the freezer after I took a spoonful and stuffed it into my mouth.

"Gloria left yet?" he shouted.

"Yeah, she left with Jackson, and I know I didn't say I would go to hear no damn band play tonight. So you did get stuck baby sitting me. I knew Gloria wasn't going to leave me alone," I mumbled, shaking my head.

"What do you mean? I didn't get stuck baby sitting you. You said that you would go with me tonight."

"Yeah right, JayR."

"No really, you did."

"Then how did you know Gloria wasn't home."

"Uh hmm."

"Don't try to lie your way out of this. Either Shelly or Gloria called you. Which one was it?"

He put his head down. "Okay, okay, busted. It was both of them. First Gloria, but I wasn't home, then Shelly called. But we already had plans to go out, so that doesn't count."

"Why didn't Shelly come and stay with me herself?"

"She has a date with Harrison."

"With Harrison! She's seeing that fool?"

"Well they just went out to the movies. I don't know if they're dating. They're going to Atlanta for a few weeks, on business."

"Seems like everybody has a date but me."

"What am I? Ground steak?" JayR grinned.

"No, but you're my brother."

"Half-brother."

"What?"

"I'm your half-brother."

"What does that mean?"

"I'm only your brother when you need me, and you only

need me half the time."

"Be quiet. Let's go."

"Yes, ma'am."

We pulled into the parking lot of the Mystic Brew Coffee Shop. I sat in the car for a few seconds to catch my breath and gather good thoughts.

JayR got out and came over to my side of the car. He opened my door and I slowly slipped out, almost in a trance. I couldn't understand what made me wait for him.

We walked silently to the front door of the coffeehouse and peeped inside. The place was small and jammed with people. "I didn't know this many people like to drink coffee so late at night," I said to JayR, trying to act as if I were interested in his choice of outings.

"I didn't know that my friend's band was so popular. Hold on a minute," he said and walked away.

I couldn't believe my eyes. There on the stage was a pint-size drummer with tiny little feet and a big drum set perched in front of him. Another pint-size man played a saxophone, and a three-foot bass player was playing his ass off standing on top of the crate that coffee comes in.

"Oh, hell no!" I remarked just as JayR grabbed my hand.

"What's wrong?" he asked.

I can't believe I gotta sit her all night and listen to Tiny Tim and his miniature friends playing those instruments that they know damn well are too big for all three of them put together. That's what I was thinking, but what I said was, "I have to use the restroom."

JayR gave me a funny look like I had said something wrong.

"That's not what you were thinking."

"How do you know what I was thinking?"

"You're rubbing the bridge of your nose."

"Damn," I said and looked away.

"Febe."

"What?"

"Would you like to be alone with your thoughts?" he remarked with a big Colgate smile.

"No," I replied getting an attitude.

"Good, because if I wanted to be alone, I would have come alone."

I rolled my eyes and looked around the room. "Are we gonna sit down or stand all night?" I asked. "I'm not in the mood for no damn chipmunks anyway, and I sure as hell don't want to stand all night to listen to them."

That Colgate smile faded, and he replied, "We have a seat over here next to the band. You don't have to stand all night. And just because they're small doesn't mean they sound like chipmunks," he said and walked ahead of me. I followed him and took my seat at an empty table on the far right side of the dimly lit room. His eyes seemed to glow as the tiny trio played their rendition of "Let's Get It On" by Marvin Gaye.

We sat across from each other. JayR smiled and bobbed his head. I didn't grin, but I didn't frown either. I wasn't giving him any slack, because I knew I didn't say I would do this tonight, so he was gonna have to take what he got.

What the fuck was his problem? I thought. As he smiled at me again.

I started to say something but stopped, and cleared my throat as nervousness began to creep into my head, yanking on my thoughts. I had to control my thoughts because they were getting away from me.

A little more silence stood between us. He looked at me and folded both hands on the table, licked his thick black lips and asked "Febe, why are you so hard?"

"What!" I answered with frown lines in the middle of my forehead.

"Why are you so hard? Ever since I met you, you've been cold, hard, and heartless toward me. What did I do you?"

"Nothing," I said and rolled my eyes. He was right. There was a time or two, okay maybe three, that my hardness pissed him off, but that's me.

He didn't say anything for a while. We just watched the band get ready to play another song.

Then he turned to me again. I huffed and puffed.

"What now?" I asked.

"Tell me about the bag boy at the Piggly Wiggly," he said.

"What?" Who told you about the bag boy? And he isn't a boy, he's a man."

"Shelly told me. Now you finish it."

"Why?"

"Because it sounded funny to me."

I looked down at my hands. "What do you want to know?" I asked.

"Why did you hit him?"

"I told that son of a bitch I didn't need any help, but he was insisting on putting my bags in the back of the car. He kept shouting at me to give him the bags. So I let him have the bags and my fist right across the lips. I dropped that son of a bitch right to his knees," I said with a giggle. "I put my bags in my car and drove away."

"Then what happened?"

"When I got home and told Gloria what happened she was pissed off and called the store to check on the man. The manager was pissed off as well. He wanted to talk to me. He told me not to come back to that store."

"Then what?"

"I told him that I would burn that bitch down. Then Gloria snatched the phone from my hands, apologized for my behavior, and sent the bag boy some money, flowers, and an unsigned card, of course."

"Do you go back to that store?"

"Every chance I get."

He had a much different reaction than what I received from the others. He almost fell on the floor laughing his butt off. "I guess when you say no, it's no." He chuckled.

"If you can remember that, then we can be friends." I remarked.

"Febe, I wish you weren't so guarded and knew how to be open and feel free."

"I can never be."

"Why not?"

"Because I feel that someone or something is always waiting to hurt me."

He stared at me. "I won't," he mumbled softly, and turned his head.

At that moment I saw the man Nikkei had described to me. Tall and dark with big almond eyes and thick eyebrows. His hair was cut close to his head with sideburns that flowed in a thin line down his face and around his mouth and chin. He wasn't that gorgeous, like she described, but I guess you had to look at him with real sister eyes to be able to see what she saw, because I just didn't see it.

But he was nice and polite just like Nikkei said. I would give her that. Not intimidating at all, more fascinating and interesting. But, he was a man, and sooner or later they all turn on you, I heard an inner voice say, as I traced the scars on my left hand. I blinked to keep from frowning as my mind brought up the memories of last night's dream and the thought of my fading future slipping from between my fingers.

"Febe, what's wrong? You're not having a good time?" he asked.

"Yes." I answered quickly. I think I'm gonna be sick on this roller coaster ride call mood swings. Up and down, yes and no.

"Well not from the look on your face."

"What look?"

"That don't-mess-with-me-expression. It's written all over your face. It's such a hard expression for a lady."

"There you go with that hard word again. It's just my expression, take it or leave it."

"Okay, don't get upset, just trying to make conversation. I'm sure you have a lot on your mind. I know that you're going through some changes in your life, and after that bag-boy story, I can sympathize with you," he said with a chuckle.

"Are you studying to be a comedian?" I asked.

"No, why?"

"Just asked." I tried to focus on the band, but it became hard to concentrate on the lyrics.

My thoughts kept drifting. Suddenly I had an acute awareness of my appearance. JayR was making me feel uneasy with the intensive look he had. I brought my hand slowly to my face.

"Febe," he said, "you don't have to hide your scars, not from me."

He brought my hand down to the table. I closed my eyes and bit my bottom lip softly. What the hell, I thought to myself. This feeling was unreal. I know I let him touch me months ago in the car, now this. I jerked my hand away.

"You want a drink or something?" he asked looking past me, as if I had hurt his feelings.

"Water is fine." When he walked away, I slammed my hands down on the table. Something was surging through my blood, setting it on fire. I needed the water to put this flame out in a hurry. But what I really wanted was to be able to talk to Nikkei about her brother.

JayR returned to the table, walking on the opposite side of me.

"Here you go. I had the lady put a cherry in it for you."

"Why?"

We looked at each other and said in unison, "Nikkei."

"You got it! She said you like stuff in a glass."

"She told you that?"

"Yep." He winked.

His smile brought down the tension a few notches, and I smiled back.

"Febe, I have to say something."

"Go on, I'm listening," I said, putting the cherry into my mouth.

"It's something about you, and please forgive me if I offend you, but you're so mysterious and dark, and even puzzling, you're positively difficult to figure out, it's driving me insane. I have never met anyone like you. Even when Nikkei was telling me about you, I thought she was making you up. But Shelly confirmed what Nikkei had said. You are very mysterious and secretive."

"I'm not offended," I replied and looked away. He was making me nervous, so I kept my distance like he had the plague or something. But something inside of me was trying to get me to make a move, take advantage of his amazement with me, but I was rooted to my seat.

I mean my butt was fused to that plastic chair, and I had no idea what was surging through my head.

JayR sat back and took in a large portion of the stale air, exhaled, and twiddled his thumbs.

He definitely wanted to say more. He couldn't keep his eyes on his friend's band, and I could see him staring at me from the corner of my eye.

The silence, the waiting for the big question, "Do you remember anything?" was working the hell out of my nerves. The Tiny Trio was rocking the place, but it was too damn quiet at our table. I wanted to make some noise. His quietness was driving me insane. I wanted to leave, but something about him was compelling me to stay.

Then the damn band took a break, forcing us into a ridiculous amount of nervousness. I smiled as I saw the three men jump off the stage. But my smile faded when JayR's eyes met mine. My heart turned over in response, suddenly I had to fight an overwhelming need to touch JayR. He seemed to be peering at me intensely. He was really starting to make me nervous, staring at me with something in his eyes that I couldn't put my finger on. Then his eyes dropped from my mine and slid down my neck to my shoulders, toward my scared breasts. My body felt heavy and warm. My pulse skittered alarmingly. The thudding of my heart drowned out the noise in the background.

"Do it."

I blinked slowly, fighting whatever I was feeling. I gathered the saliva in my mouth and swallowed.

"Do what?" I asked.

"Excuse me?" he replied.

"You said do it. What do you want me to do?"

"Febe, I didn't say do it. I was listening to the band."

At that moment I begin to hear the band. I remembered seeing them leave, but not return. "JayR, swear to me you never said do it."

"Febe, I don't need you to do anything for me, but if you ever need me to do something, I'm here. I know that you've got some heavy stuff on your mind. I can help if you let me. I'm very good at that sort of stuff. I have two sisters, you know."

"No, I'm fine, thank you," I said and turned my attention to the band.

"Come on, Febe, let me help you," he said again and grabbed my hand.

Air jetted from my nostrils. Tiny veins stood at attention on my forehead. A moment of stillness surrounded me. I tried to suffocate my irritation, but I was starting to get pissed off. Something was going on, and I needed to get control of it.

"JayR, I'm not like other women. I'm not the person to take a joke, and I don't care for the bullshit. I'm sure that Nikkei told you that. I'm making an exception because of the family thing. I need a lot more time to get used to talking to you, confiding in you."

"Trusting me," he said.

"Trust, never."

He sat and stared at me. His eyes were truly glued to my face, examining me like I was a specimen that he had just discovered.

The scars that lined my cheek and the one above my eyes and across my upper lip felt as if they were standing out twelve inches from my face, and I couldn't hide them from his prying eyes. I wondered if he could tell that my face held so much anger, so much hurt, and so many damn years of pain. I kept trying to look away, trying to keep my attention on the band. If I didn't, the way JayR kept looking at me, I was liable to punch him right in his face, and forget about brotherly love.

"Febe!" I heard him shout, forcing me out of my somber mood.

"What!" I snapped, blinking.

"I was asking if you wanted to leave and go someplace a little quieter?"

Fuck that, I thought, any quieter and he can put me in the ground. I shook my head. "It's two in the morning. I have to go home."

"Okay, let me say bye to my friends, then we can leave."

"I'm gonna call a cab."

"No. You're acting strange again. I'll take you home."

"JayR, I gotta get some air," He grabbed my elbow and his touch felt like fire. I could barely see my way to the door. I stumbled into the night air, where the sky was dark and the stars were burning bright. I took a deep breath, after he let go of my elbow. I felt a chill and I shivered a little. He took off his jacket and gave it to me.

"Are you sure you don't want to go someplace else?" he asked again. "This place isn't far and you can see forever," he said, smiling, taking my hand as we approached his car.

I was holding back my thoughts, keeping them submerged. But they began creeping up, seeping through my pores. There was too much bitterness in my soul for me to take the bullshit. My chest tightened and I pulled my hands away from him, not forcibly but just enough for him to get the point. I didn't understand what I was feeling when he touched me, and my thoughts burst through and the words spilled out. "I don't need to see forever, JayR, I only need to see past each day."

The phone rang, just as we entered the dark house.

"Are you gonna get that?"

"Uh," I answered still dazed at the information he had given me.

"The phone, Febe. Are you gonna get the phone?"

"Yes." I fumbled for the button on the speakerphone and pushed it. "Hello."

"Is JayR there?" the familiar voice on the other end asked.

"Yeah, man, I'm here," JayR shouted.

I left him alone and went to use the bathroom, change clothes, and take more meds, because I was starting to hear that crazy voice again. I didn't want to eavesdrop, but I did. Besides JayR wasn't speaking softly like his conversation was private or something.

"JayR, it's Slim. We found Lydia's husband."

"Where is he?"

"Get this man, he was driving a truckload of adult toys, to New York."

"Slim, that's perfect. You know what to do. Who's with him now?"

"Crazy Jimmy."

"Okay, give Jimmy this gig."

"Crazy Jimmy and a truckload of vibrators. Are you insane?"

"Give Crazy Jimmy this one, Slim. Call me back with the details."

"Okay, JayR."

"Hey, Slim, any word on that Indian guy?"

"Mohammed?"

"Yeah, Sulee's husband."

"No man, no word. He must be in hiding. The nurses in his office said he hasn't been in for weeks now."

"Find him."

"Why we gotta go and fuck with this man JayR? He's gone."

"Listen, Febe wants him found. Sulee is a big bag of nerves, and it drives Febe crazy."

"You care for that girl, don't you?"

"Yeah, man, I guess I do."

"Man, that girl is something else," I heard Slim say. "Do you see how much enjoyment she gets when we're working."

"She's on fire for life, and I love that about her." JayR chuckled.

"Well you need to let her know that her fire for life is burning bright in New York; Galveston, Texas; and we got a small army in Ohio. I don't think she knows what she's started."

"As long as everybody remembers we couldn't save Nikkei, but we took the oath to try and help the other Nikkeis of this world."

"Preach on, Brother JayR." Slim chuckled.

"Did you talk to Anthony?" JayR asked.

"Yeah, man. That fool ain't gonna touch Lisa no more. I know he's learned his lesson."

A short silence passed before Slim spoke again. "Man, you and Febe should have been there for Rachel's husband. I thought he was gonna pass out. He pissed in his boxers, I mean worse than Ronny."

"Well Ronny pissed in his pants every time we showed up." JayR chuckled.

"What about Keno?"

"Oh, I gave him the gig with that dude on the east side. He said the man was trying to strike a deal with him, but he had nothing Keno could use."

"Didn't that fool just get out of the hospital a few days ago?"

"Yeah, man, but he went and beat his wife up again."

"And."

"And Keno took another bite out of his ass. Say, JayR, I gotta run. Crazy Jimmy has got this fool doing whiskey and tequila shots the Mexican way"

"The Mexican way?"

"Yeah, he's pouring the liquor down his throat and shaking

this fool's head."

"Okay, Slim, take care and drop me a line regarding Alex, and let Crazy Jimmy be creative with that truck full of dildos."

"Alright, JayR, peace out. Hey, hey, I'll keep the hawk out for Mohammed. But what you want us to do with him when we find him?"

"An eye for an eye, and a tooth for a tooth."

Chapter 25

"What's that?" Gloria asked as she placed the tea bag in her cup.

"JayR sent me some information."

"In the mail? Why didn't he just bring it to you? He's here all the time."

"He's out of town right now, some sort of emergency."

"Umm, one of those special trips, I bet." Gloria winked.

I shrugged. "I don't know, I didn't ask."

"Are you okay?"

"Yeah, why?"

"JayR was talking to Shelly, he said that you were acting weird when you guys went to the coffeehouse. It freaked him out."

"I don't know what he's talking about." I frowned and rubbed the bridge of my nose.

"What's wrong?"

"He made an appointment for me."

"For what?"

"Hypnosis. It helped him to stop smoking."

"Hypnosis!" she repeated.

"Yeah, we were talking about it the other night, and he thinks that hypnosis might help me to stop wiggin' out. He also said it might help with my memory."

"Are you going to do it?" Gloria asked.

"I don't know, maybe I should try it. I've tried everything else and I'm still left with a bagful of bad dreams and bits and pieces of memory like a jigsaw puzzle."

"Well, if you ask me, I think you should try God before you go off half cocked letting somebody put a spell on your mind."

"Thanks for the info but I want to try this first. Let's go to the bookstore and research it."

Gloria sipped on her tea. "I think I'll pass, and you should go right in my room and read my bible, that's all the hypnosis you need."

"Well I need answers quicker than your God can give them to me."

"You should also pray for patience."

"Gloria."

"Okay, Febe, I'll stop preaching. But are you really gonna go?" she asked.

"Yeah, I think I will."

"When is it again?"

"Next Wednesday."

"Oh, I gotta meet my lawyer and Jackson. I'll reschedule my appointment and go with you."

"Oh, no, Gloria. I can handle it by myself, it's only orientation."

When I walked into the house from the orientation, Gloria was staring at me.

"So what's it like?" she asked suspiciously.

"It was simple. Nothing to get excited over."

"Were you scared?"

"Very."

"What did he do?"

"Nothing."

"Did he ask you a lot of questions?"

"Yes, but not as many as you're asking right now."

"Well give me something. You were there for four hours. You only need to go to church for one."

"I know Gloria, and I'll tell you as soon as I get these shoes off." I plopped down on the couch and she fell next to me.

"It was great, sort of fun and exciting and scary all wrapped up into one. If he could do all that he said he could, I'm in for a serious surprise."

"Did he hypnotize you? You know that's a sin."

"No, it's not a sin, and no, he didn't hypnotize me. We just talked. He went over some of the exercises that he'll be doing with me, and exercises I will need to do at home."

"So are you going all the way?"

"I don't know, I have to think about it."

"You should think about it, but in the mean time, come to church with me and talk to my pastor. He can help you before you end up in hell."

"Gloria, I've thought about your God and the answer is still no. Now let me think about this."

"What is there to think about?"

"It's not that easy to just walk out of one life into another one, Gloria."

I took her hand and looked into her eyes. "What if you don't like the new person? What if I'm a total bitch, and you can't stand me. Then where does that leave our friendship?"

"Our friendship isn't going anywhere. We are soul sisters, and we will be that way for the rest of our lives, even when we're old and gray. Besides, you are already a witch and I still love you." She smiled.

"I don't know, Gloria."

"Listen, Febe. No matter what, I'll always be here for you, and I'll always love you, even if I think you're doing the wrong thing."

I walked over to the fireplace. "But what if he makes me remember, and then I forget who you are, and Shelly and Nikkei and JayR, just like I forgot my past?"

She raised one nicely arched eyebrow. "Oh, you may forget us, but I doubt you'll forget JayR."

I put my hands on my hips. "And what is that suppose to mean? And stop batting your eyes like that, and stop pouting."

"It means, we see the way he looks at you. He'll die before he'll let you forget him."

"Me!"

"Yes, you, and don't you pretend that you haven't noticed."

"I don't know what you're talking about."

"Febe, why are you pretending that you don't like JayR? You act as if I don't know that you've been sneaking out all hours of the night to be with him."

"It's not what you think. JayR's like a brother to me."

"Well that might be the way you see it. But Shelly and I see how he looks at you, and I think it's against God for a brother to look at a sister like that. Besides, Shelly said JayR has never stayed around this long for any reason, not even for her or Nikkei."

"Gloria, let's just drop this subject and move on. JayR is a brother to me and nothing more."

"JayR likes you girl."

"Gloria, please."

"No, he really does. He took you to that concert, didn't he."

Suddenly anger rose up inside of me and I didn't know what to do. So I stormed out of the living room and headed for my side of the condo. I slammed the door behind me and sat sulking in a chair. I really didn't know what I was feeling for JayR. Sometimes I wanted more, but then again I couldn't shake this resentfulness I had toward him because he's a man.

Gloria shouted through the door. "Okay, Febe, whatever you say. It's dropped. I'm sorry. I didn't mean to get you so upset." She knocked several times before I answered.

"What!" I yelled, through the closed door.

"When are you going to see the hypnotist again?"

I swung the door open. "What!"

"When are you going to see the hypnotist again?"

"Wednesday, Gloria, why?"

"I would like to go with you."

"Fine." I started to slam the door, but she stuck her foot in.

"What?"

"If it doesn't work, will you please try my God?"

"I'll think about it."

CHAPTER 26

Wednesday morning, Gloria drove me to the hypnotist's office. Her mouth was moving a mile a minute about her God.

"Make a left at the light. It's the pale yellow building on the right. Right here." I snapped.

"Where do I park?"

"Pull behind the building and park in any stall."

"I won't get towed, will I?"

"No, Gloria."

"Febe, what kind of place is this? It looks rundown."

"It's fine, Gloria."

"Well, it doesn't look fine. It looks like street people live in here." She said as she secured her car.

"Just go up the stairs. It's the first door to your right."

"Can we pray before we go in?"

"You pray, I'm going up."

The right side of Gloria's lip raised just a little. She wasn't happy about this at all.

"Stop making those faces."

"I can't believe you actually saw someone in this building."

"Gloria, it's not that bad."

"What was JayR thinking? This place is a dump."

"Just open the door and go inside."

"I don't want to touch that doorknob."

I reached in front of her and opened the door.

When we entered the room, Gloria's mouth fell open.

"Wow! I didn't know what to expect when you opened the door, but whatever it was, it surely wasn't this."

"It's beautiful, isn't it?" I smiled. "You shouldn't judge Gloria."

"You're right, I shouldn't judge."

Gloria walked around the room in amazement. "His plants are so healthy and the carpet is so white. Oh my, a baby grand piano in the middle of the floor," she shrieked.

"Yeah, he plays sometimes," I answered as I stood by the cozy fireplace. Gloria walked over and warmed her hands.

"It's very nice," she mumbled. Then her attention went to the wall. "What is that a picture of?" she asked as she tilted her head.

"If you squint you can see baby whales."

"Oh, wow, I can see them." She grinned.

"You see, Gloria, you should never judge a building from the outside."

"I guess you're right. But why does he hide it like this?"

"He said it keeps the burglars away. If the building is old and ragged, then people figure there is nothing worth anything inside."

"Well I guess he's got a point." Gloria raised one brow.

"Besides, the rent is low for a tattered old building."

Gloria turned to me. "Do you think he couldn't make it as

a psychologist and became a hypnotist?"

"Gloria."

She shrugged. "Well that's what some doctors say about chiropractors."

"That's not true."

"It's not?"

I looked over at the grandfather clock standing in the corner. A cold chill ran down my spine. It was eleven-thirty, and I knew he would be coming around the corner any minute. I sat on the almond colored chair next to the fireplace. I tried to hide the fear behind my shades, but Gloria saw right through them.

She sat down next to me, put her arms around my shoulders, and held me.

"I know it's scary, but it's your choice."

"Don't start preaching to me, Gloria."

"Okay, I won't." She smiled. "Maybe if nothing else, he can stop those nightmares."

"I know, Gloria, but I'm still scared. I don't know what to expect. I mean, I know what he's gonna do, but what's gonna come out of it?"

"I thought he told you what to expect."

"He did, but he also said that each person is different."

"It's gonna be alright, and I'll be right by your side holding your hand, and praying for you."

I gave her hands a little pat, and she smiled at me. Then we heard the doctor whistling as he came down the hall.

I forgot to mention one thing to Gloria about the hypnotist. I thought I'd wait for her to find out, and that's when he magically appeared. All three feet, four inches of him. When I saw the look on Gloria's face as she stood to greet the hypnotist, I thought I was going to pass out laughing.

"Hello, Febe," he said, sounding like one of those guys from the Wizard of Oz. "I'm glad you kept our appointment. After last week I thought I had scared you away," he shrieked in his chipmunk voice. "And this must be your sister, Gloria." He reached for her hand.

She turned and looked at me over her shoulder. I pinched her on her side. "Stop staring," I said softly.

"Follow me please," he said, turning his back to us.

Gloria whispered in my ear. "What is it with JayR and these short people? First the concert, now the hypnotist. Oh, and let's not forget about the painter. I thought he would need to stand on my shoulders to reach the first step." Gloria chuckled.

"Gloria, they're in a band."

She shrugged. "Sorry."

We entered his office, and the hypnotist hopped up on the chair next to a black leather couch. He motioned for me to have a seat on the couch, as he took out a pen and paper. Gloria sat in the corner to my right. I had never gone this far back into his office, I thought, as I slid down on the cold couch.

He had many pictures of himself on the walls around the room. Over his fireplace was a picture of his band, all decked out in their tuxes. Then I noticed that he was standing, sitting, or riding a tiny horse. Hell, I didn't know horses came that size, but apparently they did. My eyes met Gloria and she swallowed her giggle, put her head down, and coughed.

"My pictures are there to show people that you can do whatever you put your mind to. If you believe it, you will achieve it," he said.

I cleared my throat and turned to the hypnotist. "How long have you known JayR?"

"He looked at me over the top of his glasses. "Oh, I've known JayR a very long time. He helped out once when I was in a fight. This cat must have been four or five feet tall. Big guy." He motioned with his hands.

"JayR came to your rescue?"

"Well actually he came to the other cat's rescue. I had that guy by the neck. I was trying to bite a hole to the other side."

Gloria and I sat in amazement, our mouths wide open. Then Gloria started the chain reaction of laughter. We all were laughing at the thought of the tiny hypnotist around someone's neck and JayR pulling him off. We laughed for a long time at that one. He told other stories to get me comfortable before starting the process.

"Okay, Febe, let's get started."

I took a deep breath, held it in, then exhaled.

"Are you ready?" he asked as he clicked on the tape.

I looked over at Gloria. She winked, and I smiled.

"Yes," I answered.

He scribbled something on his note pad. "Do you understand what I'm about to do?"

"Yes."

He pushed a button and soft music filled the room, the lights dimmed, and I could smell strawberries or bubble gum, something fruity.

"Now I want you to relax, concentrate, and listen."

I concentrated on the sounds and smells in the room. I began to relax and absorb the suggestion from the tape.

"Okay, Febe, like I told you, repetition enforces suggestion so I'm going to say a few words over and over. Find a spot and focus on the sound of my voice." He began to speak slowly. "Fear, anger, hate." The more he spoke the deeper his voice became. "Peace, love, happiness." He started to sound like Barry White.

"Count, Febe, count from one to ten and up again."

"One. . .two. . .three. . .four. . .five. . ." My eyelids were too heavy to stay open, my scalp loosened and my face relaxed. There was a stimulating sensation traveling down my neck, pulsating at my shoulders and gyrating through my back muscles. I deeply wanted to rest. I began to float to the ceiling. At one point I felt vulnerable, and I didn't like it, but I continued to concentrate.

"Febe—." his voice was so deep, I thought he was inside my head—. "feel your body go limp. You must begin to sort out the wanted from the unwanted impressions. Your mind is constantly concerned with sounds. Your brain is constantly flashing images, and you are constantly blocking them with sounds. You can break the spell. You can't remember because it's too painful to remember."

"Yes, it is." I could hear the voice in my head.

"Your dreams are your reality. You know the outcome, and you have to end the pain. Focus on your dreams, and you will be amazed at your overpowering strength. Focus on your dreams, on the troubles that control you. You possess a strong motivation, a desire to succeed. You are aware of what you want to accomplish. Use your imagination in a creative way to succeed. Positive thinking will find solutions. You are there, Febe. Feel your surroundings. Look at your surroundings, smell your surroundings."

I could feel my breath leaving my body, my heart beating faster and faster. I felt myself running, running trying to get away. Then I saw him standing in front of me with his hands on his hips, grinning and laughing at me.

"I gotta get inside. I gotta hide," the voice screamed in pain.

"No, Febe don't go inside. Stand and fight, fight to the end. Stop running."

"No, I gotta get inside. He doesn't like it when I'm outside."

"Who doesn't like it when you're outside? Who doesn't like it? Tell me."

"Jacob! My God, Jacob doesn't like it when I'm outside. He's gonna get me. He's gonna beat me up."

"Fight, Febe. Fight back. Don't let him win."

"I can't fight him, he's too big. His hands are bigger, his feet are bigger. He's meaner. I can't fight back, I can't."

"Yes, you can."

"I'm too scared."

"You fight or you die," the deep voice demanded.

"Somebody please help me! I have to write the Texas constable a note, yeah I gotta let somebody know. I can't breathe! I can't breathe! Help me, he's gonna kill me."

"Okay, Febe, okay. I'll help you. Listen to the sound of my voice."

"I can't breathe."

"Yes, you can. You are breathing. Take small, deep breaths. He's gone. You made it inside. You're safe here with your sister, Gloria. Hear yourself count from ten to one. Slowly very slowly."

"Ten. . .nine. . .eight. . .seven. . .six. . ." I could feel my breath return to my body. "Five. . .four. . . three. . .two. . .one. . ."

"Open your eyes slowly, Febe."

I no longer heard Barry White, but Alvin and the Chipmunks. I opened my eyes slowly and turned to face the hypnotist looking down on me, smiling with big white teeth and a round dark chubby face.

My head was hurting, and my neck was burning. The tips of my fingers were throbbing. Gloria was at my side with her hands under my arms.

I walked around the couch I was supposed to be lying on, massaging my neck and shoulders.

Gloria walked over to me and put her hands on my shoulders.

I leaned my head on her hand. "What happened?"

"Jacob was chasing you. He didn't want you to be outside."

The doctor walked up to me. "Is Jacob from Texas?"

"No!" I snapped. "Jacob Scott ain't from Texas. He's from a swamp in Louisiana."

"Jacob Scott is from Louisiana?" He repeated.

"Yes! Born and raised. He moved to Texas to teach. . . foot . .ball. . ." I said, speaking slowly as I heard what I was saying.

Gloria screamed so loud she scared the shit out of me. She

jumped to a standing position like a high school cheerleader. "We know his name, we know his name!" she shouted.

My head was hurting so bad I didn't want to think about Jacob Scott. I wanted to go home, cover my head, and sleep this day away.

"Thank you, thank you, thank you," Gloria shouted again as we were leaving his office.

"I'll see you next week, Febe."

I shook my head and began to walk out of his office. Gloria bent down to shake his hand, and she had the nerve to speak very loudly. "Thank you so much for what you've done for my sister."

"Gloria, the man is short, not deaf."

"You are more than welcome," he replied in the same drawl.

"Febe, keep practicing. The results are worth the effort."

Gloria was happy and full of cheer. I was depressed and full of fear.

"I wanted to pick that man up and give him the biggest kiss, right on his tiny little lips."

"Gloria!"

"Well, I did."

"Gloria, he's short, but he still needs to be treated with respect."

"Yeah, you're right, but what are we going to do with this little bit of information?"

"We're gonna keep it to ourselves until I have time to think."

Chapter 27

"JayR, why are we standing in the dark, in the cold and the rain, waiting for Ronny to come out of some stupid neighborhood bar? He hasn't done anything to Justine" one of the crew asked.

"Yes, he has."

"What?"

"He's been pushing her around yelling and intimidating her again, so it's time to pay him a little reminder visit."

"Hey! Is that him?" one of the guys shouted.

"Yeah, that's the little punk."

"Let's get him."

"No, let's wait until he gets to his car."

"JayR, man, why we gotta wait? Why can't we kick his ass right now?"

"Because there's too many people out here."

"Where did you park his car?"

"On the other side of the building, near the back."

"Don't you think he'll know that he didn't park over there."

"Nah, he's pretty messed up, he won't remember shit."

"Okay, there he goes."

JayR stepped out of the darkness, big, bad and bold, but this time I didn't feel the excitement that was always waiting for me in the pit of my stomach whenever we went out on a gig."

"Hello, Ronny."

"Oh, shit! What the fu. . .! Who are you?"

"Don't your recognize me? I'm Prince Charming. I've come to save you on my white horse," JayR said.

"Come on, man! Leave me alone."

"You haven't been a good little boy."

"Yeah! Yeah! Man, I've been good. I haven't laid a hand on Justine.

"Oh that's not what the mirror on the wall told me."

"Yes, I've . . ."

"No, you have not."

"Oh, come on, man, please give me a break."

"Oh, don't beg, Ronny. I don't think begging helped Justine, now did it?"

"No, man, but come on. Please. Man, I can't take this. You just don't know how it feels to live like this every day of your life. You got me looking over my shoulder and shit." Ronny sniffled.

"Oh, we do."

"Yeah, man, I mean . . .damn. Sometimes I think if I just kill myself then I don't have to be a part of this madness. I just can't stand not knowing when, where, or if you're gonna show up. I mean, dang, you got me sleeping with one eye open. You act like I did a crime. She's my wife," he shrieked.

JayR's fist went into Ronny's lip. Blood streamed out of

Ronny's mouth and spilled over onto his Laker's T-shirt. He fell to the ground on one knee.

"Oh, hell, man!" he cried. "Not again, I told you I was sorry. Why you gotta torture me like this? What more do you want me to do? I only pushed her a few times.

"I want you to realize that domestic violence is a crime and you are a criminal!" JayR shouted.

"Man, if you so bad, why you gotta hide behind that dark mask?" Ronny yelled, trying to gain some strength.

"Well I can take it off, but I'll have to take your eyes out," JayR answered.

Ronny lunged at JayR with a knife, and the rest of the crew stepped from out of the darkness. Ronny began to laugh.

"Man, you gotta be shitting me. All y'all gonna kick my ass?" Ronny asked as he licked the blood from his top lip.

"Where's your little bitch?" He chuckled.

Rage rose inside of me, and I stepped out of the darkness. "Trick or treat, motherfucker," I announced striking him across his face with the brass knuckles I got from one of the boys.

"Oh, shit, girl, what are you doing?" I heard Slim shout.

JayR snapped his fingers, and Crazy Jimmy was on Ronny's ass in one second flat.

It was over before it got started. JayR snapped his fingers again and Jimmy backed off.

"Why you gotta disrespect me like this?" Ronny grunted and fell to the ground on one knee again.

"You disrespected yourself when you started hitting your wife. We are only here to give you a little taste of your own medicine."

"My father beat my mother. And it kept her in line."

"Does that make it right?" I shouted.

"What am I supposed to do?" Ronny cried.

"I suggest you start attending those anger-management classes and let that anger go, or we're gonna start visiting you twice a month..

And by the way, welcome to the club. You are now a lifetime member." JayR placed a tiny box in the palm of Ronny's hand. We left him sitting in the parking lot of that neighborhood bar, with Crazy Jimmy.

We walked back to the van in silence. I wanted to ask what was in the box, but I didn't want to get into a discussion about the knuckles.

"Hello, Anthony."

"Oh, shit man -- what you guys want?"

"Tell your partner to take a walk."

"It's okay, take a walk, I'll be fine," Anthony said slowly.

"You look so nice in your uniform, so professional."

"Yeah, man, yeah. What can I do for you?"

"We heard you got yourself a new girlfriend."

"Man, I ain't touched her!" he shouted, backing up."

"Oh, we know. We were just letting you know that she's protected under our law."

"Yeah, man, I'm good. I ain't gonna put one hand on her."

"What are your hands made for, Anthony?"

Anthony blinked frantically, "My hands are made to love her, not hurt her."

"Very good, now hold out your hands." Anthony held out both shaking hands, palm side down. JayR placed the tiny black box on top of his knuckles.

"What's this?" he asked.

"Congratulations, you are a lifetime member. Read Genesis 4:15. It will explain the ring, which will be your mark."

We walked away from another shaking man.

"JayR, what are we doing tonight with such a small crew?"

"We are only passing out a little token tonight, to let them know that we are still around."

"Still around?" I repeated

"Yeah, like when the cops make rounds in the neighborhood,

just to make their presence known."

"Oh yeah."

"That's what we're doing tonight," he answered before falling silent.

"JayR."

"Yeah."

"The doctor is still in his office," one of the guys said.

"Okay, let's roll." JayR snapped his finger.

"As we drove down the highway, I had to ask. "What's in the box?"

"Oh, this," he said, tossing one of the black boxes in the air."

"Yeah."

"Here, take a look."

I opened the box and inside was a gold ring with the letters WB.

"What's WB for?" I asked.

"Wife Beater."

"Wife Beater, JayR."

"Yes."

"Why?"

"Well one night I was talking to Gloria and she told me the story about Cain and Abel and how Cain killed Abel, his brother."

"I thought you were not a religious man."

"I'm not a praying man, but I am polite."

"Whatever, go on."

"Well anyway, she said that Cain killed Abel and the Lord put a mark on him so everyone would know what he did so that he'd be ostracized by the folks in the villages."

"And?"

"And we decided to put a mark on the abusers so the women would know what kind of man she's getting involved with."

"But what if he changes?"

"I'm sure Cain was sorry for what he did once the Lord punished him, but oh well. He died with the mark."

I eased back into the darkness of the van. I had mixed feelings regarding the punishment that was being administered to the abusers, but JayR was right. Women needed some way of knowing what kind of man she was getting involved with. I guess you can say we are omitting the element of surprise.

The van came to a smooth halt, easing me out of my thoughts.

"We're here. You coming?" JayR asked.

I eased out of the van and scurried across the lawn to the front door.

"Dr. Mohammed."

"Oh, my God, what are you doing here?" The doctor jumped to his feet.

"Sorry about the eye," Slim said. I was getting real good with voices and heights, but still no faces.

"I have nothing to do with that crazy lady no more," he whispered, flopping back into his chair.

"No-no-no, Dr Mohammed. You don't disrespect the mother of your children."

"Sorry, so sorry, but just the same I did not touch her," he responded, raising his unpatched eye brow.

"Yes, we know---hold out our hand," JayR commanded, and once again he placed the tiny box on Dr. Mohammed's knuckles.

"What is this madness?"

"Congratulations, you are now a lifetime member. Read Genesis 4:15, it will explain the ring, which will be your mark," JayR said, as he would say so many times that night.

"JayR, what is this all about?" I asked once were were inside the van heading for the next destination. "We didn't say anything about being a lifetime member. We agreed on one year if need be, and as you can see, we are only having a few repeat offenders."

"This is only going to keep them in line. It's only a reminder of what can happen, remember Cain and Abel."

"But can't this link the cops to us? There's already and investigation regarding Anthony."

"Yes, but half the policemen have one of our little reminders. Doctors, lawyers, teachers. Hell, we even got ourselves a preacher, so we have no worries."

"JayR, this is getting too big. I only wanted to teach a few abusers a lesson about living in fear."

"Febe, it's already big. Bigger than I expected it to be. Girl, you are going to redefine domestic violence. It's gonna be an eye for an eye all over this world. Febe, you hate domestic violence, but I loathe it. My sister died from it, and still I don't have a clue who killed her."

"But JayR ---"

"No, Febe. When I see these abusers walking around with the mark on their finger, it will also remind me--- no remind us, Febe -- that Nikkei didn't die in vain," he shouted, holding up a large black bag. We are recruiting men every day who have felt as powerless, as to what to do to help their mothers, sisters, or friends. We are the stronger sex and we have to protect the weaker one."

"But, JayR---"

"We have to stand up to the plate and protect those who can't protect themselves."

"So is that your little secret weapon in that black bag?"

"That's right, Febe. You hide your secrets in your heart and no one will ever find out. That's what Nikkei taught me, and that's what I do."

Once again I eased back into the darkness of the van. By the time we made it to the fourth gig, I had decided to sit this one out. Something JayR said had me thinking. Then out of nowhere, I had the answer. Easing out of the van, I became lightheaded from my revelation.

"What's wrong with you?" JayR asked when he returned to the van.

I looked up at him with tears in my eyes. "The answer to our question has been staring us in the face all this time, JayR," I mumbled.

"What, Febe?"

"In our face," I repeated, my voice trembling with pain.

"You and Nikkei are so much alike. I don't know why I didn't see it before," I said as I slid back into the van.

"What are you talking about? You are getting weird on me again."

"Nikkei. She protected her purse just like you protect that damn black sack, keeping your secrets close to you. So did she."

"Nikkei never protected her purse."

"Yes, she did. From the day I first met her, she was very protective of that purse. I bet it will lead us to the person who killed her."

"No it won't," JayR replied downhearted.

"Why not?"

"Because, we gave everything to your shelter, and what we couldn't give away, we threw away. Remember?"

"Yes, I remember." I shook my head. "But I took her purse and I think I put it in the bottom of the closet at the shelter because I knew she loved it so much. Come on, guys. We gotta go."

Chapter 28

"I know the answer is in your bag, Nikkei. I just know it," I said as I searched for her purse. "Gloria!" I shouted from the top of my lungs. "Gloria!"

"What!" She screamed, running into my room.

"Did you see a brown straw bag?"

"A what?"

"A brown straw bag. It was Nikkei's bag, her purse. I put it in the closet at the shelter, but it's not there. Now I don't know where it is. Did you happen to see it around here anywhere?"

"No, I didn't see anything. But the maid said a messenger brought over a box for a lady named Annie. It was from the shelter."

I slid to the floor when Gloria spoke that name. "Who?"

"Annie. That's who it's addressed to."

"I don't know a lady named Annie," I replied as my heart

began to race. "Where is it?"

"It's in the hall closet."

"Is it an Annie from another shelter? You and Stella are traveling from one shelter to another." Gloria asked.

"No, I've never met anyone named Annie."

"I'll go and get it." When Gloria left, all I could do was rest my head on the wall.

She returned moments later. "Well, here's the box."

Trembling with fear I took the box from Gloria. I set it between my legs, looking intently at the name. I picked it up once again. "It's light. Are you sure there's something in here?"

"Well if you shake it, you can hear something moving around in there. Are you sure you don't know an Annie."

"No, I don't know who the hell Annie is." I snapped as I tore open the box.

"Febe, this isn't a Christmas present. Take your time."

"It's Nikkei's purse, Gloria!" I frowned.

"How did Annie get her purse?"

"I don't know," I replied and dumped everything out on the floor.

"Why are you doing that?"

"We need to search through this stuff and see what we can find."

"But. . ."

"But nothing Gloria. And get that frown off your face. Besides there's nothing here but junk. Lipstick, nail file, Charlie perfume. Ain't a damn thing here!" I screamed.

"What were you hoping to find, a diary with all the answers?"

"Yes, Gloria, a diary would have been better than nothing. Something that would give us a clue."

"I only mentioned a dairy because Shelly said that Nikkei was always writing something in a book, but it wasn't a diary, more like a calendar." Gloria sipped her tea.

"Are you serious?"

"That's what Shelly said. I've never seen the book."

"Let's go over there."

"What!"

"We have a key and we know the code to the alarm. If Shelly didn't want us in, she wouldn't provide us with the ability to enter of our own free will. Is she still in Washington?"

"Yes. She and Harrison are almost finished closing the deal on the new rehab center."

"Wow, that's great." I grinned.

"Yeah, Harrison has helped this family out more than we can imagine."

"What did you say?"

"I said that Harrison has helped this family out more than we can imagine. He's a great guy."

"Hmm."

"Why the frown?"

"Oh, nothing, I just remembered something Nikkei once told me. Get your car keys. You're driving and I'll be the lookout."

"Too many movies, Febe." She shook her head and grabbed her keys.

As we approached Shelly's house, Gloria was losing her nerve. "Febe, I can't believe I'm letting you talk me into breaking into this girl's house."

"We are not breaking into her house, Gloria. We are only going in to water her plants, vacuum. . ."

"And take whatever we find that will curb your appetite to solve this mystery," Gloria added.

"Gloria, it's not that deep. Now open the door."

"Why don't you open it?"

"I'm not gonna get my fingerprints on the doorknob."

"What!" She turned to me.

"I'm just kidding, girl, now go inside."

"Febe, are you sure this is okay?"

"Yes, Gloria, and it's not a sin. Now you check the bedroom and I'll check the bathroom."

"The bathroom, Febe?"

"Yes Gloria, the bathroom. I saw on TV where someone put some very important papers in a plastic bag and concealed it in the toilet bowl."

"Too much TV, Febe," Gloria said as she disappeared into the other room.

An hour later we found ourselves sitting at the dining room table drinking cold soda, pondering over something that may not exist.

"Maybe the maid cleaned up everything, and put whatever we are looking for away." I said as I propped my feet up on the chair.

"Shelly doesn't have a maid. She cleans her house herself, and as you can see, she hasn't been doing much of that," Gloria said, passing her fingers over a mound of dust.

She hasn't been home much since Nikkei's death." I replied.

"Yeah, you're right." Gloria shrugged.

I shook my head. "Well, let's go. I didn't find what I was looking for." I sighed.

"We better take these cans with us so she won't have ants when she gets back."

"Good idea," I said, dropping my foot to the floor. And that's when I saw it, just sitting there under the chair that separated the dining room from the living room. Like it was waiting for me. Waiting for me to pick it up and open it.

"Gloria, can you please get me another soda?" I asked, keeping my eyes on the object just in case it was only an illusion.

As soon as Gloria left the room, I reached down and grabbed it and shoved it in my coat jacket and waited for her to return. It must have fallen out of her purse when I pushed it to the floor that day, I thought.

"We can leave now," I announced as I held Nikkei's words next to my warm body.

"Are you okay, Febe?"

"Yes, I'm fine."

"Are you sure?"

"Yes, I just want to go home and sleep. I'm tired and disappointed that we didn't find anything here tonight, that's all."

"Well, don't be disappointed, you tried and that's that. How about taking tomorrow off from the shelter?"

"I'm not going to the shelter tomorrow. I have an appointment with the hypnotist. Why?"

"I thought we could spend the day together or something. You've been a little distant, that's all."

"I'm sorry, Gloria. I have things on my mind, but after the appointment, we can hang out."

"That sounds great."

Once we were inside the car I took a deep breath, exhaled and asked. "What's gonna happen to me when you and Jackson get back together?"

"Febe, you don't have to worry. You're family and nothing is going to change that. If I decide to go back to Jackson, he's going to have to get used to family living with us. But you don't have to worry about that for a while. Jackson and I are a long way from living in the same house. He has to apologize, and mean it before that occurs."

"And?"

"And when he does, we are all going to move in together. I already told you that."

CHAPTER 29

I walked into Ella's office more confused than ever before.

"Febe, are you still seeing that hypnotist?" Ella asked.

"Yes," I replied softly.

"How often?"

"Once or twice a week. I have an appointment with him tomorrow."

"Are you okay?"

"Yes, why?"

"Because you're talking so slow, and you seem to be a little bit out of it."

"I'm sorry, but right now I feel like I'm sleepwalking."

"What do you mean sleepwalking?" Ella asked inquisitively.

"I mean like, I'm in a dream. Sometimes I feel like I'm not in my body, but above myself looking down."

"Okay?"

"One day, I was having lunch with JayR, and I reached out to touch his hand."

"And what's wrong with that?"

"I didn't want to touch his hand, and once he responded, I felt like I just woke up. He was burning me with his stroke."

"I see."

"What do you see?"

"I see that you are probably hiding your feelings for JayR. You want him, but you are being too stubborn to accept him."

"But that's just it. I don't want him when I'm awake, but when I'm above myself I can see me reaching out to him, and I feel like I don't have any control over it. Ella, I don't understand what's going on. Strange things are happening to me."

"What do you do when these strange things happen?"

"I call JayR."

"Why?"

"That's what I'm talking about, I don't know why. I'm losing it Ella, really I am. I feel like I have something important to do, but I haven't figure it out yet."

Ella sat quietly and stared at me, as this hollow, lifeless feeling congregated up inside of me.

"Febe, I can't say that I understand your pain because I don't, but it seems to me that your plate is full. You need to take a break."

"Take a break! What are you talking about? What would I need to take a break from?"

"From everything. The shelter, the project, the hypnotist, JayR, everything."

"You know what Ella, I'm outta here."

"Febe, wait."

"No!"

"Why are you so upset all of a sudden?"

"I don't know.

CHAPTER 30

"Febe, what happened at the hypnotist."

"She fucking woke up."

"Who woke up?"

"Go away, Gloria."

"Febe, wait! Open this door."

"Go away, Gloria. I just want to sleep."

"Febe, Stella called me and said that you were acting all weird, talking to yourself and stuff. What's going on?"

"Go away Annie, or I swear to God. . ."

"Annie? Who's Annie?"

"Go away Gloria. I don't know what's happening to me, but I feel all out of control right now, so please just go away."

"I'm calling Harrison, Febe!"

"Don't you dare call that son of a bitch, Gloria. I swear to

God if he shows up here I'll kill him. Do you hear me? I promise you, I'll kill him."

"Okay, but at least open the door."

"Gloria, please, I just need some time to think."

"Now who's being dramatic. If I can't call Harrison then I'm calling JayR and Shelly."

"Fine, call whoever the fuck you wanna call, just go away."

"Febe, who are you talking to? Answer me."

"He did this to you, I only wanted to help you, Annie."

"And you did help me, but I am strong now, and it's time for you to leave."

Chapter 31

"Who are you talking to out there, Gloria? I can hear you."

"It's me, Febe, JayR. Is someone in there with you?"

"No."

"Then please come out so we can talk. Are you okay, Febe?"

"I'm fine JayR, and I remembered everything."

"Everything?"

"Well almost everything, Gloria."

"What happened in there, Febe?"

When I opened the door the sensation was magnificent. I took a deep breath and embraced JayR. "My name is Annie Marie Scott, JayR, and I'm married to Jacob Scott from Desoto, Texas.

We were married ten years. This scar is from a knife. I didn't peel his apple right. You can come closer, JayR, I won't bite. See, this circle right here on top of my hand, this is from an ice pick, I didn't hand it to him fast enough." As I explained my scars, Shelly walked into the room.

"Shelly, hello." I smiled.

"She got her memory back, and her name is Annie." Gloria beamed.

"Where's Febe?" Shelly asked me.

"She's here, Shelly. Febe is. . .was my childhood protector."

"Your childhood protector?"

"Yes, Gloria. She protected me and has been protecting me for many years. My father used to beat me and my mother. He would lock us in a dark closet. Febe helped me through those times. She would always tell me that she was going to pay my father back for every black eye he gave me and my mother. So I named her Febe."

"Febe, I mean Annie, why did you stay with Jacob for so long?"

"I was so afraid to leave, JayR. I had nothing and nowhere to go. I never worked, and he had convinced me that I could never get a job doing anything because I was too clumsy. He had total control over me and my life. He owned me, and I owned nothing."

"Tell us about Jacob." Shelly asked.

"Jacob, my loving husband, left these scars on me. He beat me, and kept beating me. And then he stuffed me in the back of a truck, like garbage." I shook my head.

"But why?" Gloria asked.

"He only did what I allowed him to do, but Febe didn't allow him to keep hurting me. The night I told him I was pregnant, he became enraged and tried to put an end to my child's life."

"And that's when Febe emerged?"

"Yes, Shelly, she came to fight my battle."

"But now I'll fight your battles for you, and I will make Jacob pay for every black eye he has caused you. You don't have to cry anymore, Annie." JayR said taking my hand in his.

"My tears are not tears of sorrow, they are tears of joy. I am surrounded by so much love, something Jacob and his ugly ways can never take from me."

"I don't understand. Febe, Annie, whoever you are, you can't be two people at the same time."

"But, I am, Gloria. It's like Jackson when he drinks. You said he's like two different people. Some quiet people drink and become the life of the party. While some sweethearts become assholes after a few trips to the bar."

"Febe is in there somewhere." JayR smiled.

"When you're scared for years and there's no one to turn to, you become that other person. Febe took it a little too far as we all know she can do. But she was my best friend, my sister, and my protector. Gloria, please don't cry, Febe is not gone. All the good times that you had with her when she was in a good mood, that was me. All the late night movies and ice cream and kite flying were me. Febe doesn't like anything. She hated life, and I was afraid of it." Silence and tears filled the room.

"Hey, guys, don't look so sad. The best part of this situation is you don't have to put up with Febe's mouth and bad attitude. I'm the nice one." I smiled.

"So all this time I've been dealing with the bitch side of you, and it's been Febe?"

"Yes, Shelly, it has. However, she's not gone, but I know how to control her."

"How?"

"The same way you did when you wanted to wring Febe's neck when she threatened Jackson's career. You controlled yourself and so can I. My life was out of control, so Febe took control."

"So you're back in control?" Shelly asked smiling.

CHAPTER 32

"Febe, are you still leaving next week?"

I slid the twenty pound turkey back into the oven.

"Yes, Gloria, I am. I've told you a thousand times, this is omething I have to do, and stop worrying about me. I'll be fine."

"Have you told JayR?"

"Told him what?"

"That you're leaving."

"Gloria, I'm not leaving for good. I'll be back."

"When are you going to tell him?"

"I don't know, maybe tonight. Are you finished with the pecans?"

"Almost. Next time let's just buy them already shelled, and why lo we have to cook Thanksgiving dinner anyway? Last year we ate out."

"Last year I didn't know how to cook a turkey. Now put the ecans down and talk to me." Gloria gently placed the large yellow bowl down on the table.

"Now tell me, why are you about to cry?"

"I don't know. I just don't want you to end up staying out there."

I walked over to her and gave her an assuring hug. "Oh Gloria, baby, I'll be back. I'll never leave you, unless some tall, dark bald headed, handsome, good-looking man comes along."

"You mean JayR." She chuckled.

"Now what would give you that idea?" I responded with a chuckle of my own.

"Promise me that you'll come back to us."

"I promise, Gloria. I'm coming back to my family. My parents are dead and I don't have any sisters or brothers. So you're stuck with us, for life."

"Us!" she said lightly.

"Yes, Febe and me."

"Don't say that, it creeps me out. I still don't understand two people living in one person's body. Shelly said it can't happen."

"Well, call me a medical miracle."

"So why don't you want us to call you Annie?"

"Oh, but you can. I will answer to anything but anger."

Before Gloria had a chance to respond, the doorbell rang.

"Well that must be your tall, dark, and handsome man coming in right now." Gloria smirked.

"I have to finish getting dressed. Move, move, move."

"Getting dressed?"

"Yes. Is Jackson coming tonight?" I shouted from the other side of the room.

"Yes."

"Good. I can't wait to see him," I yelled back into the room.

A few minutes later I heard JayR say, "Febe, are you making yourself pretty for us?"

I didn't answer him, and I didn't have to. When I emerged from the bedroom, JayR's mouth fell open, and the noise level in the room ent from a twelve to a minus one in two seconds flat.

"Oh, my God." JayR smiled and reached for my hand. "Febe, ou're beautiful." His voice held a rasp of excitement with a slight tinge f amazement mixed in.

I didn't want to blush, but I did. "Thank you. I did try."

"Well don't try any harder, girl. Dang."

"JayR."

"Okay, okay, easy on the compliments." He winked, raising oth hands in the air.

Then suddenly he snatched me into his arms. The way he wisted, and whirled me around, I thought the tight black dress vas going to slide down to my knees. "Febe, you've never wore nything that tight before."

"Shelly, I'm not hiding my anguish any longer. It's all over. 'his body has a story to tell, and I will let it talk to anyone who vants to listen."

"Well, it seems to be talking to JayR," Gloria said with a big mile.

"I think it's saying something to me too," Jackson said, kissing Gloria on her cheek as he entered the room. She elbowed him slightly n his ribs.

"But I can't hear what it's saying." He smiled.

"Well the show is over," I announced and walked toward the kitchen. "JayR, would you please take the turkey out of the oven and et it next to the ham on the table?"

"Your wish is my command," he said smoothly. As he slid passed me, his hand lightly brushed my butt, making electricity un threw my body, and I felt dizzy.

"You okay?" He smiled, catching me in his arms.

"I'm fine, but you gotta keep your hands to yourself."

"Yes, my dear," he said with another wink. I followed him into he kitchen, giggling like a schoolgirl.

"I can't help but look at you, Febe," he whispered in my ear once we were in the kitchen.

"Why?"

"Your face is so peaceful. You don't have that stone-cold, far-away expression anymore. You're just not the same person I met in the hospital."

"No, I'm not that person. I never was that person. She was me. You were looking at Febe. I'm Annie, remember."

His voice was low and smooth. "I knew behind those scars was the world's most beautiful woman."

"Harrison is here," Gloria announced.

"Hey, are we gonna eat?" Jackson shouted. "I can't stand the smell any longer."

"Yes Jackson," I shouted in return. "Everyone take your seats."

"Gloria, aren't you gonna pray first?" JayR asked.

"I thought you weren't a praying man," I replied.

"I ain't, but you're living proof that there is a God."

"Amen!" Gloria shouted.

"Then let me pray," I announced. "Let us bow our heads. Father, thank You for surrounding me with such beautiful people, who took me in and nursed me back to health. When your heart is filled with darkness you can only see darkness. But now that my heart has been given another chance at peace, by You, I can see all the beauty that You have put before me, and for that, I thank You. Amen."

JayR praised my cooking, along with everyone else. After dinner the men all resembled stuffed pigs as they sat around the TV with an expensive glass of brandy, trying to keep their attention on us and the football game at the same time.

"I didn't know you could cook so good," Shelly said as we put the food away.

"Why haven't you cooked like this before?" Gloria asked.

"Gloria, I didn't know how until a few weeks ago."

"Oh yeah, that's right," she replied.

Shelly tapped me on the arm. "I have to tell you something."

"What?" I turned to her.

"My brother likes you."

"You think?" I smiled.

"Well," Harrison said, interrupting our girl talk. "I don't know bout the rest of you, but I'm sort of glad that Febe's gone. Annie is a nuch nicer person and she keeps to herself."

The three of us stared at him.

"Well now that my foot is in my mouth, I'll go and see the guys." Ve silently followed him.

"Jackson, where did you get that ring?"

JayR choked on his drink, and his pecan pie almost fell in his lap.

"Yeah, man, that's a nice ring," JayR jumped in.

Harrison reached for Jackson's hands. "What are the initials or? Shouldn't it be JM for Jackson Maxwell?" He chuckled.

"No, it's a club. It stands for We Belong."

Gloria sipped on her drink. "We belong to what?"

"It's an organization for men who help other men through lifficult times in their lives. This ring is given to us as a constant eminder of love for ourselves, as well as others. I'm a lifetime nember. The organization is very large, and you can't find anything out about it. It's as close-lipped as the Masons, unless you want to oin."

"Yeah, man, I know it's large. I was just messing with you. 've seen a lot of men wearing that same ring. I was up in Chicago t a physicians conference and saw a few men with that same ring on. Even the doorman at the hotel was sporting one. I pointed it out to a colleague, and he said that it's a big thing in New York. You an't even get any information from them, and don't try to take the lamn thing off, they go into a raging fit. I don't understand it." Iarrison shook his head.

"It's not for you to understand. Just know it's a good thing.

The men have paid a very high price to wear this ring."

"Yeah, but what's the purpose?" Shelly asked.

"It symbolizes that each person has a right to live in harmony. May it be man, woman, or child. They all have that right," Jackson said, reaching for Gloria's hand.

"You preach it to them, Jackson," Gloria said, taking his hand. "It sounds like we need more of those organizations around to help a lot of people," she added, kissing him on the lips.

"Why are you so knowledgeable on this subject, Jackson?" Harrison asked.

"I take my membership seriously."

"That's stupid." Harrison replied.

"What's stupid?" JayR rose to his feet.

"JayR, let it go." I said, as the tension began to build.

"No, Febe, I want to know. What's stupid about that Harrison?"

"Well first of all," he stood, "you have all these men running around showing off their club ring like they're in some kind of fraternity or something. But instead, it's some stupid organization that some crack brain schemer thought of to make weak men join and follow him. Then he feeds them a bunch of crap that this ring symbolizes a person has the right to live free. Hell, we know that by the amendments."

"And you have a problem with that?"

"No, Jackson, I have a problem that men are so weak that they need someone to tell them that a ring symbolizes strength. The stupid part is an organization like that exists."

"Oh, did they turn down your application Harrison?" Gloria asked, breaking the tension that was building on JayR's face.

"Excuse me, Harrison, but I do have something to say." Jackson stood and Harrison sat down. "I'm sure each man who wears this ring will have a different story to tell about why he belongs to this organization. But I have only mine to share tonight." He turned to Gloria.

"This ring is a constant reminder of who I used to be, and for that I am sorry, Gloria. Even if I take off this ring tonight, it will still be there to remind me that my hands are made to love you."

JayR jumped up and turned toward the door.

"What's wrong?" Shelly asked.

"I don't know. I thought I heard something."

"It's the sound of love and happiness," I said.

I think it's the sound of bullshit coming from Jackson," Harrison said, taking another sip of his brandy.

"I like it," Gloria announced with a kiss to Jackson's lips.

JayR followed me back into the kitchen. "Do you remember the ring?" he whispered in my ear. His warm breath sent chills up my spine. I swallowed a mouthful of nerves and was about to turn to kiss him on his full dark lips when all hell broke out in the living room.

"Everyone, remain calm!" Four guys walked over to where JayR and I were standing, and put JayR's hands behind his back, with handcuffs.

"What in God's name are you doing?" I shouted.

"Febe, don't do anything. It's okay. Calm down." JayR shouted back.

"But what are they doing?"

JayR looked up into a black mask. "Can I please have a moment alone with her? You can keep the handcuffs on." The guy nodded and we walked back into the kitchen.

"You may not remember these guys."

"But I do," I cried. "I do."

"Then you know it is no use fighting with them. It's only going to make matters worse. I'll go with them and find out whatever I need to know by morning."

"Are they going to give you a ring?" I asked.

"Febe, no. It's a misunderstanding, that's all."

"But why are they here?" I asked. "Did you order a checkup on Jackson tonight?"

"No, I didn't order anything," JayR said angrily.

"Okay, that's enough. Let's go!" a man said.

We walked back into the living room, where the men proceeded to shackle JayR's feet and wrap this strong gray tape around his arms and shoulders.

Shelly jumped to her feet screaming and yelling at JayR, like he was a criminal.

"Shelly, please don't. I didn't do anything wrong."

"JayR, I just can't believe this. I told you to never bring your work into my life. I told you that your lifestyle would get us all killed someday. Now look at what you've done. You've brought these thugs into our home on Thanksgiving Day. What the fuck you gonna bring us on Christmas, the Mob!" she yelled.

We all stared at Shelly stunned because we'd never seen that side of her.

"Shelly I. . ." JayR tried to continue, but Shelly held her hand to stop his words from getting to her.

JayR stood near the door. I didn't know what to do. I knew the crew was there for a purpose. Then I herd Febe say, "See, told you all men are alike."

We have a message from Nikkei to Harrison."

"Me?" Harrison replied.

"Oh, my God, Harrison," Jackson uttered softly.

That's when my heart fell on the floor. Our living room was filled to the brim with men in black from the top of their heads to the bottom of their feet. I looked at JayR and he looked at me. I closed my mouth sharply and looked away. The tallest man spoke and I recognized his voice right away.

"Nikkei sends her gratitude for helping her family out so much." He held a book in his hand.

"That's Nikkei's," Shelly mumbled softly.

He unfolded the papers. "Thanks for getting Shelly's center off the ground and running smoothly, and thanks for referring so many people to her place. Thanks for keeping JayR out of jail, and thanks for those long talks when he had no one else around. Thanks for bringing Gloria and Febe into our lives. I thank you for it all."

Everyone began to give Harrison a standing ovation for all that he had done for this family. But my heart was not at ease, I could feel something was wrong.

The man held up his hand to quiet the room. "To my sisters and brother. If you are reading this letter you are no longer in debt to Dr. Paul Harrison. He's paid in full." Two men went over to Harrison and escorted him to the middle of the living room floor. "I paid him with my life."

"She's lying. I never touched her! I never put a hand on her!" Harrison shouted as the crew was dragging JayR out of the house by his ankles.

The tall guy repeated again, "She paid with her life." He then hit Dr. Harrison so hard the entire room gasped for air.

"She's lying." Harrison repeated, touching his bloody lips.

One of the men pulled out a tiny green box. I wasn't sure, but what he held in his hands was not a good thing. I took a step back and bumped into another crewman. The tall guy opened the box very slowly and stared inside.

"A picture is worth a thousand words," he uttered softly while shaking his head. Two crewmen pulled Harrison to his feet. He took out the pictures and stared at them, searching, investigating them for something. Maybe he held it in his hands for a few moments to diminish the dramatic effect the photograph might produce.

He handed it to another crewman, who gave it to me. I stared at a picture of a beautiful light skin girl with tears in her eyes and broken fingers. Harrison was written across the cast. I passed it on.

When Shelly took the picture, she gasped for air and stared. Then suddenly we heard Harrison scream. The second photo was passed around of Nikkei's swollen knee. We heard a scream and saw Harrison fall to the floor. The third picture made me gag. Nikkei's face was black-and-blue, her lips were swollen thick. I closed my eyes, because I remembered that night.

I stared as one of the crewmen's fist came out of nowhere and slammed into Harrison's face so hard his head went back, and blood flew from his mouth. His eyes fell on mine, and I winked. Well Febe winked. I stared in horror at his pain.

By the time we saw the sixth picture, the beating turned into a one-man, ass-kicking show. I had no idea where JayR was, but I could understand restraining him had to be done, or we all were going to be witnesses to a murder.

"How many pictures are in there?" I heard someone whisper.

"Over a dozen," I replied, shocked at my knowledge of what was in the box. "Damn it, Febe," I mumbled softly. She must have given the crew the box before I came back. I pressed my lips together and stared at Harrison. He was dripping blood on the white carpet.

"She was screaming for help, but too afraid to ask," Shelly said as tears fell from her eyes. "You son of a bitch!" Shelly screamed, and charged at Harrison, but Jackson held her back.

"Domestic violence is a silent killer and if you don't listen closely you might not ever hear," another familiar voice said. It was Crazy Jimmy. "My mother died because of my father's abuse," he added. "I heard her scream every night when I was a child."

A few days later I was quickly stuffing things into a suitcase. The driver was outside, and I didn't want to take this trip any more han Gloria wanted me to go. But I had some unfinished business o take care of. I had to bring closure to that part of my life.

"Febe, what did JayR say about you going?"

"Well, I never got around to telling him."

She grabbed my arm. "You didn't tell him?"

"No! Gloria, I didn't. I told you I want to do this on my own."

"On your own? You haven't seen or heard from this man in years and now you want to meet him face-to-face. Febe, he could kill you. You don't have any idea what he's been up to. He did try o kill you once, remember."

"Gloria, I know."

"What has he been doing all these years?" she asked.

"Coaching football."

"How do you know that?"

I moved her hands so I could finish packing. "A detective found him for me."

She put her hands on her hips. "Detective? You never mentioned a detective to me."

"It sort of slipped my mind."

"Febe, I know darn well it didn't slip your mind."

"Okay, Gloria. I had a friend of JayR's working on this right after I got my memory back. He found Jacob for me."

"Now Jacob's waiting for you with open arms?" she added.

"No Gloria, he's not. I just want to talk to him. Besides, I went to a psychic."

"A what?"

"A psychic, and she told me that this is something that I gotta do."

"And you believe her?"

"I'll believe a back-alley voodoo queen who freelances as a topless dancer for the blind, if she has the information that'll help me get my hands on Jacob."

"That must be Febe talking."

"Never mind, I have to go. The car is waiting for me." I started for the door. "Oh, what were you and Jackson talking about last night? You said that you were sorry to hear that."

"A friend of Jackson's is badly hurt."

"Who?"

"A judge, Phillip somebody."

"Phillip Ranch?"

"Yes, that's his name. Somebody beat the heck out of him."

"Oh, that's too bad." I said.

"Well it was only a matter of time before he got what he deserves. He used to beat his wife something awful."

"Well you know what goes around comes around."

"I guess you're right, Febe."

"Well, baby girl, I have to go."

"Please take care of yourself and come back home soon."

"I will, Gloria, and don't worry I'll be fine. Don't try to call JayR. He's out of town on business. And won't be back for a while."

"Is he looking for Harrison?" Gloria asked softly.

"Like a hound dog."

"Then he won't be calling."

"Yes, he will." I winked.

"But he never checks in when he's on one of his business trips," Gloria said.

"He never used to, but now he has me," I said, with a smile. "I don't know what it is about this man, that makes me want him so much, but I do. So just please, when he calls don't say anything about me being in Desoto, or he'll come looking for me and I don't want him there."

"What do you want me to tell him?"

"Tell him I went to a domestic violence conference. You know the one where they're trying to pass a bill so women don't have to press charges against their abusers. The DA will do that for them. Remember, I told you about that."

"No, I don't remember, but I'll do my best. Call me as soon as you get to the hotel."

"I will."

"It's a really nice place. My travel agent told me, so call me before you check in. I've arranged everything so you don't have to worry. Charge everything to the room. Jackson will take care of it."

I stopped before lowering my body into the silver limousine.

"Gloria."

"Febe, I don't want you worrying about anything. Just see that crazy man and come back home. Okay?"

"Okay, Gloria, okay."

"And don't forget to call me!" she shouted, as I closed the door and lowered the window.

"I won't. But remember, don't say a word to JayR!"

"I won't."

"Gloria, I love you."

She smiled and wiped the tears from my eyes. "I love you too, Annie."

CHAPTER 33

After the bellman left, I slipped on a pair of black Levi jeans and a black turtleneck sweater, and my black jean jacket. I tucked my hair under a black Raiders cap and pulled it through the hole in the back. I stuffed the black gloves in my back pocket, and the ski mask in the pocket of the jacket. It was time for me to come face-to-face with that monster of my dreams.

I slid into the front seat of a black Mercedes. Thank goodness for Gloria's and Jackson's connections. I took a deep breath and gave my reflection two thumbs up. I started the car and headed to my destination.

Following the long, winding road to the top of the hill, I made a left on Washington Boulevard, and a right on Avenue C. I stopped at the corner of Elgia and Corley. Something struck a nerve, and my heart started to race and my mouth went dry. I crept slowly along the street. I glanced at the car clock. It was 10:15 p.m.

I wasn't sure where I was going, but I ended up right where I needed to be, in front of Jacob's house.

I sat in the car for a moment. My stomach turned, and my heart was pounding so loud I couldn't hear myself think. Now was the time I really wanted Febe as I began to walk into the darkness toward the back porch. I missed the first step, fell and broke my thumbnail. I put my finger in my mouth to stop the bleeding, tore off the hanging nail, and continued my act of breaking and entering.

The neighbor's light from the backyard gave the place an eerie glow as I walked from room to room, trying to remember exactly what took place. I'm not quite sure what I was feeling, but when I entered the living room an image sneaked up on me and pushed me back to the wall. My eyes fell on that old orange plastic couch that I scrubbed vigorously every day.

The evil was still present in this house. I could feel it as I roamed from room to room. A sharp pain bounced through my body as the memories came flooding back.

I took a deep breath as cold sweat ran down my back. The visions were so real. I could see my body lying on the floor, crying in pain, or curled up in the corner on the bedroom floor hiding in fear.

I stumbled up the stairs into the master bedroom, holding my stomach. As oxygen forgot to return to my lungs, I could see the blood still dripping down the walls. I could hear the screams. The moans of my pain.

I blinked back unexpected tears and raced out of the bedroom, down the stairs, through the living room. I made a dash for the back door. But someone grabbed me. I drew in more stale air and fought back with all my strength, tumbling to the floor.

My foot was in his face and another in his balls. I kept kicking him, trying to kick his balls into his throat. He grabbed my legs and held me down.

“Febe! Calm down, calm down, girl. Shit! You gonna get us all caught. What are you doing in here?”

“JayR!” I shouted.

“Yeah, it's me.”

I hugged him tightly, breathing as if I just ran the L.A Marathon. “What are you doing here?”

“I asked you the same thing.”

“You first,” I insisted.

“Let's get out of here and then we can talk.”

When the cold air hit my face, I began to feel better. I picked up the wrench and screwdriver from the front seat of his rental. I threw the wrench in the back and laid the screwdriver on my lap.

I sat in silence while JayR drove me away from my past. He said nothing, only holding my hand. We drove back down the hill into a half-empty parking lot. I got out of the car to catch my breath. He walked to my side of the car and took me in his arms.

“Febe, listen we're here waiting for Jacob to come home. I told you I had everything under control. So why did you come here?”

“You didn't tell me you were coming here. You said you had to go on a business trip.”

“I did go, and now I'm finished.”

“Did you find Harrison?”

He ignored me and said, “You didn't answer my question. Why did you come here?”

“I came to see."

JayR's jaws tightened. “See what?”

“I needed to see him. I wanted to see him face-to-face. I wanted to let him know that I was alive.”

“And what type of reception were you expecting? A heartfelt “welcome home, baby.”

“No!”

"Then what?"

"I don't know, JayR. I just don't know. I only wanted to see him suffer like he's made me suffer."

He surrounded me with his muscles and rocked me.

"I knew there was a little Febe left in you."

"I'm so damn tired of crying. I want this all over."

"It will be over for you very soon, but you could have jeopardized the entire mission," he said, staring into my eyes.

"What do you mean? I don't want Jacob in our lives. I don't want a monthly report on him like the others. I just want him to know that he didn't win."

"He's gonna know, Febe, I promise you that." He kissed me on my forehead. "Your wish is my command. Now get in the car. We have to go."

Moments later we were sitting in front of Jacob's house, waiting. JayR began to speak. There was a faint tremor in his voice as though some strange emotion had touched him.

"Febe, I want you to know that you are the most extraordinary, remarkable person that I've ever met. You're. . ."

He closed his eyes and dropped his head as if the words were hurting as they left his lips.

"You've been to hell and back and lived to tell your side of the story. I know that you still have some fears, and you're frightened of the unknown. But I hope in time you can learn to love me as I'm loving you right now."

I was speechless. He said love.

"Febe, did you hear me?"

"Love is supposed to be forever, JayR, and you see where forever got me. Wanting to be loved was my weakness, and I didn't play the game of love that well. I guess you can say I'm a poor sportsman."

He chuckled, and then suddenly with both hands he yanked me to him. I snapped. I had the screwdriver in my hand and I raised it off my lap, but when he kissed me with so much passion it felt as though he was inhaling my soul. I dropped the screwdriver to the floor of the car, and I swear I floated to the sky. There was something serious going on in my panties. I smiled because I knew the little girl was awake.

"I promise to take you to that special place where you can see forever and it's right here in my heart," he said, placing my hand on his pounding chest.

I bent toward him to get another kiss when someone knocked on the window.

"JayR, it's time to go. He's on his way home."

"Okay, Febe, let's roll." He smiled and kissed me again.

As we re-entered the evil dwelling of Satan, everyone took their position, and I took mine. We sat and waited for Lucifer to arrive. My heart pounded in my chest. I licked away a strong taste of terror that caressed my lips.

Then Febe spoke. *Annie, I'm here when you need me.*

I closed my eyes tight. "I know, Febe, and you will never leave me."

Never, Annie.

Chapter 34

It was a little after midnight when Jacob came into the house. I expected him to be drunk with a thick stench of whiskey filling the air, but he wasn't. He entered through the back door, set something on the table, and took his shirt out of his shorts.

He walked through the darkness, like the creature that he was, but his night vision wasn't 20/20. He should have seen me sitting at the top of the stairs. He took two slow steps up, making the stairs creak. A chill rushed through my bones.

"Did you like the flowers, Jacob?" He froze at the sound of my voice.

"What the hell?"

I stood and walked toward him, taking one creaking step after another. "Did I scare you, Jacob?"

He was quiet. "Did I scare you?" I asked again.

"No, who are you?"

"After all these years, you don't recognize the sound of my voice."

"No," he said and clicked on the light. I didn't see JayR or the crew anywhere.

"Oh, that's right. I'm sorry, you never heard me speak, you've only heard me cry." Then I began to cry just like I remembered. "No, Jacob please. I'm sorry, Jacob. I'll be good, Jacob. Don't hurt me anymore, Jacob."

He stumbled off the second step and bumped into the wall. He was much older than I remembered. There were many lines around his gray and black mustache and on his forehead. He still had that greasy black curly ponytail, but he was almost bald on top. His stomach hung over his gray mesh gym shorts, and he still had that damn gold tooth.

"Oh, my God, Annie! You're alive!"

I walked right up to his face. I could smell the chili dogs and whiskey on his breath. "Yes, Jacob, it's me." My heart was racing and my palms were sweating. I passed my finger across Febe's handiwork on his face. "Nice scar," I said.

"Annie, I don't know what to say. I'm so sorry, baby. I was going through some things in my life that I didn't understand. You don't know how sorry I am. I was in a different mind-set back then. But I got some help and I'm better now. I changed my life around, I go to church. I've been baptized."

His voice was shaking, and I knew he didn't like me being this close to him, invading his space. His face incited something in me, like a rake being dragged across concrete, nails on a chalkboard, or the sound of a screaming child, his demonic words pierced my ears like a hot poker.

I walked into the living room and picked up a pretty pink ashtray. "Well congratulations, Jacob. I'm so happy that you found God."

He followed me. "I knew that you would be, Annie." He stopped speaking. "Who are these people in my house?"

"What people?"

"Annie, don't play crazy with me," he spoke sternly.

I shook my head and pointed my finger in the air with my back still to him. "No, Jacob. You are not in control of anything. Now I don't see anyone in this room but you and me. Now speak."

He cleared his throat. "Annie, what I'm trying to say is, I've been praying to God that you come back home to me, and He has answered my prayers. I prayed every night that you would come home."

"You prayed, Jacob?"

"Yes. Remember you told me that prayer changes things, and it does, because, He brought you back home to me where you belong."

"So I was right. Prayer does change things." I spun around, and with the glass ashtray I hit him across his face so hard he fell to the floor. I walked up to him. I bent over him and smiled.

His lips began to twitch. Without warning, just the way he used to do me, I took the heel of my right hand and shoved it in his nose.

He grabbed his nostrils. Blood was streaming through his fingers. "Why did you do that?!" he screamed.

"I wanted you to smell all the bullshit that you were giving me."

"It's not bullshit, Annie!" he shouted.

"Fuck you!"

Jacob jumped to his feet and lunged at me with full force, grabbing me around my neck.

But I wasn't scared because I had something for his ass that I knew would put a hurting on him for life. I had love on my side.

JayR flew into Jacob with a right fist to his jaw, sending Jacob crashing to the floor. He landed another one to Jacob's right eye, then the left. They fought by my feet. JayR on top of Jacob with his hands around Jacob's throat. Jacob was wheezing for air. I didn't move. I looked down into Jacob's face as he gasped for dear life.

"How does it feel to have your power taken away from you? Tell me, and if I like the answer, little boy, I'll let you breathe."

He closed his eyes slowly.

JayR looked up at me. I smiled.

"Release the death grip from around Jacob's neck and help him to his feet." I motioned for the crew to place the dirty white chair in the center of the living room floor. JayR stood behind me as I sat waiting for them to drag Jacob to the chair. They held his head up so I could see his eyes.

He whispered, "Annie, please, baby, you know I love you."

I put my finger to his lips and shook my head. "Strip him and stand him up."

Keno and Crazy Jimmy tore off Jacob's clothes, like a Tasmanian devil. Jacob cried and pleaded. I stood so he could see the smile on my face.

"Tie his hands behind his back."

"Please. I'm a changed man. Annie, don't let them hurt me. Annie listen, listen, what would Jesus do?" Jacob cried.

"I don't know, but I'll ask Him tonight when I pray for forgiveness."

"Annie, let me explain, I was drinking very heavily back then, drugs and shit. Annie, I don't do that anymore. I go to church. I sing in the choir. Annie, I'm one of God's children."

I held out my hand. "Blades." JayR reached into the bag and placed a double-edged razor blade into the palm of my hand.

I walked up to Jacob. "Hold his face." Jacob trembled as he eyed me walking toward him with the blade between my thumb and index finger. I could see his bleeding nostrils flaring like a dragon with each breath that he took.

I slowly and gently carved the words Wife Beater on his forehead. Blood oozed from the fresh wounds. "Why didn't you let me go to my mother's grave?" I said, forcing his head back with my finger, bouncing it off the wall.

"I'm sorry, Annie, I really am."

I pushed his head back again. "That's not an answer, Jacob. Why didn't you let me go to my mother's grave?"

"Because. . ."

"Because what?" I shouted, making the still room jump.

"Because. . ." he mumbled.

I dropped to my knees in front of his wilted dick, and I picked the foul thing up between my fingers and placed the blade at the tip of the hole.

"Why didn't you let me go to my mother's grave?" I shouted again through clenched teeth, trying to remain calm because I was feeling some kind of rage that I knew was Febe. I focused on the tiny drips of blood that began to ooze from the thin slices on his forehead.

"Because she's not dead!" he screamed out in pain, wiggling back and forth. I held the blade in position letting him slice himself with each jiggle of his hips "She's not dead!" he cried. "I just saw her yesterday."

"I want the rum."

"Febe, no."

"JayR, 151."

"Febe, listen to reason. No rum."

I turned to JayR. I felt steam rising from the top of my head, and I was breathing fire.

"Give me the rum now," I uttered each word very slowly. JayR's eyes widened. Then he went into the black bag and placed the large brown bottle of one hundred and fifty-one proof rum in my hand. I turned back to Jacob.

"All these years, Jacob, you let me believe my mother was dead. Why?" I screamed. "Why!"

"Control, Annie. That's all, control." He dropped his head.

I was shocked. My anger and rage slipped away. I felt as pathetic as he looked.

"What did I ever do to you?" I asked pitifully.

He was silent, then he slowly raised his head. "Nothin Annie. You were weak. You gave me control, and I took it."

JayR jumped in his face. "She didn't let you take a dam thing, your punk ass stole it. You saw someone weak, and yo took advantage of it."

I grabbed JayR by his large biceps. "No, JayR. He's right. allowed him to abuse me because I was weak, because I loved him He only did what I allowed him to do." I took a deep breath.

"Where's my mother, Jacob?"

"Let me go and I'll tell you?"

"Jacob, always trying to strike a deal." I laughed.

"Well you know how it is," he smirked.

I stepped into his space. "This is how it is: If you don't tel me where she is, I'm going to slice you from ear to asshole, take my time until your screams are muffled cries. Until the devil i hell begs me to set you free. Now where is my mother?"

Jacob licked his lip and looked from one shaking head t another.

"Tell her where her mama is!" JayR shouted. Jacob jumped and stared at JayR for a moment. "She's at the Stonewall Retiremen Home," he answered looking away.

"You put my mother in an old folk's home?"

"After you left she had a stroke. I thought I was doing you a favor."

"The favor would have been to never have married me," I shouted.

"Someone make contact and get Annie's mother," JayR commanded.

"Where are the pictures?" I asked.

"What pictures?" He repeated.

"The pictures that you took each time you beat me. You told me you were going to have them framed as a reminder for me to be good while you were away. So where are the fucking pictures? I'm getting tired of this game, Jacob."

"I destroyed them!"

JayR snapped his fingers. "Search." The crew began its hunt.

"I was trying to be nice, but now you are forcing my hands."

Jacob shouted, "Annie, you almost cut my dick off! How are you trying to be nice?"

I moved my finger back and forth in front of his face.

"No, no, no, Jacob. You are not in control. Now where are the pictures?"

"I told you, I destroyed them."

"Well I don't believe you so I'm gonna torture you until I feel better, and I feel pretty damn bad right now.

Ten years of hurt, Jacob, ten long agonizing years of pain." I unscrewed the top on the rum and carefully poured some of the strong liquid into the cap.

"Oooouch! Damn it, this shit burns like hell!" I shouted as the rum covered my broken thumbnail. "Where are the pictures?"

"Annie, I don't have any pictures." He cried. "Please Annie, don't hurt me anymore."

Slim and Crazy Jimmy held Jacob's arms, and I slowly poured the bottle of rum on the tiny razor slits, setting his manhood ablaze.

Jacob jumped around the house like a fish out of water. They couldn't hold him. He hopped on one foot cussing and shouting, praising God and praying. They tried to hold him down, and I tried to pour more, but he had a grip on his dick so tight, if they continued to pull his hands away, he would have ripped his balls off.

"Let him go! Let him go!" JayR shouted. "This man has suffered enough."

"What?"

"Febe, that's enough. You're gonna kill him."

"So. One dead black man is just another statistic. Nobod is gonna miss him."

"But he's a human being, and we don't kill. Put him in a tu of water, and clean him up."

I threw the bottle down and stormed out of the house. Jay followed behind me.

"Febe, you are not angry at me, so calm down and listen.

We don't take another human life. If you kill him, he's jus dead. You will be doing him a favor. We can make him live in fea just like the others, but we can't kill him. You've engraved Wif Beater into his forehead, which is better than the rings. So th world will see him for what he is."

"I want the pictures."

"He doesn't have the pictures."

I took a few steps closer to JayR and touched his broad chest "Can I ask him one more time, JayR? I know he's lying. Please."

"Febe?"

"JayR, I'm only gonna ask one question."

"Okay, let's go back inside and wrap this thing up." H smiled hugging me so tight I exhaled in his arms. When w entered the house, Jacob was sitting on the couch squeaky clean Wet, cold, and shaking.

His hands were in his lap. JayR and I sat down in front of him

Jacob looked me in my face, and then turned his eyes t the wall. "What happened to you, Annie? What happened to m sweet, shy little Annie?"

"I was sweet, but never shy. You beat me into submission Now JayR has your sweet little Annie, Jacob, and you have Febe You do remember Febe, don't you Jacob?" I said, pointing to hi scar. "She's here Jacob. For every black eye that you've given me she's here with a vengeance. Now if you don't want to meet Febe again, I suggest you tell us. Where are the pictures?"

"I don't. . ."

I pulled JayR's .357 from my side pocket and pointed it at Jacob's face, cocked to kill. JayR patted his breast pocket, then searched inside his jacket holster.

"Damn," he mumbled. "You are getting better, Annie." He smirked, shaking his head. "I can't help you, man, even if I wanted to. It's ready to fire."

"I ain't worried. If you kill me, the lawman is gonna have your ass so deep in prison, your alter ego won't be able to find you. So do what you gotta do, sister," Jacob said laughing.

"Well that's where you're wrong, Jacob. I have the battered woman's syndrome on my side. I'll get off in no time. Now where are the pictures?"

Jacob looked away, then back at me. "In the other room." He pointed.

JayR pointed in the same direction. "Show us." Jacob got up and slowly walked into the other room, like he had a stick up his ass. He moved the couch from the wall and lifted up the edge of the green shag carpet. Under the matting in a plastic bag were photos of my battered past.

Jacob handed them to me. I gave them to JayR, who took them out of the plastic bag and cringed with tears in his eyes. "You put dates on these damn pictures. You are a sick bastard."

Jacob kept his eyes glued to the floor. I stood with my back to both of them. I didn't want to let Jacob see me cry.

JayR turned to the crew. He shouted his command and the crew fell into position. I turned to see what was going on.

"Crew!" JayR shouted. "Unmask." I turned to face them as JayR did a military turn and revealed his face to Jacob. A lump formed in my throat. I brought my hands to my mouth.

"JayR, why are you revealing the crew's identity?" I asked.

JayR took me in his arms. "I'm going to give him the dignity of seeing the faces of the men who are going to hunt him down every day of his life.

Someone is going to be watching you," he said to Jacob. "Every move you make, they will make two. Every breath you take, they will take two. For every black eye you have given her they will give you two."

CHAPTER 35

I was sitting on the balcony, sipping hot butter rum tea, looking out over the tiny city.

JayR silently entered the room with the key I left at the front desk. I kept my gaze on the city. "What happened after I left?" I asked.

"The crew tried to convince Jacob the safest place for him was in prison. We can't get to him there."

"Or?"

"Or we'll hunt him down and beat him like the dog that he is."

I stood and turned to face JayR. The expression that was on his face would have sent me running for the hills, but I didn't move. I couldn't move.

"Let me hold you tonight, the way you want to be held." His words wrapped around me like a blanket.

"I'm scared, and my heart is beating in my chest and. . ."

"Fear no more, sweet Annie." His arms encircled me, an held me tight. The heat from his fingers felt like they were goin to leave blisters on my skin. His lips sent slivers of a lovable sen sation racing through my blood.

I wasn't sure what I was supposed to do with the hurrican that was growing between my thighs, but I knew I was willing t wait out the storm.

"JayR, I. . ." He placed his lips on mine, and I wanted t faint. I didn't because I also wanted to be awake for whatever wa going to come next, so I fought against the urge that was forcin my eyes closed. But I lost.

JayR reached for the CD player and stopped Sade fron singing. The room went still. "I'll be your security blanket tonigh You don't have to be afraid of the quietness anymore."

His sweet kisses felt like whispers, as he led me to the be and eased my throbbing body under the cool sheets and slid i beside me.

We laid in each other's arms and he began rocking me Rocking all my fears away. My insides melted like ice cream.

"JayR?"

"Yes."

I reached over and turned on the light. I removed my T shirt, and laid down before him naked, exposing everything that was hiding, inside and out. He stared in dismay. Looking down a the road map of my life. Silent tears fell from his eyes and hit m body like scalding-hot water from a faucet.

One agonizing drop after another, he traced my scars with light touch of his fingers. When he held me in his arms so tightl and cried, all the pain left my body, and I truly became free.

For the first time in my life I felt the power of love enter m body, my soul, and my heart when our bodies fused together an we became one.

Tears, so many tears, began to flow. The tighter JayR held me and the slower he rocked, the harder I cried.

"Hush now, Annie," he said. "Because my love doesn't hurt."

He turned out the lights, picked up the phone, and broke the organization's number one rule.

"Kill him."

OTHER NOVELS BY C.F. HAWTHORNE

HOMELESS LOVE

Attorney Nina Moore has to choose between the love and respect of her father or the love and happiness she's found in the arms of Franklin Agustus Brooks a homeless man.

TEARS IN MY JOY

Samantha finds that living is not all peaches and cream when her mother forces her into a life of prostitution and drugs, but through Samantha's tears she still manages to find joy.

COMING SOON